Triple Barrel

Jeff Norburn

Dedication

This novel is dedicated to the love of my life –
my gorgeous, wonderful, funny, & brilliant wife Melody

And to my children - Diandra and Rylan.
Two pretty great kids who have become two exceptional adults

Thank you for your love and support

Chapter 1

Monday October 17, 2016

Ana Marshall heard a ping and glanced down at the screen mounted on the dashboard. She missed the days when the ambulance radio crackled to life and a human spoke to them. Those days were gone. In order to minimize the clamor on the radio most of their communication with dispatch was done silently now through the CAD, or Computer Aided Dispatch.

She turned to her partner, Rick Lebeck, who was at the wheel of the ambulance. "MVI, one patient, Code 2, George Oliver High School parking lot."

Rick turned right out of the Mount St. Joseph Hospital parking lot and into rush hour traffic. "I know where that is."

She programmed the address into the GPS anyway. She wished she could turn on the lights and siren but nowadays most of their calls were Code 2 to minimize the number of ambulances involved in high speed crashes. A Code 3 was reserved for life threatening calls and most of those went to the Advanced Life Support cars leaving the Basic Life Support teams, like Ana and Rick, stuck in traffic. It sucked. There were few things in life Ana loved more than responding Code 3.

4

"Fives are on the scene," she said and pressed the touch screen, letting dispatch know they were en route. Not long ago she would have used the radio to tell dispatch they were '10-8'. Now she pressed a finger to a glorified iPad. Sometimes technology was a buzz kill.

She was glad to be on the job though. She'd been off work on medical leave for a few weeks and today was her first shift back.

"Was a pedestrian hit?" Rick asked.

"Doesn't say." The CAD provided them with patient details if they were available but in this case it wasn't sharing much.

The school wasn't far from the hospital and despite crawling through Vancouver city traffic it would only take a few minutes to be on scene.

"I can't see someone getting hurt in a parking lot MVI unless a pedestrian is involved."

There was no point speculating but Rick did it anyway.

"We'll see when we get there," she said.

"Fives are there?"

"That's what the CAD says and it doesn't lie."

Fives were cops. Firefighters were sixes. In emergency services, everybody had a number.

A few minutes later, Rick pulled the ambulance into the school parking lot and stopped near a police cruiser. Ana could see a battered orange pick-up truck in the dimming early evening light about 100 feet away at the base of a grass slope facing the lot, its front end smashed into a concrete barricade.

It appeared the truck had come down the grass slope from the road above and crashed into one of the barricades that surrounded the lot. She stared up at the top of the hill where at least one police cruiser was parked, presumably at the place where the truck had left the road. The cruiser's red and blue lights pulsed over the hillside.

Rick got out the driver's side door and walked over to a cop who was leaning against a police car near the entrance to the lot. Ana went around to the back of the ambulance and opened the door. She heard Rick start a conversation with the cop.

"Hey Ray. What have we got?"

Somehow Rick knew the name of every cop in the city.

"High speed chase," she heard Ray say. "Stolen truck. Probably a tweeker. Goes off road up there, comes down the hill and slams into the barricade."

"Just one patient?"

"Yup."

"He conscious?"

"Yeah, cuts on his head, leg's fucked up, but he's breathing."

"You guys do any first aid?"

"We made sure he was alive. Other than that, we left him for you."

Ana finished unloading the stretcher and walked over to Rick and the cop. She pushed the stretcher alongside her, a first aid jump kit with a hard collar and an oxygen unit on top of the grey blanket.

"We need you with us," Rick said to Ray. "In case he starts flailing."

They stopped when they got close to the pick-up. The driver's side window was open. The driver was a stringy looking guy in his mid-twenties, wearing a grimy t-shirt that was two sizes too big for him. He rocked in his seat, mumbling with strange intensity.

"Hey buddy, how you feelin'?" Rick asked. "I'm a paramedic. My name's Rick. We're here to help. This is Ana. We're together."

'We're together', she thought. It was a strange thing to say to a patient. She wondered if it was intentional.

The driver continued mumbling, showing no sign that he'd heard Rick.

She turned to Ray, "Do you have the truck keys?"

The cop was slightly overweight and looked like he was in his mid-forties. He held up a key ring. "Of course. We got his keys and frisked him. He's unarmed."

Rick moved to the truck window and spoke to the driver. "Can you tell me what hurts?"

The driver pressed his head against the steering wheel, closed his eyes and muttered incoherently. Rick opened the truck door and Ana moved up with the stretcher.

The pick-up had crashed into a barricade directly beneath an overhead light. It was starting to get dark but she could still see inside the cab. The driver's face was bloody from what appeared to be superficial cuts to his head. Ana glanced down and could see that he had an obvious tib/fib compound fracture on his right leg. The bone was jutting out, pressing against his blood-stained jeans like a tent pole. They'd need to examine him properly to determine what other injuries he had. There was no doubt though that he was high on something. He should be in agony but he appeared blissfully unaware of that.

"I want you to keep your head still," Rick told him.

Ana lifted a plastic hard-collar off the stretcher.

"We're going to put a collar on you to keep your neck from moving, ok?"

Rick placed a gentle hand on the man's shoulder. As soon as he touched him, the driver freaked out. He screamed and swung his arms wildly as if he'd been attacked. A flailing arm struck Rick on the side of the head and he jerked back. Ana stumbled away from the truck, tripping on the pavement on the far side of the barricade. Rick turned, saw that she'd fallen, and moved quickly to her side.

"I'm fine," she said, embarrassed and a little irritated.

He helped her up and they backed away to the ambulance. She heard the driver slam the door shut and saw Ray move deliberately toward the pick-up truck, his service revolver out and by his side.

The driver slapped at the door lock, hitting it multiple times, eventually managing to get the locking mechanism down. He rolled the window up and screamed incoherently at them, his eyes wild.

"Calm down buddy," Ray said, levelling the gun with both hands. "Open the door."

Ana saw a second cop come forward with his gun out. He must have been in the cruiser because she hadn't noticed him before. He was considerably younger than Ray and looked barely old enough to drive, let alone enforce the law.

The driver's head dropped out of sight temporarily. When he popped back up, she saw he was holding something in his hand.

"Gun!" Rick said. "He's got a gun."

"Slow down," Ray said evenly. "It's not a gun. He doesn't have a gun. Everyone stay calm."

Ana looked closely and saw that it wasn't a gun. It was an orange, battery operated power drill. The driver held it up, grinning dementedly at them, and pressed the trigger. She heard it whir and wondered why someone would have a power drill in their truck.

"Put it down," the second cop yelled.

The cops separated, one on each side of the truck, pointing their guns at the driver through the front windshield. The driver whirled around, manically depressing the drill's switch, pointing it like a gun back and forth at the two cops. They seemed at a loss for how to react.

After a while the driver appeared to grow distracted, staring at the drill as if hypnotized by it, turning it over until the bit was pointed toward his chest. And then, without warning, he squeezed the trigger and rammed it hard into his ribcage.

"Jesus!" Rick said.

The driver pulled the drill out, the bit covered in blood. He grinned and drove it into his chest again.

The second cop moved quickly to the passenger side door and opened it. "Drop it," he yelled, pointing his gun at him.

The driver turned to face the second cop, pulled the drill out of his chest, and pressed it to his temple.

8

"Don't do it," the second cop said. "Put it down."

The situation was absurd, Ana thought - two cops threatening to shoot a man to stop him from drilling a hole in his own forehead, but that was how things were on the streets.

Ray signaled to his partner and moved to the driver's side window. He pounded his fist against the glass. The driver spun around to face him, the drill still pressed to the side of his head.

Ana watched the young cop holster his weapon and slide into the vehicle on the passenger side while the driver was distracted. The young cop grabbed the driver's arm and tried to pull the drill away. She couldn't see much as the two men fought over the drill. Then she heard the second cop scream.

"Fuck!" Ray yelled.

He moved quickly, holstering his gun and pulling out a steel baton. He swung the baton into the driver's side window causing it to shatter into tiny pieces. The second cop continued to howl in pain while Ray drove his fist through the open window, pounding the driver repeatedly on the side of the head.

"Let go!" he screamed. "Let go of him you fucking piece of shit!"

Ana shifted position so she had a better view into the cab. The driver grabbed a hold of the young cop's arm and sunk his teeth deep into it. The second cop used the elbow of his other arm to jab at the driver's head. Finally the second cop managed to free his arm and scramble back across the passenger seat. He fell out the passenger door and landed on the grass on the other side of the truck.

Ray, flushed with rage, unlocked the truck's door and grabbed the driver in a choke hold. The man at the wheel couldn't have weighed more than 120lbs. Ana cringed as Ray dragged him from the vehicle, broken leg and all, and dropped him unceremoniously on the grass beside the barricade, the lower part of his right leg twisted in a grotesque, unnatural position.

The second cop came around the front of the pick-up, holding his bleeding arm. Ana went to his side.

"Fucking guy bit me," the young cop said.

"Let me take a look at it," she said, getting him to sit on the edge of the barricade.

"What if the fucking guy has AIDS or something?"

"I guess you'll die then," she said.

"What?"

She smiled. "Relax. I'm fucking with you."

The young cop didn't look amused. "That's not funny."

"If I were you I'd be more worried about Hep C. Have you had shots?"

"I—I don't know."

"We'll get you checked out," she said. "I'll be right back."

She walked over to Rick. The driver was face down on the grass beside the truck. Ray had rolled him onto his stomach and cuffed his hands behind his back. The driver craned his head up, twisting his neck to look around.

Rick looked at Ana and shrugged. "Not sure there's much point in putting a collar on him now."

Ray came up to them. "You looking after my partner?"

Ana nodded. "We'll clean it and bandage him up. He needs to go in and get it looked at though."

He motioned to the driver. "What about him?"

Rick shrugged. "We'll pack 'em up the best we can. We'll need your help getting him on the clamshell and tied down."

Ray nodded.

Rick turned to Ana. "How are you holding up?"

She grinned. "This is the most fun I've had in weeks. God I've missed this shit."

Chapter 2

Gavin Taylor tried to remain as still as possible, hoping he gave nothing away.

"All in," he said, keeping his voice level.

"We have a player all in," the dealer said.

"How much is it?" asked the other player in the hand, a middle aged Chinese man.

Gavin held his breath and tried not to blink. He stared straight ahead, not making eye contact with anyone. He could feel his pulse throbbing in his neck and hoped the Chinese man didn't notice or that if he did, he didn't know what it meant.

The dealer counted Gavin's chips. The other player had a huge stack of chips in front of him and Gavin knew with a quick glance he could easily estimate how much had been bet. The Chinese man was stalling, Gavin thought, trying to get a read on him.

"$788," the dealer said.

It was a decent sized bet into a pot of roughly $1,200.

The other player counted out the chips he needed to make the call, taking his time, staring at Gavin like he was an exhibit in a museum - or a zoo.

The tension was killing him. He repeated the word 'fold, fold, fold,' silently in his head, as if he could telepathically make the man bend to his will.

If only he had that kind of power.

"Call," the Chinese man said.

Gavin felt his heart sink. He waited, expecting the other player to turn over his cards.

"You're first to show," the dealer said.

Gavin knew that. He just didn't want to.

"I'm pretty sure you have me beat," he said, without turning over his cards.

The Chinese man stared at him. "I want to see them."

Gavin sighed. If he mucked, the other player would win without showing his hand so he turned his cards over, showing the bluff.

The Chinese man smiled and turned over his cards. He had bottom pair. A weak hand but better than nothing, which was what Gavin had. It was bullshit, Gavin thought. There was no way he should have made that call. The fucking guy obviously didn't know how to play poker.

The dealer pushed the chips over to the Chinese man who added them to his already massive stack of chips. Gavin felt sick. He should leave the casino. He'd already lost $2,000 which was money he couldn't afford to lose. Forget the alimony and child support he owed, he'd hired a man to kill someone and he didn't have the cash to pay for the job.

He pushed his chair away from the table, stood, and scanned the poker room. He loved being inside a casino. In particular, he loved the clatter of chips as nearly 200 players simultaneously riffled, stacked, and restacked their chips. He felt a rush of adrenalin. People were winning and losing money all around him and he desperately needed to be a part of that.

He still had $1,500, thanks to another payday loan and cash advance on the only credit card he had that hadn't been cut in half by a judgmental cashier. If he wanted to make his money back, the best thing to do was to buy-in at a table with higher stakes. Maybe his luck would improve.

He walked over to the only $5/$10 table in the poker room. A slight Chinese man in a uniform approached him. It seemed to Gavin that almost everyone at the River Rock Casino was Chinese.

"5/10?" the man asked.

Gavin nodded and was led to a seat at a table with six other players. He sat down, pulled out his wallet, and laid fifteen $100 bills on the table. The money was scooped up and replaced with a tray of green and red chips. He stacked them, noticing that his stack was smaller than everyone else's at the table. It looked as if most of the players had bought in for the full $3,000 table maximum and had been adding to their stacks ever since.

He posted a $10 bet, something he was required to do as a new player at the table unless he wanted to wait until it was his turn to be in the big blind. But Gavin had no interest in waiting. He came to play, not to watch other people play.

He thought of himself as an intuitive player. He didn't think about pot odds, implied odds, or expected value calculations. He didn't like math. It was too much work. Instead he trusted his gut and made decisions based on how lucky he felt.

Gavin signaled a waitress and ordered a diet coke. He needed to watch his weight if he ever planned to get laid again. His sexual prospects weren't good given that he was in his mid-forties and spent almost all of his time indoors. Most of the food he ate came in a cardboard box or a foil wrapper and rarely ever expired.

The cards were dealt and Gavin carefully lifted the corners of the two cards in front of him. He'd been dealt the king of hearts and the

JEFF NORBURN

three of spades.

There was no indication that his luck was changing.

He was first to act in the hand and checked, tapping his fingers lightly on the table. His forced bet of $10 was effectively the same as calling so if no one raised the pot, he might get a look at a cheap flop.

Of course, with his luck, that didn't happen. Everyone folded until a player across from him, a young guy barely old enough to play in the casino, raised the bet to $40. Everyone else folded except the player to Gavin's right, who was in the big blind. She was an overweight woman, who looked to be in her 50s. She said nothing but flipped one green chip and one red chip across the line, calling the raise.

Gavin had shitty cards but decided he had an opportunity to make a move. The set up was perfect for a 'squeeze play,' to try to get the other two players to fold.

"Raise," he announced.

He waited, in part for dramatic effect and in part because he was terrible at math and needed to figure out how much money he should bet. Eventually he pushed 5 green chips across the line.

Since Gavin hadn't said the amount, the dealer clarified for the table. "The raise is to $135."

Action was on the kid. He was one of those guys who tried to grow a beard but only managed to grow massive amounts of neck hair while his face remained mostly hairless. He wore the requisite hoodie, mandatory poker attire for anyone under the age of thirty. The kid was silent for a solid minute and then said "Raise to $500."

Gavin felt like he'd been kicked in the stomach.

The player in the big blind quickly mucked their hand. Gavin did his best to give the impression he was faced with a tough decision.

Finally he shook his head and said, "Alright, I believe you."

He tossed his cards into the muck, grimacing, and stared longingly at the chips he'd lost like they were children he'd never see again.

14

Not seeing your children again was something Gavin could relate to. He had a 15 year old daughter that he'd probably never see again, at least not if she had anything to say about it. You'd think that if your daughter refused to talk to you that you could stop paying child support but apparently it didn't work that way. Your offspring could disown you and post all kinds of shit about you on the internet but you still had to pay for all their crap.

His daughter, Ashley, wasn't speaking to him on account of the whole 'alleged pervert situation', which was really just a big misunderstanding.

Gavin had been trying to be a good father by attending one of Ashley's volleyball games when he found himself sitting beside one of the other fathers. The two men struck up a conversation and talked about the usual things; sports, cars, and women. They were both divorced so it was only natural that they'd scope out the moms in the stands and a few of the teachers.

And that was when Gavin made the comment that was completely blown out of proportion and had gotten him into so much trouble.

"You know," he said. "Some of those girls down there look pretty damn hot."

Gavin probably should have paid more attention to the man's facial expressions, perhaps then he would have stopped. But he didn't and went on to say, "Sometimes when Ash has her friends over at my place, man, those girls wearing their shorty shorts, with their little titties all perky and everything, I can't help but get a chub, you know?"

That was when the guy lost it. He lunged at Gavin, taking wild swings and screaming at him, telling him to stay the hell away from his daughter, which was stupid because his daughter was a total woofster. Super Dad got a few shots in but the other fathers promptly pulled him off and the police were called.

Word got around the school quickly that Ashley's dad was a

perv. Gavin didn't think that was fair. It wasn't like he'd groped someone or dropped trou. He'd just pointed out what was obvious to anyone. Some of those girls - not all of them, but some of them - were damn hot.

The next thing he knew there was a social media page called 'Ashley's Perv Dad'. People posted all kinds of shit on the site, calling him a pedophile which was completely untrue. He wasn't turned on by kids, for Christ sake. These were fully developed girls and he hadn't touched any of them. He'd simply noticed that some of them had rockin' bods and who could blame him for that? It wasn't against the law or anything.

But apparently he'd ruined his daughter's life. She wouldn't talk to him and of course her mother was livid. She already had plenty of reasons to hate him. Unfortunately for Gavin, she was just one of three ex-wives he had to deal with.

Damn, he needed his luck to change.

♦

An hour later Gavin took a sip of Diet Coke and turned up the corners of his cards, revealing the 6 of clubs and the 8 of clubs. They weren't good cards but it was the kind of hand that had potential to make a flush or a straight.

"$40," he said, casually dropping a green and three red chips over the line. He was feeling confident after getting lucky and taking down a big pot a few hands earlier. He had a stack of almost $3,700 in front of him. He'd come to the casino with $3,500 so he was up $200 on the night and he could feel the momentum shifting.

Everyone folded to the player on the button who quickly announced a raise to $150.

He was an overweight, unshaven man in his fifties, wearing a ball cap and sunglasses. Gavin had noticed that he was a tight player, playing only a few hands, but playing those hands very aggressively.

The players in the small and big blind quickly mucked their cards and the action came back to Gavin who called the raise.

The dealer rapped the table, turned over three cards and spread them out on the felt. Gavin could barely contain his excitement. There were two clubs on the flop, a king and a seven. He had four cards to his flush. If he hit one more club he would almost certainly win the pot.

He was first to act and stared down at the table, thinking hard. He struggled with the math, trying to figure out how much money was in the pot and how much he should bet.

"$300," he said, sliding 12 green chips over the line.

Ball Cap was silent for a long time. Gavin willed him to call. He knew the club was coming. He could feel it. This was going to be a huge pot and he needed it. His life was seriously fucked up, and not just because an entire high school thought he was a pervert or worse. He was being blackmailed on two fronts and in danger of losing his job and going to jail. If he wanted to get himself out of the serious shit he was in, he was going to need cash, $7,500 to be exact.

"Raise," Ball Cap said. He counted out a stack of chips and pushed them over the line. "$700."

Gavin didn't stop to consider his options. His only thought was that he wanted to make the pot bigger and then win it all. "Raise to $1,200."

He hadn't finished counting out the bet when Ball Cap announced that he was all-in. Gavin didn't think about it. He snap-called and flipped over his cards as if he had the stone cold nuts.

Ball Cap turned over pocket kings and shook his head. Gavin knew he was worried. If a club hit, he could lose the hand even though he'd flopped a set of kings. Ball Cap had more chips so Gavin was the player at risk. There was nearly $7,500 in the pot.

The dealer turned over the jack of clubs and Gavin squealed like a little girl.

"It figures," Ball Cap groaned. "Why do these fucking donks always hit their shit on me? Every time."

Calling someone a 'donk' or a 'donkey' was supposed to be an insult but Gavin loved being called a donk. No one ever called you a donk when they won a hand. If someone called him a donk it was because he'd won a big pot.

He barely noticed the dealer turn the final card, the river, anticipating the huge stack of chips being pushed his way but when the hand was over, the dealer pushed the chips to Ball Cap.

Gavin stared down at the table and saw that the river was the seven of diamonds.

Shit.

Ball Cap had made a full house. Gavin's flush was no good.

In one fell swoop, he'd lost the last of his money. A $7,500 pot was gone because of the random turn of a card. He needed to win that pot. Not because he owed all of his ex-wives money. That was par for the course. Pissing off an angry ex was one thing. Pissing off a hired killer - that was a much bigger problem.

Chapter 3

Ana and Rick stood beside her Pontiac Sunfire in the station parking lot. It was dark and had started to rain lightly. Their shift was over and Ana wanted to go home but Rick was not cooperating.

"Are you sure you're OK?" he asked, not for the first time.

She had wondered in recent weeks if Rick had feelings for her, a situation that had resulted in some increasingly awkward conversations. They'd worked together for nearly four years and while she liked him, she had a hard time thinking of him as anything other than a coworker. Now that she was single and her world had been turned upside down, she didn't know if she was ready for another relationship anyway.

Even if she were, she couldn't understand why someone like Rick would be interested in her. She'd met some of the women he'd dated and as far as she could tell, they were much prettier than she was. The best Ana could say about herself was that she was 'athletic-looking'.

Were there men out there, she wondered, looking for a broad-shouldered woman with child-bearing hips and the cardiovascular system of a racehorse?

She didn't think so and she was ok with that. She would simply carry on with life as a single mother.

"I'm fine," she said.

"I want you to know I'm here for you."

She sighed. His eyes were so earnest and filled with concern, she wanted to punch him. "The best thing you can do is treat me like everyone else," she said.

Rick frowned. He wasn't a big man but he was in good shape and impeccably groomed with a neatly trimmed beard and short, brown, heavily-gelled hair. She hadn't seen him shirtless but she suspected his chest had been duly manscaped.

"You need someone to talk to."

"I've got a counselor to talk to," she said, more tersely than she intended. She tried to make up for her harsh tone with a small smile. "I'm ok Rick, really, I am."

She'd been off work for nearly five weeks on medical leave due to stress. She'd shown weakness and that bothered her. She didn't like to be reminded of it.

He stared into her eyes, something no other man she knew did. Men might stare at a woman's body, notably her cleavage, but rarely were they willing to look a woman in the eye. It was as if they thought eye contact would cause their heads to explode.

Not Rick though. He wasn't like any man she'd known.

"I wasn't there for you before and I should have been."

She stared down at the car keys in her hand. "You don't need to worry about me." As soon as she said the words, she immediately wished she'd chosen them differently. She knew what he was going to say before he started to speak and held up a hand to cut him off. "I know you worry about me," she said and smiled wearily. "But I'm ok – so knock it off."

She suspected he was smart enough to know that he was getting on her nerves but even a metrosexual man was still a man. In

20

her experience, when she told a man to 'shut the fuck up' for some reason they thought she meant, 'keep talking, you almost have me convinced.'

He nodded and smiled weakly. There was an awkward silence and she felt bad. He meant well and, if she was being honest with herself, he had a point. She'd needed help before. She'd seen some horrible things on the job and they'd left their mark.

The way she'd always thought of it was; she put those memories in glass jars and stored them in a locked cupboard in her mind. If she took the jars out, the memories inside were distorted by the glass and she felt separate from them, as if they were no longer part of her. Most of the time, she kept them hidden and locked away.

When her marriage fell apart and her father died shortly afterward, she visited the cupboard more often, sometimes leaving it unlocked. She'd start crying for no reason and found herself calling in sick for work because she couldn't get out of bed. She couldn't sleep and when she did she had nightmares.

And then there was the little boy who had fallen from an apartment balcony. That was in May, nearly five months ago. She'd seen dead children before of course; it was part of the job, but she was in a fragile state of mind and the boy was five years old, the same age as her son.

And he looked so much like Braden.

She tried to place the image of the dead boy into one of the jars but she couldn't. Gradually the other jars started to break and the memories of things she had so carefully locked away, were free to drift into her mind and consume her until she couldn't function anymore.

Since then there'd been counselling sessions where she'd learned coping skills. And they wanted her to take medication, the modern world's solution to every ailment, but she refused. She'd been off work on medical leave for weeks but she was back at work now and she felt whole again - without the help of a selective serotonin reuptake inhibitor, thank you very much.

Rick looked down. "I guess I overstepped."

She leaned in and gave him a quick kiss on the cheek, just above his beard. She was slightly taller than he was, but at 5'10" she was taller than a lot of men.

"Thank you for caring," she said.

He smiled, displaying irresistible dimples, and she couldn't help but think how handsome he was. He was a little too 'put-together' for her tastes but he had gorgeous blue eyes.

"I'll let you go," he said.

She watched as he walked to his ridiculously impractical convertible sports car. It was a black Audi R8 that he'd told her he'd bought used for just under $170,000. It was the kind of car that she imagined would be driven by an overcompensating asshole, except she knew Rick, and he wasn't an asshole.

A pathetic man-baby maybe, but not an asshole.

He could be annoying but he was sweet too, she thought. And he looked good. Somehow his navy blue uniform looked as neatly pressed as it did at the start of their shift.

Ana slid behind the wheel of her red 2005 Pontiac Sunfire and wondered if she could ever fall for a man who used product in his hair, whitened his teeth, and waxed all manner of body parts. It would be a dramatic change from the type of guy she was usually attracted to.

Considering how well her past relationships had turned out, maybe change was what she needed.

Chapter 4

Tuesday October 18

Ana woke to the sound of knocking. She glanced at the alarm clock and groaned. It was 1:54 am.

It occurred to her that she should probably be scared. Someone was outside her Burnaby townhouse in the middle of the night and she was a single woman, alone with a small child. Being scared would be a normal reaction. Perhaps under different circumstances she would be frightened but she had a pretty good idea who was at the door and she wasn't scared of him.

He just made her sad.

She climbed out of bed and slipped a cheap terry-cloth robe over her pajamas. The knocking had grown more urgent and the dog was barking. She hustled down the stairs and went to the door.

"That's enough Lukin," she said sternly to the dog and bent over to pick him up. She pet his thick white fur and he stopped barking. Lukin was a 2 year old Japanese Spitz, a small dog that looked like he should be pulling a miniaturized arctic sled.

She peered through the peep hole. No surprise. It was her younger brother.

She left the chain in place, opened the door as far as it would allow, and whispered through the opening, "What do you want Steve?"

"Let me in," he said, his voice much too loud.

"Keep it down. You're going to wake Braden."

Not to mention the neighbors, she thought.

"Oh, right, your little man." He sounded like a total stoner. "Is Little Dude sleeping?"

"It's the middle of the night," she said, keeping her voice low. "Of course he's sleeping."

"Right. Little Dude's got school and shit in the morning."

"What do you want Steve?"

"What makes you think I want something?"

"Are you high?"

"No, no," he said. "I wouldn't come here if I was high."

Of course he wouldn't, she thought. He had no reason to drop by if he was high. He only came if he needed money so he could get high.

"Look at me," she said. "Open your eyes."

He leaned his head into the narrow gap and opened his eyes comically wide.

She sighed. "Move your head back."

He did and she closed the door and removed the chain. "Just be quiet," she said and let him in.

He kicked off his shoes, a dirty pair of sneakers with one sole that flapped loose, having nearly come apart from the rest of the shoe. Steve was 4 years younger than she was but he looked older. He was pale, thin, and dirty, with tangled shoulder length hair. He looked like a drug addict, which wasn't surprising since that's what he was.

She stood at the door and watched him walk through the living room of her modestly furnished town house. He took a seat at the badly-scratched and crayon-doodled kitchen table. She felt a deep sadness, remembering him as a child. She thought of the tweeker in the orange pick-up and how easily she could get called one day to respond to an OD, only to find her baby brother suffocating on his own puke.

She set Lukin down and followed Steve into the kitchen where she automatically started to make a cup of coffee. In the old days she would have made a pot but now she had one of those individual pod machines that suited her swinging-single lifestyle. She wasn't sure who she was making the coffee for, she just was.

"So Sis," Steve said. "How's it going?"

"Why are you here Steve?" The answer was obvious even though she knew he wouldn't ask for money yet. They had to do the dance first.

"Can't a guy just drop by and say hi to his sis and her Little Dude?"

"At 2 o'clock in the morning?"

"Oh shit," he said. "If I'd known it was that late I wouldn't have come. I thought it was ...you know.....midnight or something. But...shit... two...that's not cool, is it?"

He was giving her a headache already. The coffee maker finished brewing.

"You want a cup of coffee?" she asked.

"Yeah, sure. Thanks sis. You're too good to me."

She thought about that and decided he was right. She was too good to him. In fact they all were. She wasn't the worst offender though, not even close. That award belonged to her older brother Marko. He was the real soft touch.

"Cream? Sugar?" she asked.

"No cream. Lots of sugar."

She placed the steaming cup of coffee on the table in front of him and then poured a glass of water for herself from a pitcher she kept in the fridge. She thought about having a cup herself but decided against it, holding out hope that she'd get some sleep tonight.

"Has anyone told you that you look like shit?" she said, putting the pitcher back in the fridge.

"Just you." He leaned back in the kitchen chair. "That's why I'm here. I crave the warm embrace of family."

He slid his hand under the waist band of his dirty jeans and aggressively scratched. She frowned and he slid his hand out sheepishly.

"Sorry," he said. "I got an itch."

She sighed and sat down at the table across from him with her glass of water. It was time to do the dance. She told him he needed to get into a program. He lied and said he was getting into one any day. Eventually he got around to asking for money and she told him she couldn't give him any. She was a single mother, struggling to pay the rent. She'd stopped giving him money years ago but that didn't stop him from trying.

There had been a time 4 or 5 years ago when he might have gotten her to give him money. She didn't believe the lies he told then either but he could wear her down with his charm, a skill he no longer had - although he didn't seem to realize that. Apparently he didn't understand that his sunken eyes, plaque covered teeth, and horrific body odor made it all but impossible for him to charm anyone, except perhaps other likeminded drug-users with a similar aversion to personal hygiene.

"How's Little Dude?" he asked, after the dance was over.

"Do you even know his name?"

"Sure," Steve said. "You said it tonight, it's something...I don't know. I just call him Little Dude. It's hard to keep that shit straight, you know."

"You're a piece of work Steve," she said, getting up from the table. "But you can crash on the couch if you want. I have to work early, day shift, and get Braden to daycare. If you stay you'll have to get up early and leave with us."

There was no way she'd leave him alone in her house while she was at work.

"Cool. How early we talkin?'"

"Six."

He grimaced. "No wonder I don't get a job. Real life sucks."

"Some of us deal with real life every day little brother. Like I said, you're welcome to stay if you don't mind leaving with us in the morning."

He glanced down at the beige faux-suede couch and then up at the flat screen TV on a stand against the wall and said, "What the hell. A little z time'll do me good. Maybe I'll even shower in the morning, get cleaned up and looking respectable and shit."

Ana thought that was a great idea. He'd still have to put those disgusting clothes back on after he showered but it couldn't hurt to wash the skin underneath, not to mention his hair.

She got him a pillow and blanket from the linen closet, cringing inwardly as she did. The blanket she could wash but the pillow could never be used again and should probably be incinerated in the interest of public health.

"Thanks sis," he said, taking them from her.

She put the coffee cup and water glass in the kitchen sink and then went to the door to set the chain.

"Goodnight little brother," she said. "You're a pain in the ass but I love you."

She went upstairs and checked on Braden who was fast asleep in his room. It was 2:55 am. She could still catch three more hours of sleep if she was lucky.

She fell asleep almost immediately and was dead to the world until the alarm woke her at 6 am. She wasn't used to the early mornings yet. It occurred to her that if she was finding the early mornings hard, it'd be far worse tomorrow night when she worked her first night shift. She forced herself out of bed and stumbled like a zombie down the stairs.

27

She noticed right away that Steve wasn't on the couch, in fact, the blanket and pillow looked as if they hadn't been used. She glanced at the door and saw that the chain was undone. He must have left right away, she thought. It wasn't until she looked back at the couch that she saw the obvious. She should have noticed right away but more importantly, she should have seen it coming before she went to bed.

Her TV was gone.

Chapter 5

Gavin Taylor was disappointed to see Marko Milanovic standing at his office door, or more specifically, he was disappointed to see that Marko Milanovic was still alive. You can hire people to do a job, he thought, but you couldn't always count on them to do it in a timely manner. Of course, Gavin couldn't really complain on account of the fact that he didn't have enough money to pay the hit man anyway. He probably should be relieved, he supposed. The longer the killer took, the more time Gavin had to come up with the cash.

"Got a minute boss?" Marko asked.

Marko was in his early fifties. He'd lost his white collar job when his company downsized and had ended up here, loading trucks at an electronics warehouse for slightly better than minimum wage. He should be looking forward to 'Freedom 55' and sucking piña coladas on a tropical beach somewhere but instead he was busting his hump at a shitty warehouse job.

Life was hard and then you die.

Gavin had hired Marko to work in the Burnaby warehouse even

though he had no experience doing manual labor because he looked like the kind of guy who could set aside his pride and put in an honest day's work.

It turned out that Gavin had been right. Marko was one hell of a worker.   Unfortunately, it turned out he was also prone to blackmail.

"Kinda busy," Gavin said, without looking up.

Marko came into the tiny office and shut the door.   There was barely room for the two torn vinyl chairs squeezed between the battered wooden desk and the 70s era wood panel wall.

"It's important," Marko said.

Gavin sighed.   "Can it wait?   I had a shitty night and I've got a ton of work..."

"Did you think about my offer?"

Of course, Gavin thought, that's why I hired someone to kill you.

"It's only good for a limited time," Marko said.

"Yeah," Gavin said.   "It's just that we aren't hiring anyone.   I mean, I'm with you, it's a good way to resolve the situation but I can't hire him if we don't have an opening.   We have a budget to think about."

Marko stared at him, reminding Gavin of the Chinese man at the poker table who seemed to know, just by looking at him, whether he had it or not.   Could Marko see through him too, he wondered.   Did he know Gavin was lying?

"That isn't my problem.   You do what you need to do with the budget.   Hire my brother or the video hits the web."

"It's not going to be that easy Marko.   For Christ's sake, your brother's a bloody drug addict."

"That's not true."

Gavin detected a hint of anger in his voice and smiled.   He'd struck a nerve.

"He's a recreational user," Marko went on.   "What he needs is steady work."

"Look, I feel for you.   Some of my family is fucked up too but

30

I'm not running a social service agency."

"No. You're just robbing the company blind."

Gavin winced. "I'm not admitting to anything."

"You don't need to. It's on the video.

He shrugged. "Sometimes I look the other way."

"You do more than that." Marko said, reminding Gavin of the Chinese man again, the one who humiliated him by making him show his cards.

He wasn't sure how to reply so he didn't.

"Look Gavin," Marko went on. "It's not complicated. You hire my brother or you don't and you lose your job and go to jail."

"Do I get the video after your brother gets hired?"

"You have a copy."

"All the copies I mean."

Marko smiled, showing nice white teeth. He was a well-groomed guy, clean shaven with tightly cropped greying hair. He wore clean jeans, brand new steel-toed boots and a tight-fitting golf shirt that revealed a trim, athletic body. He looked like a male model for a Viagra commercial.

"No," Marko said. "You'd just fire Steve and probably me."

There was no 'probably' about it, Gavin thought. If he had the video he'd fire Marko in a heartbeat.

"What stops you from squeezing me then? First it's a job for your brother and then what?"

"You have my word," Marko said. "I'm doing this for my brother. If you look after him you won't have a problem with me."

Gavin almost believed him. Still, he thought, murder was the better option. He just wished it didn't cost so much money to have someone killed.

"Let me talk to my boss and make sure he's ok with me hiring another guy. I think I can convince him."

"I'm not going to wait forever."

"How about if you give me until the end of the week," Gavin said, thinking that a few days should give the killer he'd hired more than enough time to take care of things.

"Don't jerk me around Gavin. Steve starts work Monday or I release it."

He nodded. "Fair enough."

Marko stood and reached for the office door.

"Say, d'you play poker?" Gavin asked suddenly.

Marko turned with the door half open. "Not professionally."

Gavin chuckled. Just because you were planning to have someone killed didn't mean you couldn't have a friendly conversation with them, particularly when the subject was poker.

"But you play?" he asked. "Hold 'em?"

"Just for fun in home games, never in the casino."

"Let me tell you about this hand I was in last night," Gavin said and told the tale of the $7,500 pot he'd lost. "That's why I'm in a bad mood today. Fucking bullshit."

Marko shrugged. "You can't win 'em all."

Gavin wasn't satisfied with Marko's response. "I had him crushed," he said, thinking Marko didn't understand the situation properly. "He hit a fucking 3 outer."

Marko furrowed his brow over frameless glasses. "Actually," he said. "The guy had ten outs."

"What the fuck are you talking about?"

"He could hit a king or any one of the three other cards on the board, including the seven. Presumably there were three of each of those still in the deck. That's 10 outs so he had about 20% equity, maybe a little more."

Gavin was confused at first but then realized Marko was right. He was an asshole, but he was right. It also sounded like he knew a lot more about poker than he'd let on.

"Even so," Gavin said, trying to salvage some of his pride. "The guy was a huge dog. It was still a major suck out."

"Sure..." Marko said, his tone condescending.

"What the fuck do you mean by that?"

"Nothing. I said sure. He had a little better than a 1 in 5 chance to hit on the river."

"Damn right. The fucking guy sucked out on me."

"Except you shouldn't have been in the hand in the first place."

Gavin simmered with rage. Who the hell did Marko think he was? "I had a flush," he said. "A fucking flush! That's a damn good hand!"

"Sure you did, after the turn."

"And before that I had a draw. I just needed to hit one club."

"Look Gavin, you can tell yourself whatever you want. You're the big-time casino poker player not me. If you ask me though, calling that big raise out of position with a weak hand against a tight player, leading out after the flop, and then 'calling off' all your chips on a thin draw, well, that's just bad poker."

Gavin felt like his head was going to explode. "What the fuck do you know?" he screamed. "You don't know shit. Get the fuck out of here!"

Marko smiled and slipped out the door.

Gavin banged an open palm on the corner of his desk so hard it hurt. Maybe he shouldn't have hired someone to kill Marko, he thought. Maybe he should kill the asshole himself.

Chapter 6

Marko checked his cell phone when he entered the warehouse coffee room and saw that he had two texts from his sister Ana. The first said:

Call me.

The second provided further elaboration:

He stole my TV. I think I should call the police.

Marko looked around the room and went to an empty table where he sat down and typed a text in response:

On a break. Ok to call you now?

He knew she was at work and he liked to text ahead to make sure it wasn't a bad time to call.

The reply came almost instantly:

Yes. Call me.

He looked around. There were only a few people in the coffee room and they were clustered at two or three tables well away from him, engaged in their own conversations. He punched her number into the phone.

"Hey Marko," she answered.

"Hey Bean." He'd been calling her Bean since she was 6 years old. As a little girl she'd been obsessed with a picture book called "Have You Seen My Jelly Bean?" about a princess who loses her jelly bean in the castle and the court jester who helps her find it.

"I think I should call the police."

"Don't do that."

"He stole my TV," she said.

"I'll talk to him. Maybe I can get it back."

"That won't work Marko. He'll have already pawned it."

"Yeah, I guess so."

"I know it's not the point, but I just bought the damn thing. Brad took the one good TV we had, along with his precious X Box."

Brad was her soon-to-be ex-husband.

"I know it's been frustrating."

"What are we going to do about him?"

"I'm working on it."

"Maybe calling the cops isn't a bad idea. It might be a wake-up call."

"I don't think that's the right thing to do."

"It might be."

"We need to help him, not turn him in."

"Tough love could be what he needs."

"Maybe one day," he said. "I want to try something first."

She sighed. "What should I tell Braden? His Uncle Steve stole our TV so he can buy drugs?"

"Don't tell him that."

"I won't," she sighed. "I'm just venting."

They were both silent for a few seconds and then she said, "It's hard to watch someone you love destroy their life."

"It won't come to that. We'll help him."

"He could have stolen anything else. Why didn't he take my

microwave? I never use that. I'm a single parent with a six year old. I need a TV."

"I'll replace it."

Her voice softened. "You can't do that."

"Yes, I can Bean."

"No, really Marko, you can't."

"I work in an electronics warehouse. I'll get a good deal."

"It's too much-"

"It's not, and I want to." He said it firmly, giving her little choice.

"I guess you do owe me after leaving me abandoned at a gas station."

Marko smiled. She liked to remind him of the time he used her as collateral for a gas can at a filling station. He was 15 years older than she was and when she was little he often took her out for ice cream or to the park. In his early twenties he was broke all the time and couldn't afford to fill the gas tank on his Ford Pinto, often adding just enough fuel to get the line on the gas gauge to rise barely above the E.

One time he ran out of gas, which was a common occurrence in those days, and they were forced to walk together to a nearby station. Unfortunately, he didn't have a gas can. The attendant said he could borrow one of theirs but he'd need to leave them something as collateral. In hindsight he could have probably used his driver's license but instead he offered to leave his sister behind.

It had seemed like a good idea at the time. He was only gone for a few minutes. But she never forgot, and as an adult, didn't miss an opportunity to harass him about it.

"If I buy you a new TV," he said. "Will that finally make up for the gas station incident?"

"I don't know," she said. "Scars like that run deep. I was only 8 years old. You can't heal a wound like that with a new TV."

"I see."

"But it's a good start."

"One step at a time," he said.

"One step at a time," she agreed and then sighed. "You know, Steve needs help, serious help."

"I'm going to help him."

"He needs to get into a program."

"We both know he won't go. What he needs is a job."

"He's not going to get a job Marko. He doesn't want one and no one will hire him anyway."

"I'm getting him a job at the warehouse."

"They won't hire him."

"Trust me. They will."

"Have you seen him lately? He looks worse. He's on meth."

"He's a recreational user," Marko said. "He parties too hard."

"I see people on meth all the time," Ana said. "He still has teeth but he looks bad."

"I'll help him."

"When was the last time you saw him?"

Marko didn't say anything. He hadn't seen Steve in weeks. Part of him knew that she was right and that his plan to save Steve was doomed to fail but he felt like he had to try.

There was a long silence and then she said, "Marko, I know you want to help him but it's complicated. You can't just get him a job and think everything will be alright."

"He needs a routine, a steady paycheck. He needs to know we care."

There was another long silence and then she said, "I love you Marko." Her voice sounded both tender and weary. "You know how naïve you sound, don't you?"

"He's our brother."

"He'll take advantage of you."

"Maybe," Marko said. Steve had taken advantage of him before and probably would again.

"Even if you manage to clean him up and get him a job, he won't keep it."

"I think he can."

"I don't know where you get that optimism from," she said. "It must come from your mother because I didn't get any of it." Marko had the same father as Ana and Steve but they had different mothers.

"It's not all optimism Bean," he said. "I've got some leverage."

"What kind of leverage?"

"Trust me. I'm going to make this work."

She started to say something but then abruptly said, "There's a call coming in. I gotta go save some lives."

"Ok. I've got to get back to work too. Those trucks don't load themselves."

"You're a good brother Marko."

They exchanged quick goodbyes and Marko disconnected the call. He glanced around the coffee room and saw that everyone had left while he was on the phone. His break was over. He sighed and scrolled through the photos on his phone until he found one of Steve and Ana when she was 15 years old and he was eleven. They were camping and had just finished having a water fight and they had their arms around one another, grinning from ear to ear. It was obvious from the photo that Ana had won that fight. She was the most fiercely competitive person he knew.

Marko blinked and felt tears in his eyes. There had been a time in his life when everything had seemed perfect. He was trying to hold onto what was left for as long as he could but lately it seemed harder to do. His sister was probably right. You could be as optimistic as you liked but that didn't stop things from turning to shit. It seemed so much in his life had done just that.

Chapter 7

Gavin spent the afternoon stewing in his office, sending texts on the burner phone Anton had given him. He'd only met Anton face-to-face on three occasions, had no idea what his last name was, or if Anton was even his real name. Anton had told Gavin to contact him only using the cheap burner phones he provided.

He was about to send another text when his phone pinged, indicating he'd received a new message. He read Anton's text and felt his blood pressure rise. It was a single word in reply to Gavin's multiple requests for a face-to-face meeting:

No

Gavin typed a message into the phone. He used a lot of abbreviations because the flip phone didn't have a proper keyboard and each letter had to be selected after scrolling through three or four options for each key.

Need 2 talk 2 U 2day

The reply came quickly:

Use phone

Frustrated Gavin stood and closed the office door. He returned to his desk, settled into his chair, and punched the number into the flip phone.

Anton answered on the second ring. "Yeah."

"This is Gavin."

"I know."

"I'd rather do this in person."

"And I'd like to fuck Beyoncé."

"Wouldn't we all," Gavin said even though he wasn't really into black chicks.

"What do you want?" Anton asked. Gavin had long suspected that Anton was part of the Russian mob. He didn't have a Russian accent but his name sounded Russian.

"Marko is still alive."

"So?"

"He's blackmailing me."

"That's your problem, not mine."

"It's a problem for both of us."

"No, it's your problem."

"My problem is your guy hasn't done the job yet."

"My guy?"

"Yes. Your guy. The guy you -" Gavin stopped - frustrated. He had hoped Anton would see the situation for what it was - a risk to their partnership. "If Marko releases that video we could all go to jail. This is a problem for both of us."

"I'm not worried."

"If we get caught, you'll get dragged into this."

"I wouldn't recommend that."

Gavin started to say something but stopped. Anton scared the shit out of him.

"Is that it?" Anton asked. "If it is, I'm done."

"No, no, wait," Gavin stammered. "I need money to pay the

guy... you know... the one you told me about... to do the job. I don't have enough cash."

"Again, not my problem."

"I was hoping you could help."

"You want a loan?"

"No, no, not a loan. I mean, we're partners, right? Marko's a threat to us. We both need him dead."

"I don't give a shit what happens to him. And we're not fucking partners. I own you."

This was not going the way Gavin had hoped. "You told me to hire someone to kill him."

"No. You asked if I knew a guy. I gave you a name and a number. If you want to pay him to so a job, that's up to you."

"You need to help me." Gavin could hear the whine in his voice but was helpless to stop it. "I'm out of options."

"No. You have options. You can kill the man yourself or give him what he wants."

"But he's blackmailing me."

"So? I'm blackmailing you. Are you going to try to kill me too?"

"No," Gavin said, completely deflated.

He'd made the mistake of thinking he and Anton were friends. He understood now that they weren't friends but he'd hoped they were business partners at least.

When he met Anton a few months ago and they'd started stealing from the warehouse, Gavin had mentioned his troubles with the 'alleged pervert situation'. Anton didn't offer any solutions to salvage his reputation but he did say he could arrange for Gavin to have a three-way with a couple of young hookers if he wanted. Gavin told him he wasn't into kids but if the girls were mature teenagers he was into it. Anton said the girls usually cost 4 figures a night each but that for him it was free. They were insanely hot and didn't disappoint.

He doubted that they were actually the ages they claimed to be,

14 and 15, thinking they were almost certainly older. But they dressed in little schoolgirl outfits and made a point of telling him their ages while they drained him of every ounce of semen his body could produce.

Not surprisingly, it had been a set up and now Anton had video footage of Gavin banging two young girls who repeatedly told him they were underage. Just like that, the extra cash he was making from the warehouse thefts almost completely disappeared. He still got a cut but it was hardly worth it in light of the fact that it threatened his job security and would land him in prison if they were caught. The workers he'd recruited in the warehouse to be part of the deal were making more than he did now, which hardly seemed fair given that he was their boss.

"I would never try to kill you Anton," Gavin said.

Anton chuckled. "It would be funny if you tried."

"You need to help me or I'm fucked."

Anton mimicked Gavin using a pathetic, whining baby-voice. "You need to help me Anton. I'm so fucked." Then back to his regular voice he said "Don't be a fucking pussy. If it were me, I'd kill him myself."

Gavin sighed. "I'd just fuck it up and get caught."

"But at least you'd be a fucking man."

"I guess so," Gavin said meekly.

"That guy I told you about, make sure you pay him. If you don't, he'll come after you, except, he'll kill your family first."

Gavin thought of his three ex-wives. If they were murdered, at least some good could come from this mess.

"And if you don't pay him," Anton went on. "You'll make me look bad. Trust me, you don't want to do that."

Gavin felt lost. "Ok," he managed to say.

"Use the phone to text me when the next pick-up is ready. Otherwise, don't call."

Anton disconnected.

Gavin stared at the phone for a few minutes and then searched 'recent calls'. He found the number he needed and pressed Send.

His head pounded. He knew now that he had two choices and neither of them involved a hired killer. He could give into the blackmail and hire Marko's brother or he could kill Marko himself. He needed to call off the hit man and cut his losses. His deposit was gone, he knew that - professional killers don't give refunds – but if he didn't cancel the contract, he was a dead man.

The phone rang and a computerized voice came over the line. "The cellular number you are trying to reach is no longer in service."

Gavin's hand shook. He tried the number again with the same result.

He stared at the phone in disbelief, his skin clammy with sweat. He dropped the phone to the desk, bent over and heaved into a waste paper basket at his feet.

Dead man puking, he thought, staring down at the trash can. He laughed, despite himself, and wiped his mouth with his sleeve.

That was him. *Dead man puking*.

Chapter 8

Marko Milanovic parked his Honda Civic in the driveway of his ex-wife's massive Point Grey home and walked to the front door. Linda had done well, marrying a dentist with a successful practice. Of course, she made good money herself as an executive for a real estate investment firm in Vancouver.

He rang the bell and a few seconds later Linda came to the door. His heart skipped a beat as it always did when he saw her. He'd never stopped loving her. What saddened him most was that he knew she still loved him.

She wore a pencil skirt with a silk blouse and had her hair up. She smiled at him and he felt that familiar ache in his chest.

"Marko," she said. "What brings you by?"

"Andy left a text book in my car," he said. "I thought he might need it."

She opened the door wider. "I'm sure he'll be glad to get it back. Come on in."

"Is he here?"

"No one's here. Just me."

Marko stepped into the foyer. He'd been there before but its excesses never failed to deflate him. The house belonged in Architectural Digest with its designer Italian mosaic tiles, coral chandelier, and floating spiral staircase.

He handed her the text book, feeling like a child.

She took it from him and set it down on an elaborate foyer table made of stone balustrades. "I mean it. Come in and talk to me. I miss you."

He nodded and she led him to the living room. He sat on a leather couch while she left to get them each a drink.

Andy was their son. He was 18 years old and in his first year of university at UBC. After the divorce 10 years ago, Linda had moved out of their modest suburban home leaving Marko to raise their son. Andy had lived with Marko until September when he came to live with his mother so he could be closer to school. The fact that Marko couldn't afford the mortgage on his house any longer was a factor in that decision as well. Marko held onto the house as long as he could after losing his job as a Sales Process Analyst 18 months earlier, racking up debt on his credit line until it consumed nearly all the equity he had in the house. He had no choice but to sell and downsize to an apartment.

Linda returned with drinks, sweeping effortlessly into the room, her red hair down. She handed him his beer, Stella Artois in a glass. She hadn't needed to ask what he drank. He was nothing if not predictable.

She set her wine glass on the coffee table and sat on the couch beside him.

"How are things going?" she asked.

He lied and said things were going well. There was no need to tell her he had a brain tumor.

"How's the new place?"

"Fine. I'm a simple man with simple needs."

"I know about that. So where are you?"

"Collingwood," he said. Collingwood was a neighborhood in East Vancouver bordering the City of Burnaby. The realtors described the area as up and coming. The building he was in had a way to go before it was either up or coming. "It's near Ana's station house. Just a few blocks away."

"How is Ana?"

"Better. She's back at work."

"That's good. I always liked her."

Marko found it hard to concentrate with Linda so close to him. The wounds had healed over time. He'd eventually come to understand that she couldn't change the way she was. He just wished it could be different, that they could be together and share a normal family life.

"How's the job?" she asked.

He took a sip of his beer. "Mindlessly boring but it's a paycheck."

"You can do so much more."

He and Linda had been high school sweethearts. Like him, she was north of fifty, but she looked as beautiful to him as the day they met.

"I guess that two year diploma from Douglas College doesn't carry as much weight as I thought it would."

She'd gone to UBC and then gotten her MBA from Queen's School of Business.

"You don't give yourself enough credit," she said. "I could make a few calls."

"You don't need to do that. I'm doing fine. I'm in the market."

He did invest in the market but it was an overstatement to say he was doing fine.

She reached for her glass. "That's good."

"I'm getting Steve a job there."

"At the warehouse?"

"Yeah, he starts next week."

She took a sip of the wine and set the glass back on the table. "Really? How's he doing?"

"Good," he lied. "He's ready to turn his life around."

"That's wonderful. I know you worry about him."

"How are you doing?"

"Good. I miss you though."

The words tore him apart. It was hard to be near her. It hurt so much but he needed her in his life. What choice did he have? She must have read something on his face because her expression changed and she looked sad.

"I'm sorry," she said. "I wish I could be the person you want me to be."

He took her hand in his. "I know."

She gave him a weak smile. "You should find a nice girl."

He thought he had found a nice girl in high school. He'd thought they were happy. It became evident early in their marriage though that they were not a good match in the bedroom. Often he was too tired to make love and when he did, he apparently lacked imagination. She wanted to have sex all the time and yet when they did, she seemed unfulfilled.

There had been affairs, after which she'd apologize and tell him that she loved him and that the other men meant nothing to her. It was just sex, she said, as if that would make it more palatable.

Counselling hadn't helped. She told him that she loved him but that she couldn't be happy in a monogamous relationship. She didn't want them to keep secrets anymore. She said they could both be free to have affairs without feeling guilty about it. It didn't need to change how they felt about each other.

But he wanted the white picket fence. He wanted the suburban family dream with backyard bar-b-ques. She was the only woman he wanted to be with.

They separated and later divorced. A few years later she married a dentist named Dieter, a tall, severe looking man who was presumably amenable to an 'open marriage.'

He sighed. "I've dated a few times. Nobody's clicked that's all."

She kissed him gently on the forehead. "Maybe one day when we're old and grey we can be together again."

Marko wasn't sure if he would live that long. He stood and managed a smile that probably conveyed more sadness than joy. "I should go."

She stood and hugged him. "It was wonderful to see you."

"Tell Andy I stopped by."

"I will."

There was an awkward moment as Marko tried to think of a way to segue into the second reason for his visit.

"Do you mind if I use your computer to check my email?"

She looked perplexed.

"My phone's dead," he lied. "I'm expecting an important email and I wanted to check for it."

"Ah, sure. Do you want to use my phone or I have a tablet or a laptop."

"You have a desktop computer don't you?"

"I guess so. No one uses it anymore. It's in the basement."

"That'll be perfect," he said. "I'll just be a minute."

Marko moved quickly to the basement stairs. He had a flash drive in the front pocket of his jeans containing video footage from the warehouse. He'd backed the file up to a cloud server and emailed it to himself but he thought it would be good if someone else had a copy as well. He thought about emailing it to Ana but then he'd have to explain the video and he didn't want to do that. In the end, he decided to download the file onto his ex-wife's computer where no one would think to look for it.

He knew he was being a little paranoid but even so, he felt

strangely comforted knowing the download was complete. He didn't think Gavin would try anything, but then again he wouldn't put anything past him either.

Chapter 9

Ana Marshall set a serving bowl of spaghetti and meatballs on the kitchen table in front of her six year old son, Braden.

"Dinner is served," she said, more for the benefit of the guest at their table, her partner Rick Lebeck, than for her son.

Braden reached for the serving spoon and awkwardly shoveled noodles and meatballs onto his plate. He liked to do it himself, she knew. It made him feel like a big boy.

"That's enough honey," she said. "Once you eat that, you can have more."

"But I'm hungry," he said.

"We'll see, sweetie." She turned to Rick and added, "Help yourself."

He smiled and moved the bowl beside his plate. "It looks delicious."

She'd invited Rick to dinner after their shift ended. She hadn't planned to, the words just came out of her mouth. She wasn't sure why. After all they'd just worked a twelve hour shift together.

"When's the TV coming home?" Braden asked.

He didn't know the TV had been stolen. Ana had told him it broke and that the TV-man was fixing it. He was six years old and didn't know that no one fixed TVs anymore. They were disposable, like razor blades, paper plates and marriages.

"Soon honey," she said. "Maybe tomorrow."

She'd been letting him watch his Transformer cartoons on her iPad and as a result, he seemed reasonably content to wait another day.

After dinner she cleaned up the dishes while Rick played Lego with Braden. He was surprisingly good with children and she was amazed by how quickly her son warmed to him. When it was time for Braden to go to bed, he asked if Rick could read his bedtime story.

She agreed and once Braden had brushed his teeth, put on his pajamas, and picked out a story book, he dragged Rick by the hand to his bedroom. Ana followed and told him she would give him a goodnight kiss after he'd had his story read.

She went to her bedroom across the hall and listened while Rick read The Grinch Who Stole Christmas to her son. Christmas was still months away but it was one of Braden's favorites. She sat on the edge of the bed, not wanting to interfere but wanting to stay close by.

Rick read the story with more animation in his voice than she ever managed when she read to her son. She couldn't remember her soon-to-be ex, Brad, ever reading to him.

When Rick neared the end of the story she stood and started toward the hallway.

"And what happened, then?" Rick read. "Well, in Whoville they say – that the Grinch's small heart grew three sizes that day,"

"My mommy has a broken heart," Braden said.

Ana stopped at her bedroom door, momentarily frozen.

"Is that so?" Rick said.

"Ah-huh, because my daddy slept with a girl who drinks like a fish."

51

Ana didn't know if she should burst out laughing or crawl into a hole.

"I'm sure you make your mommy's heart feel better." Rick's reply came smoothly, without hesitation. He carried on reading as if nothing had happened.

When he'd finished the story and the Grinch had carved the roast beast for the Whos of Whoville, Ana had no choice but to cross the hall into Braden's bedroom, trying not to show her embarrassment. She suspected she was doing a poor job of it.

Rick gave her a reassuring smile.

"Time to go to sleep young man," she said.

"Good night little guy," Rick said and stood.

Ana came further into the room "What do you say to Rick?" she prompted.

"Thank you for reading me a story," Braden said.

Ana felt a tug at her heart. She'd obviously exposed her son to more of her dysfunctional marriage than she'd realized. What kind of mother does that, she wondered. What other mental traumas had she inflicted on him?

"You're welcome," Rick said.   He nodded to Ana and then slipped out of the room.

She sat on the edge of Braden's bed and adjusted his covers. He beamed up at her, apparently oblivious to the mental scars she imagined had been inflicted on him. He chatted happily about his day and she felt a wave of emotion wash over her that was so powerful it was frightening.   There were times when the love she felt for her son overwhelmed her.

"I love you mommy," he said.

She felt herself choke up. "I love you too honey."

She kissed him on the forehead and left the room.

When she came downstairs she found Rick in the kitchen, checking his phone.

"Well that was embarrassing," she said.

He looked up and slid his phone back into his pocket. "Don't worry about it. Kids say the darndest things."

She exhaled loudly. "I need some wine."

She went to the counter and poured them both a second glass of Merlot, hers a little fuller, to finish off the bottle they'd had with dinner. Rick had brought two bottles of wine with him, one red and one white. She assumed he didn't keep cases of wine in the trunk of his car so he must have made a detour to the liquor store on his way here. It was no wonder he did well with the ladies.

That, and those dimples and gorgeous blue eyes, she thought.

They moved to the living room where they sat on the adjacent matching faux-suede couch and loveseat and stared at the empty stand where the TV had once been.

"So you're getting the TV fixed are you?" he said.

She smiled. "Not unlike Braden's goldfish that died, he'll never know it's not the same one. Marko offered to replace it."

"That's good of him."

"Yeah, well," she said. "He owes me."

"And he probably gets a good deal, working at the warehouse."

She nodded. "He says he's getting my brother Steve a job there."

"The same brother who stole your TV?"

"One and the same."

"Wow. Is it a good idea for him to work in a warehouse full of them?"

She laughed. "Probably not. I'm surprised they're hiring him."

"How did Marko manage that?"

"I don't know," she said. "He says he has leverage, whatever that means."

Rick grinned. "Maybe he's blackmailing someone."

They both laughed. The idea was ridiculous.

Lukin came out of his bed in the corner of the room and jumped up on the love seat beside Ana. She petted him and told him he was a good boy.

There was a period of silence and then Rick said. "I'm sorry about the other day, you know, pressing too hard and everything. I just wanted you to know I'm here for you."

"I know," she said. She smiled and gazed down at the glass in her hand. Without looking up, she said "You know, it wasn't just that kid who fell. I mean, that was a big part of it, but, I don't know, we learn to turn it off. We convince ourselves that life isn't so temporary, and random, and unfair, but we can't unsee the shit we see. It becomes part of us."

"I know."

She looked up and saw that he was staring at her. She felt safe, or maybe a little drunk. "You bottle it all up for so long you get numb to the point where you aren't sure you're capable of an honest emotion anymore. You think you're fine, you think you're dealing with this shit but then something knocks you off balance."

"This stuff takes a toll on us."

"It bothered me that I was so weak, that I couldn't suck it up and carry on."

"'Sucking it up' never works, at least not in the long run."

She smiled ruefully. "That's a lesson I'm learning."

Rick nodded thoughtfully and they were quiet for a while. It was a comfortable silence. She set her drink back on the coffee table and turned her attention to the dog, petting the thick white fur around his neck. After a while she looked up.

Rick was still in his uniform, impossibly pressed, neatly tucked and perfectly groomed. He was unlike any man she'd ever known. He was caring and thoughtful and empathetic. She had no frame of reference for a man like that.

"You can lean on people. You don't have to carry it all yourself," he said.

Ana nodded and downed the last of her wine. "I know a girl who drinks like a fish that I'd like to see carried somewhere."

She felt bad for breaking the emotional connection but she couldn't help herself.

He laughed but it sounded forced. "I can help with that," he said. "Is there a particular cliff I should carry her to or were you thinking I should carry her to a dumpster?"

"A cliff is good," she said, relieved he was playing along. "I mean, assuming that jagged rocks are involved."

"Obviously."

"A snake-filled pit would work too."

"I had no idea you had these homicidal tendencies."

"There's plenty you don't know about me," she said, aware that the comment sounded flirtatious. Was she deliberately sending mixed signals, she wondered, or did she really have no idea what she wanted?

He stared into her eyes. "I'd like to know more about you."

If she had any doubts about whether or not he had feelings for her, they were gone. Unfortunately she had no idea what she wanted. Clearly that extra glass of wine had been a mistake.

"Don't you have a harem of women to keep you busy?" she asked.

She knew she was deflecting. She still wasn't sure how she felt about Rick. Then again, who was she kidding? She'd invited him over for dinner. He'd read her son a bedtime story. She was flirting with him.

"I'm not seeing anyone. I haven't been seeing anyone for a while."

Ana rose from the couch, unsure how to respond, unsure how she felt. She picked up her wine glass and took it to the kitchen where she rinsed it in the sink. Rick followed her. She turned to him.

"Rick, I'm not sure if I'm ready for a relationship right now."

He took the empty wine glass from her, set it on the counter top, and took her hand in his. "That's ok," he said. "I just want you to know, I'm here for you." He smiled, a little weakly. "I should get going."

She felt relieved although she wasn't sure why. They walked together to the door and chatted for a while about innocuous things. When he left she felt a pang of regret. She wished she'd had the courage to sleep with him. God knows she needed a good lay. It had been over six months since she'd had sex with anyone.

As for good sex, she hadn't had that since college.

Chapter 10

Wednesday October 19

Ana stared at the bacon on her plate and thought that if she had to choose - bacon or sex for the rest of her life - she would choose bacon. She picked up a piece and took a bite without any feeling of guilt. One of the benefits of exercise was that she could eat anything she wanted.

It was just after 11 am. Ana and her friend Dana Becker had dropped their kids off at school, played squash at the Bonsor Recreation Centre in Burnaby and then gone to the pool for a swim and a hot tub before stopping for breakfast at a nearby diner on Kingsway.

"So you didn't sleep with him?" Dana asked, stirring a bowl of yogurt and granola with a spoon.

Dana and Ana looked similar in many ways. Both women were in their mid-thirties, athletic, tall, with broad swimmer's shoulders and long legs. The difference was that Dana was the full package in her color-coordinated designer yoga outfit, stylish haircut, and tastefully applied make-up, while Ana in her mismatched clothing, pony tail, and complete lack of make-up looked like a candidate for a make-over show.

"That's none of your business," Ana said. "But no."

"That's too bad. It would have made for more interesting conversation if you had."

Ana ate another piece of bacon. "Did I tell you that when I was off work, Rick and I went out for breakfast one morning to catch up?"

Dana gave no indication that she'd heard the story before.

"I mean, we didn't go anywhere classy like this," Ana said, looking around the restaurant. "Obviously."

The diner they were in was almost empty, likely because the food was mediocre and the restaurant had received less than stellar reviews on Yelp.

"This is pretty uptown," Dana said wryly, brushing blonde hair over her ear.

"Instead we went to this place on West 4th. Rick ordered Eggs Benedict, but not regular Eggs Benedict. This one had smoked salmon and capers and fucking organic cream cheese flown in that morning from a tiny village in the south of France."

"I thought cream cheese came from Philadelphia."

"The regular stuff might but this was fancy Dijon Cream Cheese from special French cows or something." Ana paused and dipped a piece of slightly burnt toast into the pale straw-colored yoke of a fried egg. "So anyway," she said, biting into the toast. "Our breakfast comes and do you know what Rick does?"

Dana made no effort to guess, assuming correctly that it was a rhetorical question.

"He pulls out his cell phone and takes pictures of it," Ana said.

"Oh my God, he's a foodie."

"Yeah. So I ask him, 'why are you taking a picture of your food' and he says, 'it's for my blog'."

"Wow."

"I know. I don't know if I can sleep with a guy who takes pictures of food and then blogs about it."

"He can probably cook though," Dana said.

58

Ana nodded thoughtfully. "That would be nice. And he's great with Braden."

"Not to mention, easy on the eyes."

"That too. I mean, he makes Brad look like such a….such a…."

"Shitheel," Dana finished the sentence for her.

"Yeah."

Of course Brad didn't need help to look bad. He could handle that on his own. He'd been a bad husband on many levels. Aside from sleeping around with a girl who drinks like a fish, he was selfish, inconsiderate, irresponsible and immature. He couldn't hold a job. He spent 'their' money on useless shit for himself. He came and went as he pleased without bothering to tell her where he was going or when he'd be back and when he was home he played video games like he was still in college. He spent time with Braden when it was convenient for him but he was never there for the day-to-day parenting.

So why did his cheating break her heart? That was a good question, she thought. Despite her efforts to ignore his shortcomings, on some level she knew, even then, that she had a lousy marriage. What his infidelity had done was pry at the cracks in her armor, her self-confidence.

She'd put so much energy into convincing herself that she was happy that when it was suddenly over she felt untethered, unsure of who she was. That, more than anything had drawn her to the cupboard where she kept those glass jars.

The two women ate and talked. They'd been friends since college. Both were athletes in school, competing on their university swim team. They were close and talked about personal things but Ana never fully opened up to her friend. Not really. The relationship stuff – yes - but they never talked about the things she kept in glass jars.

"Steve stole my TV the other night," Ana said.

"No shit? What the hell?"

Ana relayed the story of Steve's 2 am visit, her invitation for him to crash on the couch and waking up in the morning to find the TV gone.

"Did you call the cops?"

"No, Marko's replacing the TV. He wants to help Steve. He says he's going to get him a job at the warehouse."

"I don't know why you still talk to that little bastard. He's bad news."

Ana sighed. "He's my brother."

"You have more patience than I do. I'd rip his balls off," Dana said and took a sip of orange juice.

"From the way he was scratching them the other night they may be ready to fall off on their own."

Juice sprayed from Dana's mouth. "Oh my God! That's so gross."

They carried on their conversation, moving from topic to topic with the ease of old friends. They reminisced about their glory days in college. Ana talked about Braden and how he was enjoying Kindergarten. Dana was looking forward to going on a two week vacation with her husband and kids. They were leaving the next day for Greece and Italy. Of course no vacation would be complete without the kid's tutor and nanny.

Dana's husband, like the rest of her life, was perfect. He was smart, successful, an excellent father, a loving husband, and ridiculously handsome. Ana's friends in university were athletes and they'd all dated athletic guys who were motivated, had aspirations and applied themselves. Ana was the exception. She'd always been attracted to the slacker, musician type; guys like Brad who played in a band, had an aversion to responsibility and who took pride in looking like they'd slept in the back of a van.

Brad had been a drummer in a handful of bands since college, none of which had achieved much success. He did have one brush with greatness though. Matt Wood, the lead singer for 'The Screaming Bunnies', the band Brad was in when she'd first met him, left to form

'Jackknife Sugar-Truck', a band that today filled stadiums all over the world. Ana suspected that Brad's unwillingness to grow up was due in large part to his inability to latch onto Matt's shooting star.

Or maybe, she thought, he was just a self-absorbed asshole.

The bill came and Dana took it. She'd lost the squash game and the loser always paid.

After Dana paid they put on their coats, grabbed their purses and went outside. It was cloudy and cool but it wasn't raining. There were two types of weather in Vancouver this time of year: it was either 'raining' or 'well, at least it's not raining.'

When they reached the parking lot Dana asked, "So are you going to sleep with him or what?"

"I don't know. It's complicated. We work together."

"That's not necessarily a bad thing."

"He takes pictures of his food."

"True. And he blogs about it."

"I'm pretty sure he artificially whitens his teeth."

"So? What have you got against white teeth?" Dana asked.

Ana tilted her head, acknowledging that her friend had a point. Why complain about dental hygiene? It was time to play her trump card.

"He likes Bruno Mars," she said.

Dana winced. "My daughter likes Bruno Mars."

"She's eight."

"No man is perfect."

"No, but at least Brad had good taste in music."

"True, but he was a lousy husband and terrible in bed."

Ana raised her eyebrows. "How do you know Brad was terrible in bed?"

"It's just what I've heard."

Ana nodded. "I've heard that too."

They stopped in front of her Sunfire.

"My advice is to sleep with him," Dana said. "Email me the details."

"D'you want video?"

"Of course."

Ana hugged her. "I'm going to miss you."

"I'll miss you too but then I'll look outside and realize where I am and I'll get over it."

They said goodbye and Ana got into her car. She waited until Dana drove away in her white Toyota Prius, then she started her car and glanced in the rearview mirror. She looked at her reflection. She'd never thought of herself as attractive. She'd always been a tomboy, rarely wore makeup and had never known what to do with her straight, mousy brown hair, except put it in a ponytail.

Rick was a good-looking man who could easily find a woman who had a wardrobe that consisted of something other than jeans, sweatpants, and navy blue paramedic slacks.

She glanced down at the clock in the car and saw that it was nearly noon. She needed to sleep this afternoon before Braden came home from school. She'd spend a couple of hours with her son, they'd have dinner together, she'd drop him off at the overnight babysitter's house, and then she'd go to work for her first night shift in weeks.

Hopefully it would be uneventful.

TRIPLE BARREL

Chapter 11

Pete Pappas leaned against the wall of his East Vancouver apartment building and exhaled cigarette smoke. He wore dark jeans, leather boots and a black hooded sweatshirt under a black leather jacket - the perfect ensemble for the intimidating mother-fucker that he was.

Pete worked part time in a dollar store which didn't sound intimidating but he preferred to think of himself as a hired killer, who also happened to work part-time in a dollar store. If tonight went well, he thought, he could quit his day-job for good.

Pete regarded himself as a professional killer, although technically he'd never killed anyone for cash. He'd done it for other forms of payment like tickets to a hockey game or sexual favors, which in his opinion amounted to the same thing. Good tickets to a Canucks game cost $350 a pop. Tonight's job though would represent his first proper payday as a professional hitman, something he took very seriously.

The job was a referral from Kevin, a computer hacker he knew. Kevin had called a few days earlier and asked if he wanted to make an easy $7,500. The answer to that question was obvious. He worked in a fucking dollar store.

Kevin said he should expect a call from a guy named Gavin who would ask him to kill a warehouse worker named Marko. If Pete wanted the job he should say his fee was $10,000. He should demand $2,500 up front and another $7,500 when the job was done. Kevin would take $2,500 for the referral and Pete would keep $7,500 when the warehouse worker was dead.

$7,500 was good money for Pete, a lot more than he could make stocking shelves at the dollar store. He flicked his cigarette butt onto the concrete sidewalk and checked the time on his phone. It was 8:10 pm.

His fucking ride was late.

Pete scratched the coarse black beard that covered most of his acne-scarred face and turned his gaze back to the apartment building. Nearly every balcony was crammed with broken barbeques, kid's bikes, ratty sofas, and other junk. He spit onto the grass beside the sidewalk, picked up the backpack at his feet and wandered to the curb.

Pete had previously done some work for Kevin, mostly roughing up Johns who got out of line with one of Kevin's girls. He didn't know a lot about Kevin's business but he knew that computers were an important part of everything Kevin was into. On-line prostitution and porn websites seemed to be his main thing, but he also knew that Kevin was involved in internet scams, blackmail, and fencing stolen goods on the web. Pete had high hopes for this job, thinking it could lead to bigger things, which was why he'd recruited someone to help.

That and the fact that his '97 Chevy Lumina needed a new starter and he didn't have the cash to fix it. He didn't know how to hotwire a car so unless he wanted to take the bus home after killing someone, he needed a partner with wheels.

Kevin had been clear that the job needed to be done soon. Apparently Gavin, the guy who'd hired him, was having second thoughts. Kevin told Pete to make sure he didn't talk to Gavin until after the job was done. Pete didn't understand why, but he didn't need to. He did as he was told. He understood his role.

He was muscle, which was why he made it a priority to work out. He wasn't into the gym scene but he kept a set of barbells and a bench in his apartment. He preferred to workout at home because there was nobody there to complain if he wanted to smoke a cigarette between reps.

A maroon Chrysler Sebring pulled up to the curb. Dance music pulsed from the car's stereo, the bass shaking the car's frame.

It was about fucking time, Pete thought. He was worried that he may have made a mistake in who he'd recruited for the job but it wasn't like he had much choice. Most of the people he knew were idiots and only a few of them had cars. He swung the passenger door open.

"Yo," the man behind the wheel said. He was a huge muscle-bound mass of a man with no neck wearing tear-away track pants and a tank top. It was fucking October, Pete thought, and the guy was wearing a tank top.

His name was Chewy. It wasn't a nickname. It was his actual name. His father was a huge Star Wars fan and had named his four kids Luke, Han, Leia and Chewy. But for Chewy, sharing a name with the world's most famous Wookie wasn't ridiculous enough so he legally changed his last name from Olsen to Awesome.

Pete dropped the backpack on the floor in front of the passenger seat and climbed in.

'Fuck I hate this music," he said, turning the stereo off and closing the door. "How do you listen to that crap?"

Chewy lifted a half filled quart of chocolate milk to his lips, pounded it, and tossed the empty container into the back seat. There were at least a half dozen similar empty containers back there along with discarded protein bar wrappers, a gym bag, some clothing, and a few body building magazines.

The car smelled like stale milk and sweat.

"It gets me amped man," he said, wiping his mouth with the back of his hand. "You can put that metal shit on though if you like."

Pete ignored the comment, leaving the volume turned off. "Where the fuck have you been?"

"Yeah, sorry about that dude." Chewy pulled the Seebring away from the curb. "I was gettin' my knob polished."

Pete grunted. He hoped the knob-polishing had taken place somewhere other than the front seat of the car.

"Where to?" Chewy asked.

"Get on Kingsway and head to Burnaby."

"We're going to fucking Burnaby?"

"Head toward Burnaby. He lives in Collingwood. That's still Vancouver"

"Barely," Chewy grumbled. "Fucking Korea Town."

Pete grunted noncommittally.

"So, the plan is to rough this guy up?" Chewy said. "Fuckin' A man"

Pete hadn't told Chewy what the plan actually was. He decided it was best to keep him on a short leash and in the dark.

"Not necessarily," Pete said. "The goal is to get copies of a computer file the guy has. That's what we're getting paid for. Get his laptop, phone, tablets, discs, flash drives, whatever might have this file."

"What's on the file?"

"No idea."

"You're running the show dude. How do we know we have all the copies, if we don't even know what we're looking for?"

"We don't need to know what the file is. We just take everything it might be on."

Chewy nodded. "What if he has it on the cloud or whatever?"

"Not our problem. I have a computer guy who can deal with that. Our job is to get every device it might be on. He'll take it from there."

Pete didn't have a computer guy. It was the other way around. Kevin was the computer guy and he had Pete to run errands for him.

"Whatever man," Chewy said. "500 bucks is 500 bucks."

Pete had told Chewy he was being paid $1,000 for the job and that they'd split it 50/50.

When they got close, Pete gave directions to the apartment and they parked across the street from the building where Marko Milanovic lived. It was a dingy eyesore across the street from a car dealership and a gas station with residential units above mostly vacant retail space.

"The guy lives in an apartment so we need to keep the noise down," Pete said.

Chewy nodded.

Pete grabbed the backpack. "Follow my lead."

The two men got out of the car. Pete took a pair of leather gloves out of the backpack and slipped them on. The only other item in the bag was a roll of duct tape. The two men nodded to each other and crossed the street. Pete carried the backpack in one hand and slipped the other into his jacket pocket where he felt the weight of the .22 Ruger inside.

Chapter 12

Marko Milanovic stared blankly at the chipped Formica countertop in his kitchen and listened to the sound of the shower running. His brother Steve was in the bathroom, cleaning up.

Marko sighed. Things hadn't gone well. Ana was right. He'd been naïve.

Earlier that day he'd picked his brother up. Steve was high and the only way Marko could convince his brother to come with him was the promise of money.

He tried to talk to Steve about the job, about moving in with him, about starting a new life, but it was futile. He wasn't interested. They drove aimlessly for nearly an hour until Marko stopped to get them a burger at a fast food restaurant. But Steve wasn't hungry. He wanted money and he wanted to go home.

Defeated, but not quite ready to surrender, Marko drove to his Collingwood apartment so his brother could at least have a shower. He'd previously bought some clothes for Steve and promised him that if he showered and dressed in clean clothes he'd take him home and give him money.

The water in the bathroom stopped running. Marko glanced at the big screen TV, still in its box against a wall in the living room. He slid his phone out of his pocket and sent Ana a text. She responded immediately indicating it was ok to call. He selected her number and pressed send.

"Hey Marko," she answered. "What's up?"

"You home tonight, Bean?"

"Nope. Working my first night shift."

"Is Braden home with a sitter?"

"No. He's with an overnight sitter. Why?"

"I was going to drop off the TV."

"You don't have to do that."

"Too late, I already have it."

"It's not necessary Marko."

"It's here in my apartment. I'm tripping over it. If I don't deliver it soon, I'm going to hurt myself."

"Well, if you put it that way I guess, I don't you to get hurt."

"The sooner I drop it off, the safer I'll be."

"You have a key to my place. You can drop it off if you want."

Marko wandered over to the key hook mounted near the front door and found the one to Ana's place. It was a single key on a PJ20 key ring. He wasn't sure what PJ20 stood for but he thought it might have something to do with a band she liked. "What's your address again?"

"You know where I live."

"Sort of," he said. He returned to the kitchen and set the key down on the counter. "I know where your complex is. I'm just not positive which unit is yours."

"You're kidding? How can you not know where I live?"

"Do you know where I live?"

"You just moved. I've been in my place for years."

"I usually look for your car in the driveway."

"Jesus Marko. If Steve can find it, I would think you can."

"Just give me the address."

She gave it to him and he wrote it down on a pad of paper. They talked for a while longer. At one point Marko almost told her about the tumor but he stopped himself. He didn't want to worry anyone, at least until he knew how serious it was. Besides, if he was going to tell her, he didn't want it to be over the phone.

When the conversation ended he wandered into the living room and hit a button on the CD player. Sarah McLaughlin's voice floated into the room. He heard the bathroom door open and the sound of footsteps crossing the hall to the spare bedroom.

The spare bedroom was where Marko had hoped Steve would stay until he'd gotten on his feet. But Steve wasn't interested. He didn't care about anything except getting high.

"Don't you want a better life?" Marko had asked him.

"I have a better life," Steve said. "You just don't understand it."

"Explain it to me."

"I can't explain it to you man. You don't know what it's like to feel like fuckin' superman, to feel fucking invincible. You don't understand 'cause you don't use."

Marko realized how foolish he'd been. Steve wasn't a recreational drug user who partied too hard. He was an addict.

It was another blow for him. First he'd lost the love of his life. Then he'd lost his job and his house. His son had moved on. He knew the empty nest was the natural order of things but it still left an aching hole. On top of that he had a tumor growing inside his skull. He didn't know yet whether it was cancer or not. In his mind, he had a 50/50 chance of surviving. He might have cancer or he might not. He might live or he might not.

And so, he'd found a purpose, a reason to live. He would save his brother. Only Steve didn't want to be saved and even if he did, Marko was ill-equipped to help him.

There was one upside to the situation though, he thought. He no longer had a reason to blackmail Gavin and was free to report him and the others involved. Unfortunately, one of the others involved had a connection to his son that could complicate things. But life was like that. Nothing was ever easy.

He was about to check on Steve when he heard a knock at the door.

Chapter 13

Pete knocked on Marko Milanovic's apartment door with a gloved hand and nodded to Chewy who stood outside the sight line of the door's viewfinder.

"Who is it?" a voice asked from behind the door.

"It's Walter from down the hall," Pete said. "I think I dinged your car in the lot."

The door opened a crack, held by a chain. Chick-music was playing on the stereo, an earnest piano ballad drifting into the hallway. A trim man with salt and pepper hair appeared in the opening. Pete recognized him from the photo he'd been given.

"You hit my car?" Marko asked.

"Yeah, you should take a look at it. I'll need to give you my registration and all that."

"What did you say your name was?"

"Walter."

"Ok Walter. Give me a few minutes. I'll meet you down there."

Marko moved away from the door, presumably planning to close it.

That wasn't how Pete had planned it. He thought Marko would open the door and they'd push their way into the apartment right away. But it wasn't a problem. They could just wait until Marko came out.

Pete turned to give Chewy a signal but the big man barreled past him, knocking Pete out of the way and driving his massive shoulder into the door as it was closing. There was an audible crack and the security chain gave way, torn from the frame. The door flew open.

Pete stood stupidly in the hallway as Chewy charged at the man like an angry linebacker. Marko reeled backwards, looking confused and terrified as Chewy slammed into him, driving him to the floor.

"What the fuck," Pete muttered.

Chewy pinned the man to the carpet and pummeled him with his fists, screaming, "How d'you like that Motherfucker!"

Pete glanced anxiously down the hallway but none of the doors appeared to have opened. "Enough, Chewy, stop!" he said and stepped into the apartment, closing the door as best he could, jagged splinters protruding from the cracked frame.

Chewy jumped to his feet and kicked the man in the ribs.

"What the fuck are you doing?" Pete said.

Chewy grinned like a psychopath. "Taking care of business."

"Well, fucking stop already."

Chewy looked down at Marko and gave him another quick kick to the ribs. Marko rolled onto his side and curled into the fetal position, groaning. His face was a mess, blood streaming from his nose and split lip. His glasses lay broken on the carpet beside him.

Pete set the backpack down, pulled the Ruger from his jacket pocket and levelled it at Chewy.

"What part of 'follow my lead' don't you understand?" he said.

Chewy stared at the gun. "Chill, bro."

"What part of 'follow my lead' don't you understand?" Pete repeated.

"The dude wasn't gonna let us in."

"All we had to do was fucking wait. He was coming out."

"So? Now he knows we aren't fucking around,"

"And so does the whole fucking building."

Chewy hadn't taken his eyes off the gun, still pointed at him. "My bad, dude. Sometimes I get a little amped."

Pete took a deep breath and motioned with the gun. "Get him on the couch."

"You didn't tell me you had a gun."

"I have a gun," Pete said, deadpan.

Marko groaned, lifted his head, and spit bloody saliva on the carpet.

"What are you waiting for?" Pete said. "The guy's built like a 12 year old girl. Pick him up."

"Stop pointing the fucking gun at me. We're on the same side dude. You're making me nervous."

Pete lowered the gun.

Chewy nodded, bent down, lifted Marko onto his shoulder and dropped him on a clean, well-worn couch.

"Let's keep the noise down from now on," Pete said. "Understand?"

Chewy grunted.

Marko shifted on the couch, groaning, until he more or less managed to get into a sitting position. He wiped blood away from his brow and stared at them.

Pete moved to the coffee table and sat on the edge, facing Marko.

"What do you want?" Marko asked, his voice tight and barely audible.

Pete lifted the gun and pressed the muzzle to Marko's head. "I think you know."

"No idea."

"We came for a computer file."

Marko blinked and Pete saw recognition in his eyes. "I don't know what you're talking about."

"I think you do."

Marko said nothing and closed his eyes.

"There's no need for things to get violent," Pete said without a trace of irony. "Just give us what we want."

Marko spit blood onto the sofa cushion between his legs, apparently not concerned about the upholstery.

Pete pressed the gun harder against his head. "Where are the files?"

Marko lifted his head, with obvious effort, and stared into Pete's eyes. "Fuck you," he wheezed.

Pete turned to Chewy. "There's duct tape in my bag. Tape him up so he can't move."

Chewy looked disappointed. "I can beat it out of him."

"It'll be faster and quieter to find what we need ourselves. Tape him up."

Pete had been told that recovering all the computer devices and files was just as important as killing the man. He couldn't afford to fuck up that part of the job. He needed to find every memory stick, every cell phone, and every laptop and tablet in the apartment. Those had been Gavin's instructions but the directive had also come from Kevin who said he wanted to see all the computer stuff before it was turned over to Gavin.

Pete didn't know why, but he didn't need to. He did as he was told. And for the time being, so was Chewy.

The big man retrieved the duct tape and proceeded to bind Marko's arms and legs together.

Pete lowered the gun and studied Marko. "And tape his mouth shut too."

Chapter 14

Katie McGuire climbed out of bed and wandered naked into the living room of her tiny basement suite. She and her boyfriend Andy had made love and they'd cuddled for twenty-seven blissful minutes until he got up to go to the bathroom. Some people would say that at eighteen years of age, Andy Milanovic wasn't capable of 'making love' but Katie knew that wasn't true. She felt a connection with him that was powerful and real - even if it wasn't sexually gratifying.

She was three years older than he was, a fact that bothered her sister and most of her friends, but she wasn't troubled by their age difference. They'd only been dating for a few months but she was convinced they were soul mates.

She hadn't had an orgasm with him yet - no relationship was perfect - but she was confident that it was only a matter of time. Like other boys his age, and possibly men at any age, he lacked a basic understanding of female anatomy. He spent too much time trying to stimulate all the wrong spots while ignoring the ones that mattered.

Katie heard Andy flush the toilet and a few seconds later he came up behind her, pressing his body close to hers and cupping her small breasts. Her roommate could come home at any moment but Katie wasn't concerned.

To her disappointment, after few short seconds, he stepped away from her and wandered to the center of the cramped low-ceilinged room. He stood in his boxer shorts, staring at a painting on the wall.

"Whatcha looking at?" she asked, although it was obvious.

"This is pretty cool," Andy said.

"What?"

"The painting. Did your roommate do that?"

There were nearly a dozen paintings on the walls of the tiny Mt. Pleasant basement suite. Her roommate, Dakota, was an artist, or at least she tried to be one.

"She's a cutter," Katie said.

Andy turned to face her. "What?"

"She cuts herself, you know, with razor blades. She calls that one 'Cutting'."

The painting was abstract, as all of Dakota's paintings were. It was a mess of black and grey swirls in empty space, accentuated with rows of tiny red droplets.

Andy looked confused. "Really?"

Was it possible he had no idea that girls cut themselves, she wondered. Boys were clueless sometimes. "It's pretty common. Half the girls I know are into cutting."

She walked over to the painting and pointed. "The red drops are blood," she said. "And if you look closely you'll see a series of thin white lines running through the swirls. They represent razor cuts apparently slicing through the grey numbness of depression - at least that's how she explained it to me."

Andy nodded but appeared unconvinced. "I like it. It looks cool."

Katie frowned. Dakota was a drama queen and her paintings were clumsy and heavy-handed.

Pedestrian at best.

"She's talented," Katie lied. "Sometimes I wish I was artistic like that."

"It's cool. All the paintings are cool."

"We should get back to the bedroom. I'm not wearing anything and she could come home anytime."

They went back to her tiny bedroom, Andy ducking to get through the doorway. The bed was a single but it took up nearly the entire room. There was nowhere else to go but the bed, which suited Katie fine. They lay on top of the covers, spooning each other, his arms wrapped around her, making her feel safe. She was annoyed that Dakota's paintings had temporarily intruded on their time together but that moment had passed. Laying with him now she felt like they were the only two people on Earth. She told herself that it didn't matter that she hadn't been sexually fulfilled.

"Tell me something I don't know about you," she said. It was a game they'd been playing since they'd been together.

He appeared to think about it for a while and then offered, "I played Linus in Centennial High School's critically acclaimed production of 'You're a Good Man Charlie Brown'. I bet you didn't know that."

She sighed. "That's not what I meant. Tell me about your parents. Why did they get divorced?"

He kissed the back of her neck softly. Her hair was short and had been died bright blue. "Why do you want to know about that?"

"I want to know everything about you."

He exhaled loudly. "I don't know why. I was only eight. One day Mom moved out."

"What did your dad say?"

"Not much. He said mom wasn't going to live with us anymore but that she still loved me. That was it."

"Didn't you ever ask him why she left?"

"A few times I guess but he never said much. The most he ever said was that they wanted different things in life. My dad never says anything negative about my mom. I think he still loves her."

Andy's home life had been very different from hers and she was naturally curious about it. She couldn't fathom what it would have been like to have parents who liked each other. Of course, having parents who literally didn't try to kill one another would have been a unique experience for Katie.

"Why do you think they broke up?"

He was quiet for a long time. She could hear him breathing.

"I think it was because of me."

She turned so they were facing each other, only inches apart on the tiny bed. She touched his face and said softly, "Why do you think that?"

He rolled onto his back and was quiet again for a long moment. She ran her fingers over his narrow, nearly hairless chest.

"I don't know," he said finally. "I don't think she wanted kids. I think that was the thing that they wanted different in life. I think I was an accident, a mistake."

"But you're living with her now."

"Yeah. It's not that I think she didn't love me, if that makes any sense. She just didn't want to be a parent. In a funny way, I think now that I'm older and an adult, she feels more comfortable around me."

Katie had met Andy's mother and visited their home on two or three occasions. Their house was massive and his mother was gorgeous, super polite, and treated Katie like a welcome guest in their home. She was glad that Andy was opening up to her but at the same time she was having a hard time relating to the trauma that his mother might have had misgivings about parenthood. At least, she thought, his father wasn't in prison for murdering his mother and trying to burn their house down while he was inside.

"It's weird living there though," he said, staring up at the ceiling. "I'm always worried I'm going to move a vase three inches the wrong way or forget to use a coaster and leave a ring on the coffee table or something. My mom is so uptight. Everything has to be a certain way. She's like one of those Stepford moms. She'd freak out if she knew we were sleeping together."

"D'you think so?" Katie asked, surprised. "I thought your mom was kind of cool."

"My mom? No. She's one of those career obsessed business women that demands perfection. I think she's sexually repressed."

Katie didn't see that at all. She wouldn't be surprised if Andy's mom had some dirty secrets. It was funny how different Andy's perspective was. Katie didn't know if that was because he was a boy or because of his sheltered life experience.

She loved him but she thought sometimes he didn't have a clue.

Recently Katie had introduced him to her sister Toni, who lived in the West End with a female roommate. For some reason, Andy assumed Toni was gay, which was ridiculous. She was totally not-gay - not that it mattered - but Katie would know if she was. They were super close. She admired Toni and loved her more than anyone else in the world, maybe even more than Andy -and he was her soul mate.

Toni was the reason she was going to university. She paid for all her courses, books, and fees. Her sister had been in the military for years, serving overseas on multiple tours of duty, and now she worked at the same warehouse where Andy's father worked. Andy didn't think the warehouse paid very well but it obviously paid well enough for Toni to put Katie through school.

"I think my mother is pretty old fashioned and uptight," Andy said, still staring at the ceiling.

She snapped out her thoughts and rolled onto Andy's chest, sitting up and straddling him. She saw his eyes shift to her breasts. They were small but boys seemed to like them. She had a half dozen tattoos and multiple piercings on her body.

"I don't know about your mother, but I'm pretty sure you're not sexually repressed," she said, even though she thought he was a little uptight.

He grinned up at her. "I love you."

He'd said those words to her for the first time nearly a month ago but she never got tired of hearing them.

She gazed at him, studying his face. He was slender but handsome with short, neatly parted chestnut hair, dark russet colored eyes with tiny specs of amber, soft lips, perfect white teeth, and a gorgeous smile.

"I love you too," she said.

He stared at her earnestly. "I'd do anything for you."

She smiled.

If she could only get him to find her clitoris, she thought, then he could really do something for her.

"I mean it," he said. He sounded strangely grateful, as if her willingness to sleep with him was a debt he could never repay. "I really would do anything for you. Anything at all. That's how much I love you."

She kissed him and they made love for the second time that night, and for the second time that night, she didn't have an orgasm.

Chapter 15

"Dana thinks I should sleep with you," Ana said.

Rick had been gazing silently out the passenger-side window at the vacant lot where they were parked, waiting for their next call. He turned to her at the wheel and nodded thoughtfully.

"Dana's a smart woman. You should listen to her."

She grinned at him, appreciating his smooth response. "I told her I was saving myself for Eddie Vedder."

"The Pearl Jam guy? Is that band still together?"

She knew he was messing with her. "Of course. Best band in the history of the world."

"Next to Creed, obviously"

She was tempted to hit him. "Creed sucks."

"I don't know. I get Pearl Jam and Creed mixed up all the time."

She narrowed her eyes and gave him a cold, hard stare for a few silent seconds, letting him know that homicide was an option she was seriously considering.

"Why are you interested in me?" she asked.

"A lot of reasons."

"But we're so different."

"I don't think we're that different."

"You don't think so?" She took a sip from a water bottle she kept in the console. "What's your favorite movie?"

He thought about it for a second and then said, "Big Trouble in Little China, obviously."

She furrowed her brow. "You're not serious."

"Absolutely." He scratched his beard. "It was filmed in Vancouver."

"I think I've made my point."

"Having the same taste in movies doesn't matter. Do you know what matters to me? You're funny. You're smart. You're interesting. You're beautiful."

"Now I know you're lying."

He reached out a hand and touched her shoulder. "You are beautiful, Ana."

"I'm not beautiful," she said.

He put a hand to her chin and gently turned her face until their eyes locked. "I think you are."

She almost believed him. She felt tears welling in her eyes and cursed herself for being such a girl.

"We work together," she said. "It's complicated."

The CAD pinged.

Ana wasn't sure if she was relieved or disappointed by the interruption. Rick glanced down at the screen and read out an address on Kingsway, not far from their location.

"Code 3," he said. "Two patients. Both male. Assaulted. Fives are on scene. An ALS car is responding as well."

Ana blinked and slid the hearing-protection ear muffs on. They had a job to do. Romance, or whatever this was, would have to wait. She flipped a switch to turn the lights and siren on and pulled out of the empty parking lot.

Within seconds she felt a rush of adrenaline as they sped through city streets. Traffic was light and the few cars on the road parted like a wake, letting the ambulance speed by. She saw police lights ahead and a few seconds later she pulled the ambulance to the curb between two police cars in front of an apartment building. The ALS car hadn't arrived yet.

She flashed on a memory from when she was ten years old. Her mother had picked her up from swim practice and was driving her home. When they turned onto their street they could see fire trucks and smoke billowing across the road. Her first thought was that their house was on fire. She remembered the panic she felt as they drove closer, worrying about her father and brother, Steve. It had been a neighbor's house on fire though, not theirs. She remembered how it had melted the plastic siding on one wall of their house and how the heat had made the gutters look like grotesque icicles.

She turned off the ignition and stared uneasily at the building. For some reason she had the same feeling she had as a child, seeing fire trucks on the street where she lived.

"Marko lives around here," she said.

She felt Rick's eyes on her.

"In this building?"

"I don't know. He just moved."

"There's no reason to think it's his apartment."

She nodded. The chances of it being Marko's apartment were slim. Still, she couldn't shake the feeling.

"We better get moving," she said.

They both climbed out of the ambulance. After they'd unloaded the stretcher and their equipment, a cop led them to the elevator and up to the third floor. Another cop was waiting for them when the elevator door opened. He led them to an open apartment door. The frame was cracked and splintered, indicating a home invasion. Neighbors were standing in the hallway, kept back by police officers and yellow crime scene tape.

"There's two of them in there," the cop said. He was young and earnest. "One looks like a fatal."

"And the other one?" Rick asked.

"Unconscious in a bedroom. Someone beat them up pretty good."

Ana recognized the furniture as soon as they stepped into the room. Her eyes were drawn to the body on the floor. Two cops were working on him, doing CPR.

Her heart sank.

"That's Marko." She heard herself say the words but they felt disconnected, like her voice was coming from a TV in another room.

Rick put his hand gently on her shoulder. "I'll take him."

She nodded.

"Are you ok?" he asked.

She nodded again. "I'll check the bedroom."

A cop led her down the hallway to the bedrooms. The situation felt surreal. It was like she was floating, watching herself go through the motions. Her brother was dead in the next room but she had job to do. She couldn't think about Marko now.

She reached the bedroom and saw a naked man on the floor beside the bed. The carpet, walls, and bedspread were spattered with blood. She felt her knees go weak. The man's face was badly beaten but she recognized her younger brother Steve.

A female cop knelt by his head and looked up at Ana with relief.

"He's breathing, but it's raspy," she said.

Ana nodded, determined not to show emotion. "I'll take it from here," she said, her voice calm, as if this were just another day at the office.

The relieved cop stood and moved out of the way. Ana set her jump kit down and knelt beside Steve, her training taking over. She needed to do her job.

      Tears could come later.

Chapter 16

Chewy Awesome was at the wheel of the Sebring, driving well over the speed limit despite Pete's reminders to slow down. Fifteen minutes had passed since they'd left the apartment and Pete had been giving him directions ever since. He had no idea where they were going.

It was late and traffic was light but he wasn't concentrating on driving. His mind was back at the apartment, reliving what had happened.

Pete told him to check the bedrooms for computer equipment. When Chewy entered one of the bedrooms, a stringy-haired naked dude burst out of nowhere and jumped onto his back, screaming and clawing at his head and shoulders. Chewy felt the man's balls pressed against his back and reached around, gripped under the naked dude's shoulders, and flung him to the floor. Then he pounced on him and swung his fists until he Pete interrupted him.

"What the fuck are you doing?" Pete said.

Chewy looked up and saw Pete standing in the doorway. "The fucker scratched me."

Pete gestured with his hand. "You're making too much noise."

"But the fucker scratched me."

"Keep it up and you'll kill him too."

The words stopped Chewy cold. He stared at Pete, confused. "What the fuck are you talking about?"

"The guy in the other room, he's dead. Looks like you killed him."

Chewy stood, his knuckles bloody. "Are you shittin' me?"

Pete looked grave and shook his head. "You can check yourself but he's stone cold man."

"I just punched him."

Pete scratched his beard. "Sometimes that's all it takes."

"Holy fuck dude. I mean seriously, holy fuck!"

"That's what happens when you go ape-shit on people."

"What d'we do now?"

"What you should have done all along, whatever I fucking say."

Chewy looked at the unconscious naked dude on the floor. "D'you think he's dead too?"

Pete shrugged. "Good chance."

"He shouldn't have scratched me."

"I guess not. Now, let's get the fuck out of here." He turned and walked up the hallway.

Chewy followed, still dumbstruck. When he entered the front room he stopped and stared at the couch where the man lay, his eyes closed, his pale face swollen and bruised, smeared with dried blood.

♦

A car horn blared and snapped Chewy out of his thoughts and back to the Sebring.

"Slow down Chewy," Pete said. "You just ran a fucking red light."

"Sorry."

"Get your head in the game. The last thing we need is to get pulled over for some bullshit traffic ticket."

Pete was right. Chewy needed to get his shit together. He slowed the car and they drove in silence until Chewy asked, "You ever kill anyone?"

"A few people. It's no big deal."

"No big deal?" He stopped at an intersection and stared at Pete. "That's fucking crazy, dude. How many people have you killed?"

Pete scratched his beard. "I don't know. Five or six, I guess."

"How can you not know how many people you've killed?"

"I don't think about it much."

"I don't believe that."

Pete shrugged.

The light turned green and Chewy eased his foot down gently on the accelerator, making a conscious effort to drive slower.

"This is fucking nuts," he said. "I didn't mean to kill the guy. I just fucking punched him, you know."

"Don't worry about it."

"How can I not worry about it? Seriously dude, I killed a guy."

"Maybe two guys."

"Shit." Chewy had forgotten about the second guy. "What if the naked dude doesn't die? He got a good look at me."

"The guy looked like a junkie. He won't remember anything."

"The fucker scratched me. He's got my DNA under his fingernails."

The Sebring sailed through another red light.

"Jesus Chewy, how many times do I gotta say it? Slow down the fuck down."

Chewy lifted his foot off the accelerator. He hadn't realized how fast he was going and hadn't noticed the red light. Living a life-of-crime was more stressful than he'd anticipated.

"Turn up ahead," Pete said, pointing left.

Chewy turned onto a side street. "My finger prints are all over that apartment."

Pete ignored him and pointed to a parking lot entrance. "Pull in here."

Chewy did as he was told and steered into a big-box hardware store parking lot. The lot was huge, dark, and empty.

He thought about his situation. There was a very real possibility that he could go to jail but Pete didn't seem to be worried about it. Then again, Chewy thought, why would he? He hadn't killed anyone.

"Are you listening to me?" Chewy said.

Pete ignored him. "Pull over by those bushes."

Chewy slammed on the brakes and Pete pitched forward, slamming into the dashboard. He glared at Chewy. "What the fuck was that?"

"I said my finger prints are all over that apartment."

"So?"

Chewy was about to lose his shit. "What the fuck do you mean – so?"

"Have you ever been arrested?"

"No," Chewy said slowly.

"Then you don't have anything to worry about. The cops don't have your DNA. They don't have your fingerprints. They don't have shit. You're not in the system." Pete tilted his head. "Pull over there by those bushes."

Chewy looked around. "What are we doing? Why are we here?"

"I gotta take a leak."

"Now?" Chewy asked. "Can't it wait?"

He pulled the car up against a row of bushes and parked anyway.

Pete didn't answer. He opened the door, got out, and walked over to the shrubs where he unzipped his jeans and started pissing.

Obviously it couldn't wait.

Chewy needed fresh air and climbed out of the car. It was a cool night and he was only wearing a tank top which he now noticed was smeared with blood. A lot of blood.

Pete finished, shook, and zipped back up. When he turned around he had a cigarette between his lips and he was pulling a lighter out of his hoodie pocket.

Chewy watched him light up and couldn't help but notice, even in the dark, how ugly the guy was. Anytime he'd seen Pete with a chick, which wasn't often, she was almost always a fatty. Chewy thought it must be tough for Pete to be around guys like him who were constantly banging hard-bodies. His current girlfriend, Courtney, was blonde, tanned, and rock-hard.

A lot of it was Pete's own fault, Chewy thought. There were chicks that could probably overlook his honker of a nose and the zit-scars but the dude seriously needed to do something about his body hair. It was out of control.

Looking at Pete made Chewy feel better about his situation. He may have accidently killed someone but at least he wasn't ugly.

"So you're saying if I haven't been arrested, I'm good."

Pete took a long drag and exhaled smoke. "As long as you don't get picked up."

"As long as I don't get picked up," Chewy repeated, not finding the words reassuring.

Pete's phone appeared to have vibrated because he pulled it out and glanced at it. He typed a message, the cigarette dangling from his mouth. When he was done he slid the phone back into his pocket and looked up at Chewy. "That won't happen though because there's no reason to connect you to the dead guy."

Chewy nodded and considered this.

Pete coughed and spat on the pavement.

"So who gets the TV?" Chewy asked. He had suggested they

take the TV on their way out the door.

"It was your idea. You can have it."

"Sweet," Chewy said. "And I still get my $500?"

"Yeah." Pete said. He pulled out his phone, stared at the screen, and then looked up. "He wants us to wait here."

"Fuckin' A," Chewy said. "How long till he gets here?"

Pete slid the phone back into his pocket. "Not long."

"Sweet."

Chewy dropped to the pavement and started doing push-ups. He had energy to burn. The ground was cool and damp and the gravel on the lot dug into his hands but he felt good. He felt like Tony-Fucking-Soprano... except not a fat slob.

He pounded out a quick fifty, jumped up and started shadow boxing. He glanced at Pete. He was confused by what he saw, but the confusion quickly gave way to fear. He started to say something but didn't get a chance. The last thing he remembered seeing was the Ruger in Pete's gloved hand and the look in his eyes. He was struck by their lack of emotion.

He heard the shot, he was certain of that, and he thought he could feel the bullet shatter his skull and tear into his brain, but he probably imagined that. None of it mattered. His world went black.

♦

Pete Pappas stepped over to Chewy's body, pressed the Ruger against the big man's forehead and fired a second shot into his skull. An insurance bullet.

When he was done he looked around the vast empty parking lot for an indication someone had heard the shots or seen something, but there was none. He grabbed Chewy by the wrists and dragged him twenty feet so the body was closer to the bushes and not as obvious to someone entering the parking lot. It was a lot of work, the guy weighed well over 250lbs, and the effort triggered a massive coughing spasm that left him short of breath.

Damn, he needed another cigarette.

He realized that it had been a mistake to recruit Chewy. He should have watched a YouTube video and learned how to hotwire a car so he could steal one for the job. If he had, Chewy would be somewhere pounding chocolate milk and pumping iron. He'd still be a douchebag but he'd be alive.

Pete didn't feel bad though. Chewy's death wasn't Pete's fault. If the guy had followed Pete's lead, if he'd worn gloves, if he hadn't been stupid enough to get jumped by a naked dude with long fingernails, it wouldn't have been necessary to kill him.

At least, probably not.

The bottom line though was that Chewy was too stupid to be trusted and killing him had saved Pete $500.

Chewy hadn't actually killed the warehouse worker. Pete had done that. After Chewy left the room, Pete had pressed a gloved hand over Marko's nose and held it until he was dead. When it was done, Pete found Marko's phone and laptop and put them in the backpack he'd brought. He also found a flash drive in the front pocket of Marko's jeans and a key and a note pad with an address written on it on the kitchen counter. The key and address might not have a connection to the computer file but he slipped the notepaper and the key into his pocket anyway.

He looked down at Chewy's body in the parking lot and lit another cigarette. He took a few drags and then bent over to check Chewy's pockets, finding his key ring and wallet. He pocketed $15 in cash, tossed the wallet into the shrubs by Chewy's head, and walked back to the Sebring. He stopped and stared at the TV box in the backseat. Chewy had taken it, not realizing he would never get a chance to watch it.

Pete slipped behind the wheel of the Sebring, adjusted the seat and mirrors, and slid a piece of paper out of his pocket. The note had a Burnaby address on it. He started the engine, backed the Sebring out of the parking stall and drove slowly out of the lot. The address might not have anything to do with the computer file but he decided to check it out. Hopefully Kevin would appreciate his thoroughness.

Chapter 17

Thursday October 20

Katie was awake when Andy's cell phone rang. She reached over and picked it up from the tiny nightstand. Andy rolled over and she passed it to him.

"It's your mommy," she said, her tone playful.

"Hey mom," he said into the phone, his voice thick with sleep.

Katie traced a finger down his naked, narrow chest, sliding it under the covers.

He sat up abruptly and pushed her hand away. She was annoyed at first but she could see tension on his face and knew that the call was serious.

"What do you mean? What are you saying, Mom?"

She stared at him but he seemed unaware of her.

"Ok," he said, his voice cracking. "We're on our way. We'll meet you there."

He disconnected the call. "It's my dad," he said.

She placed her hand on his and waited for him to elaborate.

"Somebody broke into his apartment."

"Was he home?"

"Yeah."

"Oh my God. Is he alright?"

Tears welled in his eyes. "I don't think so. I don't know. Can you drive me to the hospital?"

"Of course," she said. She hugged him. "It'll be ok. I'm here for you. We'll get through this."

She was sorry about his father and hated seeing him in pain, but at the same time, she knew this was an important test. Tragedy could make or break a relationship. He needed to know that he could lean on her in his darkest hour.

Tragedy could bind a couple together forever, she thought, but only if you took full advantage of the opportunity.

♦

Ana pretended to be asleep. She wasn't proud of herself but it was necessary to avoid having a conversation with her mother. It didn't stop her mother from talking but at least Ana wasn't obligated to reply.

She was slumped in a waiting room chair in Vancouver General Hospital with her head resting on her hand, propped up by her elbow on the armrest.

It was nearly 8:00 am. Marko's ex, Linda, and their son Andy, along with his girlfriend Katie had been at the hospital earlier but they'd left hours ago. It was heartbreaking to see how devastated Andy was by his father's murder. Linda was a mess as well. In many ways their grief helped Ana keep her own emotions in check as she comforted them.

They left though after it was confirmed that Marko was dead. They barely knew Steve, so Ana was left alone most of the night with her mother. She'd done her best to be pleasant as long as she could but eventually she couldn't maintain the façade any longer and faked falling asleep. It was a better option than saying something she might regret.

Her mother was going on about what sweet boys Marko and Steven had been and how they'd always been the light of her life and that since they were dead and her only daughter didn't like to spend time with her, perhaps she should do everyone a favor and die.

The reality was that Steven wasn't dead and Marko wasn't actually her son - in fact she was only eight years older than he was and she'd done nothing but complain about him as long as Ana could remember.

She was right about her daughter not wanting to spend time with her though.

Her mother stopped talking. Ana opened her eyes, sensing that someone had entered the waiting room.

"Hey," she said.

Rick managed a small smile. "Rough night?"

She nodded.

"Who's this?" her mother asked.

"Mom this is Rick. We work together. Rick this is my mother, Marianne."

"I'm sorry for your loss," Rick said.

"My heart has been ripped from my chest," her mother said with enough dramatic flair to warrant an Oscar. "Nobody knows the pain of a mother in a situation like this. No child should die before their parent."

Ana's mother was in her mid-sixties and had unnatural looking platinum blonde hair that could use a good conditioner. She wore an overabundance of inexpensive jewelry and her make-up was both excessive and poorly applied. Her eye-liner was starting to streak under eyes that were puffy from crying and there was a pile of used tissues on her narrow lap and on the cushion beside her. Ana knew that she should feel empathy for her mother but she knew her mother well enough to know that her tears were as genuine as Ana's fake nap.

"It's terrible," Rick said. "My heart goes out to you and your family."

97

"What family?" She dabbed her eyes with a tissue. "I have no family. My husband is dead, my sons are dead and my daughter ignores me. I have no one."

Rick shifted awkwardly.

Ana stood and dutifully kissed her mother. "Steve isn't dead mom. The doctor told us that. He's going to make a full recovery. You have to stop saying that he's dead."

"You don't know," she insisted. "They beat him up, my boy. My poor little angel. He could still die. You don't know."

Ana let it pass. There was no point in arguing. Her mother had her own narrative and facts only got in the way.

"I have to go," she said. "Rick is giving me a ride back to my car."

"You're leaving?"

"Braden has school. I'll come back later to check on Steve."

"What about me?"

"Go home mom. Get some rest."

"I can't drive in my condition." She started to cry again. "How can I be expected to sleep with my son at death's door?"

Ana counted to ten in her head, then smiled weakly and said, "I'll check in on you later, after I get Braden to school."

Her mother mumbled something under her breath about how no one cared about her. Clearly, Ana thought, her mother was the real victim in all this.

Ana nodded at Rick, indicating that they should leave. He looked a little uncertain but followed Ana's lead. The two of them left the waiting room and wandered through the hospital corridors until they emerged outside. They didn't speak until they got to Rick's sports car.

"I'm not sure I can fit in that thing," Ana said, staring skeptically at the Audi.

Rick came around and opened the door for her. "With a little bending you'll fit right in."

She crawled into the passenger seat and once she was in, was surprised by how much leg room she actually had. She'd never been in a $170,000 car before. The experience was a little underwhelming. She didn't feel like she was in the lap of luxury. Presumably Rick paid what he had for the car because of what was under the hood, not for the creature comforts of its interior.

"Thanks for coming back to get me," she said.

The ALS team had transported Steve to the hospital and Rick and Ana had followed in their ambulance. After dropping Ana off at the hospital Rick had gone back to the stationhouse. A casual employee had been called in to work the rest of her shift and would cover her shift that night.

Rick settled into the driver's seat. "No problem," he said. He backed the car out of the parking space and turned to Ana. "Your mother seemed pretty upset."

"Have I ever told you about my mother?"

Rick shook his head and drove the Audi out of the parking lot.

"It's complicated," she said, although it wasn't. It was simple. Her mother was a narcissist.

"It sounds like she was really close to Marko and Steve."

Ana snorted derisively and was immediately embarrassed. She must look like a horrible person, she thought, dismissing her mother's grief.

"Sorry," she said. "I didn't mean to do that."

"No need to apologize. People say and do all kinds of things when they're grieving."

Ana paused for a moment. Rick was being supportive which was nice but he'd also missed the point.

"My mother loves drama and she loves to be the center of attention. She likes to make everything about her. I don't think she's capable of loving another human being."

"Wow."

99

"That sounds pretty terrible I guess. What kind of person says that about their mother?"

"Christina Crawford?"

Ana frowned. "You must think I'm a horrible person."

"I don't know your mother but I know you and I know you're a good person."

Ana smiled. At least he didn't think she was a monster.

When they arrived at the station Rick parked beside Ana's Sunfire. She opened her door and climbed out, something that was difficult to do gracefully from the small sports car, not that Ana had ever done much of anything gracefully. Rick came around and they stood by Ana's car. She glanced at her phone, noted the time, and told Rick that she really needed to go. She thanked him again for the ride. He smiled and nodded and then turned to go back to his car. He'd barely taken two steps when she burst into tears. She felt his arms around her and she grabbed him tight, hugging as hard as she could.

"I can't believe he's gone."

They were the first real tears she'd cried for Marko and there was no holding them back. Her body was racked with wave after wave of uncontrollable gasping sobs. Eventually the tears subsided and she took a small step back, feeling a little embarrassed, but was reassured by Rick's smile.

"I miss him already," she said softly. "Which is crazy, I know. It's only been a few hours."

He wiped a tear from her cheek, a tender but futile effort.

"He was my big brother."

"I know," he said.

"I loved him so much. Why would anyone do this? Why would someone hurt him?"

But she knew in her heart why this had happened. It seemed obvious to her that whatever had happened in that apartment, it had been because of Steve. He owed someone money or drugs or something and Marko had been caught in the middle.

"Am I a terrible person for thinking it would have been better if Steve had died instead?" she asked softly, almost in a whisper. She wasn't sure if she had said the words out loud until Rick replied.

He kissed her forehead. "You and Marko were close."

Ana realized that he hadn't actually answered her question but she thought he understood. She was relieved that Steve had survived but at the same time she knew if she saw him anytime soon, she was angry enough that she just might kill him.

Chapter 18

Katie lay alone in bed. She was exhausted but hadn't been able to sleep. Andy's father was dead. His uncle was in critical but stable condition. She wished Andy had come home with her but she understood that he needed to be with his family. But he would need her to console him today, which was why she wasn't going to class. She needed to be there for him.

That's what soulmates did.

Andy's Aunt Ana had been the one to tell them that Andy's father had been murdered. The situation was surreal, bringing back memories of her mother's death.

Katie's mother had died when Katie was 14 years old. Toni had been overseas, in the army. On that night, 7 years ago, Katie's father had come to the house where she lived with her mother in Coquitlam. He was drunk, which was the way she always remembered him. Her mother had low standards. Low standards and even lower expectations.

Katie's father had beaten her mother that night, as he often did, while Katie hid upstairs. There had been a fire that burned the house to the ground. Katie had been rescued by firefighters. Her father was charged with arson and murder and Katie wound up in foster care. In the months after the fire, Katie dreamed that one day her big sister, the soldier, would come to save her, to take her away.

Eventually she did.

It took longer than Katie would have liked, but a year later Toni came and rescued her.

She was her hero.

Katie understood what Andy was going through in a way that few people could because she knew what it was like to have a parent die as a result of violence. She lay back on her pillow and stared up at the chipped paint on the ceiling. Andy would probably phone her soon. It was nearly 9 am. He wouldn't call too early. He was thoughtful that way. But - he would need her. She was the only person who could relate, who would understand what he was going through, although their circumstances were admittedly different.

Andy's father died at the hand of a stranger, not a family member. Katie's mother, on the other hand, was killed by someone close to her, someone who was supposed to love her unconditionally.

◆

Pete woke with a raging hard-on and the pleasurable sensation - as Chewy would have said - of getting his knob polished. He opened groggy eyes and reached down and touched a mess of curly blonde hair. Kaitlin lifted her head and grinned at him. She was cute, with a round freckled face, bright blue eyes, and huge dimples.

"D'you want to come?" she asked, teasing him. Her voice had a smoky quality that drove him crazy. He swore he could get off just listening to her talk.

"You know I do," he said.

She smiled and went back down on him. It didn't take long.

When she was done, she eased up his body, settling in beside him, her arm around his chest, nuzzling and kissing his neck. He reached around and grabbed her ample ass to show his appreciation.

"Did you like that?" she asked, idly running her fingers through his chest hair.

There was nothing like an orgasm to start the day, he thought, especially when he didn't have to do any of the heavy lifting.

"You give better head than my mother," he said.

He'd never been good at giving compliments.

She lifted her head and frowned at him. "That's not funny."

"I wasn't trying to be funny."

He never tried to be funny.

She rolled away from him, onto her back, and stared up at the ceiling. "You should go down on me now."

Pete made a face. What was the point, he thought. He'd already had an orgasm.

"I would," he said. "But I gotta work."

She groaned. "You're kidding? Shit. I'm all worked up. You can't leave now."

"Not much I can do. You don't want me to get fired do you?"

He reached for his cell phone on the night stand and checked the time. He worked at the dollar store at 10 a.m., a job he hoped he could quit soon. It was 9:15. He put the phone down and turned back to Kaitlin.

She hit him in the face with a pillow. "You're an asshole, you know."

He appraised her. Chewy would have said she was fat but Pete didn't see her that way. She had a bit of a muffin-top but Pete liked that. He liked his women soft and curvy. He picked up the pillow and swung it at her, hitting her boob. They wrestled until he had her arms pinned to the bed. He knew she'd done this on purpose. Their wrestling matches always made him hard, even this soon after an orgasm.

"I hope you know what to do with that thing," she said.

"You know I do."

When they were done and getting dressed, he said, "I need you to do something for me."

"I gave you a blow job and fucked your brains out. What more d'you want?"

He liked a woman with a foul mouth. She served drinks in a bar where he was a regular and he'd seen her handle rowdy groups of men. She could cut a man to pieces with a few carefully chosen words and still get them to leave her a big tip.

"I need you to say I was here all night." It wasn't the first time he'd asked her to provide him with an alibi.

She screwed up her face in an exaggerated grimace. "From when?"

"About 8. All night."

She took a deep breath. "I would babe. You know I want to but I don't think I can. I worked until 11 last night and then some of us went out for something to eat and when I got home April and Warren were practically doing it on the couch. I kinda walked in on them. They'll remember that."

April was her roommate. She was far too skinny for Pete's tastes. Her boyfriend Warren was a massive douche bag who sold auto parts or something.

"Shit," Pete said.

After killing Chewy he'd gone to the address on the note paper which turned out to be Marko's sister's place. She wasn't home. There was no sign of a desktop computer and she presumably had her phone with her but he found a tablet and took it. By the time he met Kevin to turn over the phone, laptop and tablet, it was nearly 1 a.m. He ditched the Sebring and arrived at Kaitlin's apartment around 1:30, hoping he could say he'd been there all night.

He realized now that he should have given this more thought.

"Sorry, I can't help," she said. "What d'you do last night?"

"Nothing you need to worry about."

"You didn't kill anyone did you?"

He stared at her. "Why would you say that?"

"Don't look so serious. I'm just fucking with you."

Pete frowned. He liked his women curvy, horny, and foul-mouthed, but he didn't care much for Kaitlin's humor.

"Don't joke about shit like that."

"Lighten up Pete." She came over to him, wearing a baggy t-shirt and nothing else. She lifted her arms to wrap them loosely around his neck and her shirt rose above her waist. "You got your rocks off – twice. Cheer up."

He could feel the weight of her breasts against his chest and when she kissed his neck he thought for a moment that he might get hard again.

"I gotta go," he said. "I'm already late."

She looked up at him. "I have no idea what I see in you."

He didn't know either. They'd been having sex for a few months but they'd never gone to a movie or out for dinner. He just came over once in a while to fuck her. Or when he needed an alibi. Or both.

He broke away from her, collected his t-shirt from the back of a chair and started to put it on.

"I think it's the chest hair," she said, watching him pull the shirt over his head. "I like a manly chest."

She obviously wasn't into him for his money, he thought. He finished dressing and she followed him to the door.

"Thanks for the fuck," he said. Pete liked that she didn't expect him to say anything romantic. He reached around and spanked her naked ass. "I'll see you around."

"Maybe you will and maybe you won't."

He pulled her close and kissed her hard. He could tell she was surprised but that she liked it too. The truth was, he really liked Kaitlin.

"Maybe I'll be back tonight," he said.

She cupped his crotch and grinned. "Are you sure you don't need to give that thing a rest?"

He felt his dick move and knew she felt it too. "What do you think?" he said.

She grinned. "I guess not."

He spanked her bare ass one more time and stepped out into the hallway. The building was dingy and the carpet hadn't seen a vacuum in months. He walked to the exit and thought about the night before, feeling a pang of regret.

Not for killing Chewy, that didn't bother him.

He felt bad about the dog though.

Chapter 19

Rick woke to the sound of his cell phone ringing. He usually turned his phone off when he was sleeping during the day but he'd left it on in case Ana called. He reached for the phone on his night stand and read the display. It was her. He answered.

"Rick," she said, sounding relieved. "I didn't know who else to call. They broke into my house."

He was still sleepy and it took some time to process the words. "Ana, what are you talking about? Who broke into your house?"

"They killed Lukin."

"What?" It took him a moment to remember that Lukin was her dog. "Someone killed your dog?"

"Can you come?"

"Of course, I'll be right there. Are you at home?"

"Yes."

"Are you safe? Have you called the police?"

"The police are here."

"I'll be there as fast as I can."

Rick lived on West 22nd in Vancouver and on a weekday morning it would take nearly 45 minutes to get to Ana's Burnaby townhouse.

He drove like a madman in the Audi R8 whenever there was an opening in traffic but there weren't many of those. The Audi had a 4.2 liter V8, all-aluminum alloy 32-valve engine with a fuel stratified injection system but none of that mattered when you were stuck in a traffic jam.

Forty minutes later he pulled up to Ana's townhouse. There were three police cars parked outside and he saw Ana in the carport talking to a police officer. Rick parked and walked over to them.

She looked relieved when she saw him and stepped away from the cop who slipped back into the house. Her eyes were bloodshot and her cheeks were damp with tears. They hugged and she thanked him for coming and suggested they go for a walk.

They didn't go far, wandering through the townhouse subdivision, sometimes doubling back the way they came. Rick didn't ask questions. He let her talk.

She said she'd gotten home and at first she hadn't noticed anything different except that the dog hadn't come to greet her. She called Lukin's name. He didn't bark or come so she went looking for him. She found him by the back door. Apparently they'd strangled him, probably because he was barking. That was when she called 911.

"It might be the same people who killed Marko who did this."

"Why do you think that?"

"Marko had a key to my place. It sounds like its missing."

"Oh my God."

"What if Braden had been home last night?" she said.

Rick nodded gravely.

"They could have a key to my house."

"You should get the locks changed," he said, glad to be able to offer practical advice.

"I will."

"I know a guy who'll come right away."

Rick was a paramedic but he made most of his money in real estate and property development. He knew all the good contractors.

"I don't want to stay here tonight."

"You don't have to."

"There's nowhere Braden and I can go except a hotel I guess."

"You can stay with me."

"I couldn't do that."

"Sure you can. I'm working tonight. I have lots of room. You and Braden are welcome to stay as long as you need to."

"I don't know what to say Rick. Dana's gone. Marko's dead. I don't have anyone else."

He was apparently her last resort but he didn't mind. He was glad he could help. He also knew with more certainty than anything he'd known in his life, he was falling in love.

Chapter 20

Gavin Taylor was in full panic mode. He was also starving. He had no food in his freezer, no beer in his fridge, and no money for either. He was completely broke after his big loss at the casino on Monday night. He'd maxed out his credit cards and had already taken out multiple payday loans that were going to consume all of his next paycheck.

To make matters worse, he was pretty certain that Marko was dead and that the hit man he'd hired would come looking for his $7,500 fee. He'd heard on the news that there had been a home invasion last night in Vancouver that left one man dead. There had also been a body found in a big-box hardware store parking lot in Burnaby. Gavin assumed that one of those bodies was Marko and he was even more certain when Marko failed to show up for work.

Gavin needed a plan. The trouble was that he didn't do his best thinking on an empty stomach. His roommate had food but he wasn't willing to share, choosing instead to let Gavin starve. He probably wouldn't care if Gavin got tortured and killed by the Russian mob.

Gavin rented a three bedroom house in Coquitlam with George

Richardson, another divorced dad. Each dad had their own room and they used the third bedroom when one of them had their kids sleep over. The other guy's kids slept-over on a regular basis while Gavin's kid hadn't set foot in the place since the volleyball incident.

Despite the fact that George's rug-rats were always crawling around the place, somehow he was the bad roommate. George complained nonstop that Gavin left his porn magazines lying around where his kids could find them, that he didn't do his share of the chores, and – one time – he didn't clean up properly after he'd jerked-off on the couch. What pissed Gavin off the most was that George refused to acknowledge that Gavin had tried to clean up his mess, he'd just missed a few spots.

His roommate's biggest complaint though was that Gavin was always stealing his food which was why he stored it all in his room. He'd even bought a full sized fridge for his bedroom which he kept padlocked in addition to the lock on his bedroom door. The guy was fucking paranoid.

The end result was that Gavin had no choice but to forage for food on his own which was why he was in the staff lunch room at the warehouse. The workers were all working, as they should be, unaware that their supervisor was going through their lockers in search of food or cash. Most of them locked their stuff up but a few were too lazy or trusting and Gavin netted $22 in cash, mostly coins, along with a stash of cookies, snacks, and cold pizza.

He slipped back into his office and stashed his bounty in a desk drawer. He ate the cold pizza first and was digging into his drawer for a cookie when his phone pinged, indicating a text message.

He didn't recognize the number but the message was clear.

Job complete. Wire money. Instructions to follow.

Gavin stared at the message and felt sick. He put the cookie down. The phone pinged again and instructions to wire $7,500 followed. The first $2,500 payment had been done the same way, except the account codes were different this time.

He could pretend not to have seen the text. That might buy him some time but as he stared at the message he started to get annoyed. The guy expected to get paid but he hadn't given Gavin the computer files yet and that was the whole point, wasn't it?

He typed:

Need files b4 pay u

The reply was swift:

Computer files have been dealt with

Nice try shithead, Gavin thought. He typed:

No deal - no files no pay

His phone rang seconds later and Gavin thought he might puke. He stared at it, not wanting to answer but knowing he couldn't avoid it. It wasn't like he could pretend he didn't notice his phone ring after texting only a few seconds earlier. He answered the call.

"Hello," he said, trying to sound cool.

"I want my money." It was the voice of the man he had spoken to before. He even sounded like a professional killer.

Gavin did his best to muster whatever confidence he could, trying to sound tough. "You'll get it when I get the computer files."

"I took care of them. Job's done."

"That wasn't the deal. I get the files."

"The files were destroyed."

"I need proof. You can't expect me to take your word for it."

The voice was menacing. "Are you saying I'm a liar?"

"No, no. Of course not." Gavin heard the whine in his own voice and winced.

"What kind of proof do you want?" the man said.

Gavin had no idea but he had to say something. Almost anything was better than 'I don't have the money to pay you' which would almost certainly get him killed.

"I want Marko's phone and laptop and whatever devices he had the file on."

There was a long silence.

"Fine. I'll bring them over. Let's get this done."

"No, no, no – you can't do that. I'm at work. There are people here."

"Then go somewhere else."

"I can't," Gavin said. He needed to buy some time. Even a few hours would help. "I can meet you tonight."

"Where?"

That's when Gavin got an idea that could make this all go away. "D'you play poker?" he asked.

"Why?"

"We could play heads up. Double or nothing."

"You want to play poker for the money you owe me?"

"Yeah," Gavin said. "Heads up. You win, you double your money. I win, I owe you nothing. What d'you think?"

"I think you're a fucking idiot."

"You could double your money."

"I'm not playing poker for money you fucking owe me. I'll give you the phone and laptop and you pay me, 9 o'clock at the No. 5."

The No. 5 was short for the No. 5 Orange, a strip club in East Vancouver.

"I don't know if I can do that."

"You can't afford not to."

"Ok, I'll be there. How will I recognize you?"

"I'll find you," he said and disconnected the call.

Gavin thought he might pass out. Why did things like this happen to him, he wondered. It was as if the world was conspiring against him. He was just trying to live his life and get ahead but there was always a set-back. The sad thing was that so much of it was beyond his control. It wasn't his fault that a father at Ashley's volleyball game had misinterpreted what he said, or that Marko had tried to blackmail him, or that a guy at the casino had sucked out on him and he'd lost the money he needed to pay Marko's killer.

Life just wasn't fair.

Chapter 21

It was just after 1 pm when Ana parked her Sunfire in the driveway of her mother's Burnaby split-level house. The cloudy morning had given way to sunshine and it was uncharacteristically warm for October. She walked to the door of her childhood home and knocked.

Her mother answered the door in a black skirt and an animal print silk blouse, dabbing her eyes with a tissue.

"Where have you been?" she asked.

No 'it's nice to see you Ana'. No 'Thank you for picking me up Ana'.

Ana had learned through the years that it was best not to engage her mother by directly answering her questions. She had no interest in explaining that her house had been broken into or that she had found her dog strangled to death.

"I'm here now mom," she said. "Let's go." She turned and walked back to the car.

Her mother had phoned shortly after Ana had dropped Braden off at school and said that she had nearly gotten into an accident on the way home because she'd been crying so hard.

"It isn't safe for me to drive in this condition but I really want to see Stevie." She burst into sobs. "Who knows if he'll ever wake up again? If he does, he'll want to see his mother."

Ana sincerely doubted that. It had been a long, stressful morning and she'd had little or no sleep in the past 24 hours so she wasn't in the best frame of mind to spend time with her mother.

But what could she do? She was her mother.

They got into the Sunfire and drove in silence for a few minutes which was a relief. The fact that it was sunny didn't seem right to her. It was as if the weather was refusing to acknowledge that Marko was dead. People were out walking and cycling and enjoying the rare opportunity to be outdoors this time of year. It felt obscene to her but at the same time she knew that families were touched by tragedy all the time and that the rest of world moved on, oblivious to their pain.

"Where's Brad?" her mother asked.

Ana snapped out of her thoughts. "I have no idea."

Her mother had done nothing but complain about Brad while they were married but the moment they split up her mother decided he was a 'good catch' and that Ana had been foolish to let him get away.

"Does he know what happened to Steve and Marko?"

"Honestly, I don't know. I haven't talked to him in a while."

"He was a keeper Ana. You were lucky to have him."

Ana said nothing. She could feel her mother staring at her.

"A sturdy, big-boned girl like you can't afford to be picky," her mother said.

Ana held her tongue, knowing that if she said anything, she'd start something she didn't have the energy to finish.

When they arrived at the hospital they were told that Steve was awake and they could visit him. Ana wasn't sure if she was ready to see him yet.

"You should see him first," Ana said. "I'll get a coffee."

She could tell that her mother liked the idea of having a special status that entitled her to visit Steve before other family members did, not that anyone was lining up to visit him.

Ana found a coffee shop on the hospital main floor, ordered a latte and drank it while flipping through the Province newspaper. She couldn't remember the last time she'd read the paper. It felt vaguely nostalgic, like she'd gone back in time before the internet and 24 hour cable news.

When she returned to the waiting room she found her mother sitting alone. She glared at Ana as if she'd been set afloat on an ice drift.

"You were gone a long time."

Ana ignored the comment. "Did Steve fall asleep again?"

Part of her hoped that he had. It meant that she would have an excuse not to see him right away. She wanted to talk to him and find out what happened in the apartment but she was angry with him and wasn't sure she was ready to hear him make excuses.

"No. He's awake. The Hat Squad came to interview him."

"The Hat Squad?"

"The police but they call themselves IHat."

"It's IHIT mom. It's an acronym for Integrated Homicide Investigation Team."

Her mother looked embarrassed. "I'm sure they said IHat and one of them had a hat on."

Ana sighed. "Maybe there are two units and IHat is investigating this case."

Her mother seemed satisfied with Ana's concession. "Whatever they're called, they kicked me out. His mother! They said they needed to talk to him alone."

Ana nodded.

The police were with Steve for at least 30 minutes; 30 painful minutes that Ana spent with her mother in the waiting room listening to

118

her talk about how Steve had a gentle soul and how he had the spirit of an artist and how no one in the family understood him like she did. Her mother made no mention of how Steve was a drug addict who had lied to them all, or how he'd borrowed, coerced and stolen money from them that he'd never repay. Not a word was said about how he had missed his father's funeral. No suggestion was made that maybe, just maybe, it was his fault that Marko was dead.

"That man who picked you up, are you sleeping with him?" her mother asked without segue.

It unnerved Ana to realize that she had the same tendency to ask deliberately provocative questions to provoke a reaction. It was disturbing to know that she had this in common with her mother.

"He's my partner. Whether we have a relationship beyond that is none of your business."

Her mother shrugged. "I thought so. I don't care for him."

"You don't know him."

"He looks like a Nancy Boy."

Ana cursed herself for taking the bait. She stood. "I have to go."

"You haven't seen your brother yet."

"I have to pick Braden up from school. I'll come back and visit."

"You can't just leave me here."

"I can drive you home now or drive you home later this afternoon when I come back. I'll bring Braden."

Most grandmothers would be thrilled to see their grandchildren. This was not the case with Marianne Milanovic. She found grandchildren, as she had found her own children, to be a horrible nuisance.

"I guess I'll stay," her mother said, reaching for the tissue box.

119

Chapter 22

Pete was in the stockroom at the dollar store opening boxes of Halloween decorations when the door opened and two men stepped into the room. Pete could tell just by looking at them that they were cops.

"Mr. Pappas?" the first cop said. He was Chinese.

Pete nodded.

"I'm Detective Yang." He tilted his head slightly to his partner, a stocky, balding man with a Greying cop-stache. "This is Detective Munroe."

"We're with the Integrated Homicide Investigation Team," Munroe said.

"What's this about?"

"Is there somewhere we can talk?" Yang asked. He was a slight man and looked to be in his mid-thirties.

Pete looked around the back room of the dollar store. Kewal, one of Pete's coworkers was unpacking a box in slow motion, trying to pretend he wasn't listening to Pete's conversation with the two detectives.

"We can go out back I guess. I could use a smoke anyway." Pete turned to Kewal. "I'll be outside."

Kewal nodded and the three men went out the back door onto a concrete loading dock. Pete lit a cigarette. Hopefully it would help calm his nerves. He was playing it cool but his brain was firing on all cylinders, trying to figure out how the detectives had found him so quickly. Pete assumed that because he was known to hang out with Chewy and because of his criminal record there was a chance the police would come talk to him, but he hadn't expected it this quickly. He mentally kicked himself for not having his alibi locked down.

Munroe noted that they would be recording the conversation, Pete agreed, and the cop turned on a small recording device, stating the date, time, location, and a list of those present before they began.

Yang started the questioning. "When was the last time you saw Chewy Awesome?"

Pete was impressed the cop kept a straight face when he said Chewy's name. "Shit," he said. "I don't know. A week maybe."

"You weren't with Mr. Awesome last night?"

"No. Why would you think that?"

"Where were you last night?"

It was the question Pete had been dreading. "Home," he said. It wasn't a great answer but it was his safest bet.

"Were you alone?"

He put a hand to his chin and stroked his beard. "What's this about?"

"Were you home alone or was someone with you?"

"If you answer my question I might answer yours."

"That's not how this works Mr. Pappas." It was Munroe this time.

Pete shrugged. "I was alone."

Yang resumed the questioning. "Can anyone verify your whereabouts?"

"Not that I know of."

"No one saw you enter your building? You didn't order a pizza? You didn't log onto your computer or order a movie on pay-per-view or talk to your girlfriend?"

Pete shook his head. "Nope."

"What did you do all night?"

"Nothing," Pete said, exhaling smoke. "I worked out."

"Worked out?"

"I have some gym equipment. A bench and some free weights."

"Did you do anything else?"

"I jacked off, then I went to bed."

"When you masturbated, was it to porn on the internet or was it on TV?" Munroe asked.

It didn't appear to have occurred to the cops that Pete's comment was sarcasm. He had to be careful though. He knew they could track his internet use and if he said he watched TV they'd trip him up by asking what shows he watched, on what channel and at what time.

"I use my imagination."

"What time did you go to bed?"

Pete shrugged. "Ten I guess."

"That's pretty early."

"It was a weeknight." He scratched his beard. "I had to work in the morning. I'd hate to lose my job here at the dollar store."

"What time were you home last night?"

"I don't know. Six I guess. I never went out."

"So you were home for four hours before you went to bed. Were you working out that whole time or was that four hours of jacking off?" Munroe asked.

Pete kept his voice level. "I made something to eat. Then I cleaned up the kitchen, then I worked out, then I had a shower, then I jacked off, and then I went to bed."

"You think you're pretty funny don't you?" Munroe asked.

"Not at all," Pete said.

He never tried to be funny. Sometimes people thought he was joking when in reality he was just an asshole. The line between humor and being an asshole was a thin one.

"You didn't see Mr. Awesome last night?" Yang asked.

"I just told you. I was home alone."

"Any idea why Chewy's girlfriend told us he was with you last night?"

Pete shrugged.

"She told us Chewy had a job with you last night. He was going to make a little money. Any idea what that might have been?"

Pete felt two sets of eyes on him, watching for his reaction. He stayed cool. The mystery of how the cops came to interview him so quickly was solved.

"Chewy lied," he said.

"Why would he do that Mr. Pappas?"

"My guess is he was banging some chick on the side and told his girlfriend he was with me."

"How long have you known Mr. Awesome?"

Pete had to think about it. "Maybe two years."

"Are you close friends?"

"He was just a guy who was around sometimes. We hung out in the same bar with some of the same people."

They asked questions about the people Pete and Chewy hung around with and the bars they went to. Pete answered their questions and gave them names. They asked Pete to account for his whereabouts from the time he woke up until he went to bed.

"Any idea who Mr. Awesome might have been with last night if not you?" Munroe asked.

"I don't pay much attention to Chewy's love life. We have different taste in women."

"How so?"

"He likes muscle-chicks. The ones that look like dudes in bikinis and high heels."

"And you're not into that?"

Pete shook his head. "Not my thing."

"Have you ever been in Chewy's car?"

Changing the topic without warning seemed to be a favorite interview technique for the detectives. "Yeah," Pete said. "Lots of times. It's a Sebring. Piece of shit."

"You sound like you don't like Chewy much," Yang observed.

Pete thought about that. He didn't like Chewy but he didn't like most people.

"I don't know," Pete said. "I don't really think about it. The guy was just around. He was alright I guess."

"I notice you're using the past tense," Munroe said. "'The guy was just around' and 'he was alright'. Why is that?"

"Because he's dead obviously or didn't you know that? It's all over Facebook. His girlfriend created a memorial page."

"You don't seem upset by that."

Pete shrugged.

"Are you upset?" Yang asked.

"Let me tell you a story about Chewy," Pete said, dropping his cigarette butt on the concrete and crushing it under his boot. "A group of us went to Granville Island for some reason in the summer - I don't remember why - but we got hungry and went to the food fair. Chewy decides he wants fish and chips so he goes to the fish and chip place and guess what he does?"

The cops watched Pete with curious expressions on their faces but apparently they weren't interested in trying to guess.

"He asks them to melt cheese on his fish," Pete said. "They don't have cheese, obviously, because 'who the fuck puts cheese on fish?' But Chewy is expecting this and pulls out two slices of Kraft-fucking-cheese from his pocket, individually wrapped in plastic, and insists they melt it on his fish. The fucking guy carried two slices of processed cheese around with him all day. Then he sits down with us and wants to eat his fucking cheese-fish. I got up and left. It was fucking embarrassing."

"What's your point?"

"I'm just saying... people die every day. Is the world really going to miss a guy who puts cheese on his fish? I don't think so."

Chapter 23

Toni Little looked over her shoulder and put the forklift in reverse. After a few months of working in the warehouse she'd grown oblivious to the incessant beeping sound the lift made. When she'd backed up enough to turn around, she stopped the forklift and was about to move ahead to load the pallet of DVD players into the trailer when she saw her supervisor, Gavin Taylor, waving at her like an idiot from across the aisle.

Toni waited while Gavin made his way to the forklift. He was a soft 250lbs and looked ridiculous in an absurdly small safety vest.

"We need to talk," Gavin said.

Toni held up her hands, indicating that she was in the middle of doing something.

"Leave it for now," Gavin said. He motioned for her to get off the forklift.

Toni turned the lift off and hopped down. He was her boss after all. "What do you need?" she said.

Gavin looked around. "Not here. In my office."

She sighed and they walked to Gavin's office where she sat on one of the torn vinyl chairs between the desk and the wood panel wall.

Gavin took off the fluorescent vest and hung it on a hook beside a battered filing cabinet, closed the door and dropped his girth into a well-worn office chair behind the desk. The room smelled vaguely of stale vomit.

"What's this about?" Toni asked.

"We're being blackmailed."

"What?"

"There's a guy out there trying to blackmail us. He's got video footage."

"I thought the cameras were taken care of."

"They are... they are," Gavin said. "But this is different. Its amateur video, shot with a cell phone. He wants $7,500 or he says he'll release it."

"How'd he get the video?"

"I don't know."

"Is it someone who works here?"

Gavin looked impatient. "I don't know, I don't fucking know." His hands shook. "It doesn't matter. We need to do something about it."

"What did you have in mind?" Toni asked slowly. She wasn't sure where Gavin was going with this.

"Isn't it obvious?"

She stared silently at Gavin, waiting, letting him know it wasn't obvious.

"You need to kill him," he finally said.

Toni narrowed her eyes. "What the fuck? You want me to kill someone?"

"Would you rather pay him $7,500?"

"What are you talking about?"

127

"That's your choice. Pay him or kill him."

"Why is this on me? You're the ring leader."

"We're in this together. You're all over that video."

"Maybe so, but I don't see why this falls on me. Why can't you pay him or kill him if you think that's what needs to be done?"

"I can't. I'm in deep with the Russian mob. I'm tapped out."

Toni raised an eyebrow. "The Russian mob?"

"I'm up to my neck in it. You have no fucking idea."

Toni didn't know what he was talking about. There was no Russian mob in Vancouver. Gavin was an idiot.

"Maybe you don't have the money to pay him but you could kill him."

Gavin shifted uncomfortably in his seat. "I thought of that and... you know... I think it'd be better if you did it."

"I'm sure you do." Toni said. "Before we do anything, I want to see this video."

Gavin exhaled. "I don't have it anymore."

Toni leaned forward. She was a woman, but she was fit and muscular and knew she could intimidate a lot of men. Men like Gavin. "Why not?"

"I deleted it."

"You're shitting me?"

"No." Gavin's voice became a loud whisper. "It was on my computer. He sent it to my work email for Christ sake."

"You could have saved it on a flash drive or something."

"You don't understand the pressure I'm under," Gavin said, clearly growing agitated. He was more disheveled than usual and his face was getting red. "I can't have that shit on my computer. I fucking can't."

"Take it easy," she said. Gavin claimed he was some kind of shit-hot poker player but Toni couldn't imagine how that was true. He hid his emotions like a thirteen year old girl.

"I don't think you understand. This is serious fucking shit."

Toni took a deep breath and waited for Gavin to get it together. In her opinion, this was not 'serious fucking shit'. Toni had been to Afghanistan. She'd seen 'serious fucking shit'.

When Gavin calmed a little, Toni asked, "Why should I kill the guy? Why not Grant or Bobby? They're in this too. Why do I get the honor?"

"I just thought... you know... you had experience." Gavin sounded like a child being punished. "You were in the army. I figured you probably killed people before so it wouldn't be a big deal ... you know... to kill one more."

She narrowed her eyes. "There's a big difference between killing in combat and murdering someone over stolen TVs."

"Yeah, maybe... I mean, I know it's morally wrong and all that, but you know how to do it at least." Gavin pointed at himself. "Look at me. Do I look like I know how to kill someone?"

Toni had done two tours in Afghanistan but contrary to what Gavin had assumed, she'd never killed anybody. She was willing to do it though, under the right circumstances. She thought of her sister Katie and her dream of going to college.

"What's in it for me if I do this?"

Gavin looked confused. "We get rid of the blackmailer."

"That benefits all of us. I'm the one taking the risk. What do I get for my efforts?"

"Now you're trying to blackmail me?"

"It's not blackmail Gavin. I'm taking the risk. I need to be compensated for that."

"Like what?"

"A bigger cut."

"Jesus, Toni. You're killing me. I already owe the Russian mob. They have me by the fucking balls."

"Do you want me to do this or not?"

Gavin stared at her but didn't say anything.

"From now on I take half," she said. "You and the other guys can split the rest any way you want."

Gavin sighed. "Grant and Bobby aren't going to like that."

"Then they can kill the guy."

"Alright, alright. Just get it done."

"And I want direct contact with Anton."

Gavin looked flustered. "I can't do that. He'll only talk to me."

"Tell him this is the way it is or the deal is off."

"Fuck. You might as well put a gun to my head." Gavin pressed a finger to his temple. "Alright, alright, but it has to be done tonight. He's expecting me at the No. 5 at 9. You like strippers don't you?"

Toni hadn't told anyone she worked with that she was gay but they assumed it anyway. It annoyed her that she fit whatever stereotype men like Gavin assumed about gay women but after eight years in the military, she was used to it.

"It all depends on whether or not they can dance," she said.

Gavin grinned, like the fucking pervert he was. "Maybe you can get a lap dance while you're there."

She stared hard into his eyes.

He looked uncomfortable and broke eye contact, glancing down at his desk. "He'll have a laptop and a phone and maybe some other computer shit to give us in exchange."

"That doesn't make any sense," she said.

"What doesn't make sense?"

"Why is he giving us laptops and phones? It's weird."

"The video is on it," Gavin said, as if Toni were too stupid to understand.

"So? The video could be on a hundred devices. It can be on servers, on a cloud, or he could have emailed it to a thousand people. It doesn't make sense for him to give us his fucking phone."

Gavin sighed. "Just bring it to me and I'll worry about that."

It was irritating to have Gavin talk to her as if he were some kind of computer savant and she was a backwater hick with no idea how technology worked. But she held her tongue. Nothing Gavin said made any sense.

"So he gives you the phone and laptop, and then when he leaves, I follow him and kill him."

"Fuck no. I'm not going to be there. You take care of it."

"That won't work Gavin. I don't know what he looks like. He's expecting you, not me. How am I going to know who to kill?"

"I-ah-I don't know."

"How have you been communicating with this guy?" Toni asked. "You said you got an email from him. Is it just email or have you talked or texted with him on the phone?"

Gavin seemed taken aback by the question. "Ah – both I guess. I talked to him once and he texted me a couple times on the phone, the one Anton gave me."

"I'm going to need that cell."

Gavin looked alarmed. "Why?"

"I'll need to text him so I can draw him out."

"I don't know..."

"Just give me the fucking phone Gavin."

"Why don't you tell me what you want me to text to him and I'll do it?"

Toni leaned in. "Why don't you kill him yourself? If I say I need your phone, I need your phone."

Gavin squirmed in his seat. Finally he said, "Ok, but I have to delete some personal shit off of it first. Come get it at the end of your shift."

"As long as the guy's number is still there," she said. "I need that."

"It'll be there."

"Maybe I'll learn something about our blackmailer."

131

Gavin looked alarmed. "There's nothing to learn. You just need to kill him."

Toni stared at Gavin. There was something fucked up about this whole thing, she thought.

"I'll kill him," she said, even though she had no plans to kill anyone if she could avoid it. She wanted to see how things played out. The only thing she knew for certain was that she couldn't trust Gavin.

Gavin appeared mollified. "Ok. D'you know how you're going to do it... I mean... d'you know how you're going to kill him?"

"Not yet."

"You should make it look like an accident. The guy's connected to the Russian mob. If they think we killed him that might not be good for us."

She seriously doubted that the blackmailer was connected to the Russian mob.

"You can't just whack a 'made' guy," Gavin went on. "It'd be better if he got... you know... hit by a bus or if he fell down a flight of stairs or had the radio fall in the bathtub, something like that."

Toni shook her head. She was always amazed when she met people in the civilian world who, if they'd been born anywhere else on the planet, would have been dead decades ago. Here in North America, people like Gavin led long useless lives even though they were, by any reasonable standard, too stupid to live.

"I'll see what I can do," she said.

Chapter 24

Pete Pappas got off the bus on West Broadway and walked a block until he reached an office building. He wandered into a marble lobby, found the directory, and scanned it for the company he was looking for. A few minutes later he stood in front of a frosted glass door on the third floor. The lettering on the door read Hiro P Consulting Group.

He opened the door and found a typical office filled with workstations, except each station faced a wall and had multiple rows of stacked monitors. It looked like a NASA control center. No partitions separated the work stations and a large open space occupied the center of the room. There was no receptionist at the counter and there appeared to be only one person in the office.

Kevin Hofstede jumped up from a leather office chair and bound toward him with the effusive confidence of a car salesman.

"Pete," he said. "I'm glad you found us."

Pete shrugged. "You gave me the address. There are signs everywhere. Why wouldn't I find you?"

"You're a funny guy." Kevin opened a small gate on the reception counter to let Pete in and then reached out his hand. Pete felt awkward but shook it.

"Sit down, sit down," Kevin said, directing Pete to one of the many computer workstations.

Pete looked around, feeling out of place. He'd talked to Kevin a few times before and he'd met him in person, but he'd never had a one-on-one meeting like this. He made his way to the nearest work station and leaned against the corner of the desk.

"Everyone else is gone," Kevin said. "Do you want a drink or anything?"

Pete didn't answer. He was confused. When Kevin had given him the address and said he wanted to meet here, Pete had assumed he would find a seedy office squirrelled away behind a massage parlor or something. This office looked professional - respectable. The furniture and fixtures were new and contemporary. Pete would have preferred to meet in a dingy basement office under a laundromat. This was not a world he felt comfortable in.

"What is this place?" Pete asked. "It looks like a legit office."

"It is."

"So it's like a front?"

"I guess you could say that, but not really." Kevin grinned. He was a fair-haired, lanky, good looking guy in his late twenties or early thirties. He didn't look like a computer geek or a criminal. He looked like the star of the college basketball team. "Mostly I'd say this is part of the machine, part of the enterprise that makes me money. It's the legit part that I pay taxes on. Heck, I even have business cards."

Kevin walked purposefully to the front door and locked it.

"But if you have all this," Pete said, looking around. "Why -?"

"Why do I engage in criminal activities? Because it's profitable. More profitable than all this. And most of the time it's fun."

Pete nodded. "It looks like you're doing all right."

"My parents love all this. They don't understand the first thing about computers but they like being able to tell their friends how successful I am." He clapped his hands together. "What about that drink? D'you want a beer?"

"Ah-sure."

"If I start talking to my parents about a SYN flood, DDoS attacks, or TCP and UDP packets, their eyes glaze over. They don't know what we do here and they don't care. Not really. What they understand is that a nice office equals success and that a child's success means they didn't screw up as parents. This office validates their whole fucking lives."

Kevin disappeared into a back room and returned with two microbrewery beers in bottles. Pete accepted the beer and took a hard pull. He thought of his parents and his successful siblings. Pete was the only one of four siblings who hadn't gone to college. He was the only one who hadn't become a respected professional like a doctor or a lawyer. He was the only one who was a fuck up.

"Who's Hiro P?" Pete asked.

"Hiro Protagonist," Kevin said and dropped back into his office chair.

The name was clearly supposed to mean something to Pete. He stared at Kevin.

"Neal Stephenson? Snow Crash? Hiro Protagonist?" Kevin prompted.

Pete shook his head. He had no idea what Kevin was talking about.

"He's a character in a book." Kevin said, sounding defeated, like he'd been trying to explain something to someone who didn't speak the language and had finally given up.

Pete nodded. He hadn't read a book since Lord of the Flies in the eighth grade, and even then he hadn't read most of it, just the parts where one of the kids got killed.

Kevin took a long swig and fixed his eyes on Pete. "So let's get down to it then."

"Down to what? I thought I was here to pick up the computer stuff from last night to give to the warehouse guy."

"Nope," Kevin said.

"I thought you were done with them."

"I am done with them. I needed to know if a file was saved to a cloud server or emailed to anyone. It had been uploaded to a cloud server but I was able to delete it."

"Great. So, I can give him the stuff?"

Kevin laughed. "Shit, no. I destroyed them."

"What are you talking about? I need them to get paid. This Gavin dude wants them."

"Gavin's an idiot. We can give him any laptop and phone and he'll never know the difference. For Christ's sake, the guy thinks I'm a Russian mobster named Anton."

Pete felt his pulse pound in his temple. "Won't he check them?"

Kevin grinned. "He couldn't crack the password, let alone find anything once he was in. He's stalling."

"Stalling?"

"For time."

Pete stared at him. "I don't understand."

"He probably can't pay you."

"What the fuck? You're talking in riddles." Pete leaned forward. "I just want my money."

"I'll give you a little background that might clear things up."

"It fucking better, because nothing you're saying makes any sense."

"I met Gavin a few months ago. He had money-problems. I played poker with him a few times in the casino. He might be the worst player I've ever seen. He loses, every time. So I'm talking to him, and it turns out he's a supervisor at an electronics warehouse and I suggest he could make some money if he was willing to steal shit from the warehouse." Kevin shrugged. "Turns out he's open to the idea. He gets me in and gives me access to the warehouse's computer network. I do my thing and now I can adjust inventory numbers and override security cameras. Gavin recruits a small crew and we start stealing shit. It's working fine, not super profitable but we're making money, and then one of the workers at the warehouse figures out what Gavin is up to and tries to blackmail him with a video he took with his phone."

"Marko. The guy I killed."

"Right. Gavin doesn't want to give him what he wants and asks yours truly, Anton, for a referral so he can hire a professional hit man. I thought of you."

"That's great but it doesn't do me any good if he can't pay."

"There's still an upside to all this. He's scared shitless of me. I have this whole persona going where he thinks I'm a Russian mobster. Seriously. It's fucking retarded. He has no clue. There is no Russian mob in Vancouver. We have the Hell's Angels, the Red Scorpions, and the United Nations Gang. The guy watches too much TV."

Pete felt himself grow agitated. "I don't give a shit about any of that. I want to get paid."

"I know, I know, but like I said, he's scared shitless of me and he thinks you're a professional hit man with mob connections, so he's even more scared of you. Trust me, if he can, he'll find the money."

"This is bullshit. I might get paid, if he can find the money. What if he can't?"

"You'll get paid. Don't worry about it. We're getting bogged down in the past. I want to talk the future, what we do next. This warehouse venture, it isn't working out."

"You lost me again."

Kevin put the beer down on the desk. "The warehouse thefts were a mistake. It was fun, but its high risk, low return, and way too time consuming. It's time to shut that shit down."

"What are you talking about?"

"There're too many people involved. When the warehouse guys get caught, and inevitably they will, maybe they try to give me up, maybe they don't. They don't know who I am, but still, it's a risk."

"I'm not following."

"Marko, the man you killed, he was a liability. Just like Gavin is a liability."

"You want me to kill him?"

Kevin smiled. "And you said you weren't following."

"If I kill him, how does he pay me?"

Kevin sighed. "There's a good chance he was never going to pay you. The guy's a degenerate gambler."

"So, what, I don't get paid?"

"That's not what I'm saying. Look, I wanted the blackmailer dead too. As Anton I convinced Gavin that he needed to take responsibility for that, and if he pays you – great. If not, I'm good for it. You'll get paid."

Pete nodded, non-committedly.

"Do you still have the gun you used on the muscle head?" Kevin asked.

Pete patted his pocket. "It's right here."

"Good. After you kill Gavin, leave it behind with Gavin's finger prints on it."

"Guns aren't cheap," Pete said. He was getting tired of taking the fucking bus, let alone trying to find cash to buy a new gun for a job no one had paid him for.

"I'll look after that too."

"No offence, but I haven't seen shit yet."

"We'll fix that. When are you meeting Gavin?"

"Tonight at 9."

Kevin looked thoughtful. "Push it back to tomorrow night. I have a gig for you tonight if you're interested. Unrelated to the warehouse thing."

"I can't keep waiting to get paid."

"I'll pay you for the job tonight." Kevin smiled. "And if Gavin doesn't come up with the cash he owes you before you kill him, like I said, I'll cover that too."

Pete tilted his head from side to side, like he was working out a kink in his neck. "And I get paid for killing Gavin too I assume."

Kevin lifted an envelope off the desk and handed it to him. "That's for tonight."

Pete opened the envelope and saw that it was filled with twenties and fifties. He didn't know what the job was but it didn't matter. He'd do pretty much anything for that kind of cash.

"If Gavin doesn't come through tomorrow," Kevin added. "I'll cover the $7,500 promised for that and give you the same for taking care of Gavin."

"Alright. I'm in."

"One more thing. I want you to do something for me." Kevin stood. "I don't how to say this without insulting you so I'm just going to lay it out there."

Pete stared at him.

"You look like an Islamic terrorist."

"I'm Greek."

"It doesn't matter. People notice you. They remember you. When they see you they pay attention because they think you're going to plant a fucking bomb or something. You need to blend in."

"People take one look at me and they know not to fuck with me."

"They'll know that anyway. Just shave. That's all I'm saying."

Pete grunted. He couldn't believe it. The dollar store didn't give a shit what he looked like but to be a criminal, he needed to shave.

Chapter 25

Ana was exhausted but knew it would be hours before she'd have a chance to sleep. She picked Braden up from school and the two of them headed to Vancouver General Hospital, even though what she really needed was a nap.

"Mommy is taking you to the hospital because Uncle Steve is there and Grandma wants to see you," Ana explained even though she doubted that her mother had any interest in seeing Braden.

"Is Uncle Marko in heaven with Grandpa?" Braden asked. He was secured in a car seat in the back of the Sunfire. Braden complained about the car seat all the time. He told her that some of his school friends didn't use a car seat or a booster seat anymore. Their parents let them use a seat belt and sit in the front.

Of course, Ana thought, their parents hadn't seen nearly as many car accidents as she had.

"Yes, Uncle Marko is in heaven with Grandpa." She felt tears welling in her eyes and blinked them away.

"But not Uncle Steve?"

"No. Not Uncle Steve. Uncle Steve is in the hospital."

He thought about that for a moment and then told her that his friend Ryan's mom was in the hospital. Then he told her about how another boy at school had a cat who had kittens, and how another boy brought a Batman action figure to school, and how his teacher, Miss Kirby, said he did really good with his alphabet. A conversation with a six year could be exhausting. The abrupt shifts in topic could be disorienting even for someone who'd had more than an hour's sleep in the last day.

When Braden paused for a moment, Ana said. "Do you remember Rick from the other night? He came over to our house?"

"Uh-huh."

"He invited us to come stay at his house tonight. Does that sound like fun?"

Braden was clearly not convinced that this was a good idea.

"He has a really big TV. We can watch one of your movies and have popcorn."

She was a little embarrassed that she had resorted to bribery so quickly.

"OK," he said, reluctantly.

"Mommy packed your bag with your toothbrush and your PJ's."

"Can Lukin come too?" he asked.

Oh my God, Ana thought, the kid was determined to make her cry. "No honey. Lukin can't come."

"Oh." She could hear the disappointment in his voice. "Won't he be lonely?"

The tears came. She couldn't stop them. She reached for a tissue from a box on the passenger seat, dabbed at her eyes and blew her nose.

"What's wrong mommy?"

She took a deep breath. "Mommy's just sad, honey."

"Because Uncle Marko went to heaven?"

They were stuck in traffic at a red light. Ana turned to face her son, realizing there was no point in trying to hide her tears. She reached back and touched his hand.

"Yes honey. Mommy is sad because Uncle Marko went to heaven."

She had no idea how she was going to tell him about the dog.

◆

When they arrived at the hospital they found Ana's mother sitting in the waiting area, reading a magazine. She was uncharacteristically excited to see Braden. There were, after all, people in the waiting room and she had a role to play.

"Braden, my sweet little angel, come give your Grandma a hug."

He paused for a moment. He wasn't used to this version of Grandma, the one who noticed him when he wasn't making too much noise or giving her a headache.

"Go on honey," Ana prompted.

He wandered over shyly and she wrapped herself around him and ruffled his sandy blonde hair and told him he was getting big. After her mother had finished another Academy Award worthy performance, Ana asked if Steve was awake.

"I don't know. I thought I would sit out here for a little while and let him rest. I think it tires him to have company all the time."

Ana knew her mother was the one who needed a break. How would she catch up on the latest Kardashian scandal if she didn't take the time to read about it?

"I was getting hungry," her mother went on. "But I didn't bring my purse so I haven't been able to eat anything. I wasn't expecting to be left alone here for hours."

It had been less than 90 minutes since Ana had left the hospital.

She sighed and pulled a $20 bill out of her purse. "Why don't you take Braden for a snack while I check on Steve?"

She could see a flash of horror on her mother's face at the thought of being left alone with a six year old. Ana wasn't thrilled herself at the prospect of leaving Braden with her mother but how much damage could she do in 15 or 20 minutes? She didn't want Braden to see Steve in his current condition. She also wanted to talk to him alone.

"I suppose," her mother said slowly.

There wasn't much she could do. There were people watching.

♦

After they were gone, Ana found Steve's room. There were four beds in the room, two empty and one shielded by curtains. Steve was awake in the fourth bed, staring out the window. His face was swollen and bruised, making him barely recognizable. An IV tube ran to his wrist and his ribs were taped.

He turned when she came in. "Hey sis."

"Hey." She took a seat beside the bed. "How you feelin'?"

He groaned. "I could use more drugs."

"I think you've had more than your share," she said with a smile. So often she forgot the 'old Steve' who was bright, funny, and artistic. He used to draw, albeit usually demons, dragons, and skulls, but he was talented. Ana was the jock and Steve was the artist.

He stared at her earnestly. "I'm going to get clean."

She'd heard that before but she was still glad to hear him make the promise. Maybe some good would come from Marko's death.

She put her hand on top of his. "I'm glad. I want you to know that I'm here to help."

"Thanks sis."

They talked for a while about innocuous things and then Ana said, "How did it go with the police?"

143

Steve nodded and then winced as if the movement caused him pain. "I couldn't tell them much."

"But you told them what you know?"

"I guess."

"What do you mean – 'I guess?"

"I don't know."

"You want them to find the people who did this, right?"

Steve looked confused. "Yeah, sure."

Ana felt anger creep in. "You don't sound like you're sure."

"I am. I do."

"Steve, you need to be straight with us on this."

"I am being straight."

"Who did this to you?"

"I don't know."

"You don't know?"

He looked genuinely confused.

"You're saying you don't know who killed Marko?" Ana asked.

"I only saw one of them. The guy was built like the Hulk. He was huge."

"Why did they come to the apartment? What did they want?"

"I don't know."

"Were they mad at you? Did you owe them money? Did they want drugs?"

Steve shook her hand off. "What are you talking about?"

"They were after something."

"This had nothing to do with me."

The empathy Ana had felt for Steve evaporated. She stood. "You need to tell the police what you know about the guys who did this."

"I don't know anything about them. This had nothing to do with me."

"Don't lie to me Steve."

He turned and stared out the window. "If that's what you think

– just go. Get the fuck out of here."

"It's an addiction Steve. That's what led to this. You need to be straight about what happened. We need to find the people who did this."

He shook his head, still staring out the window, not looking at Ana. "Thanks for visiting sis. Thanks for your fucking concern."

Ana stared at him, tears in her eyes. She couldn't do it anymore. She couldn't listen to his denials and excuses. "You need help Steve. I can help you but -"

"Fuck you."

"He was your brother."

"Get the fuck out."

She turned and started toward the door. When she reached the hallway she heard him shout after her. "It was Marko they were after, so fuck you! Fuck all of you!"

Chapter 26

Gavin sat at his desk, deleting text messages on the burner phone. He was worried about Toni. Women, as far as he was concerned, fit into one of three categories: fuckable, unfuckable, and highly fuckable. Toni though was in a different category entirely. She was 'scary as shit'. He felt like he'd made a deal with the devil to buy some time and the clock was ticking. He didn't want to lose control of the situation by having Toni deal directly with Anton and he definitely couldn't afford to have her take a bigger cut of the payout.

For Christ sake, he thought, Toni was a woman. She didn't need the money. Gavin, on the other hand, had three fucking ex-wives who were sucking him dry.

Once again, life wasn't fair.

The solution however was clear. Gavin needed to find someone to kill Toni after Toni killed the man he'd hired to kill Marko.

Like most things in life, he thought, his problems could be solved with a generous infusion of cash. Before the bad beat on Monday night he'd been on a roll. If the Poker Gods hadn't fucked him over, he would have left the casino with enough money to pay the hired killer. Instead, he was broke and had no choice but to make the deal with Toni.

His phone pinged. He was reluctant to look at the message. He expected bad news but when he read it, he smiled. His luck had changed. The killer wanted to move their meeting to tomorrow night.

He had a day's grace. Tomorrow was payday so he could load up with some new payday loans and hit the casino after work. A big win could go a long way to solving his problems.

♦

Ana stared at the mirror over the sink in the ladies restroom and decided that she looked presentable enough after an extended crying jag to venture into the world again.

What was happening to her, she wondered. She'd always been able to control her emotions, at least in public, but lately she'd become an emotional basket case.

It was difficult to see Steve in pain but she was frustrated that he wouldn't take responsibility for what happened. Even so, she'd reacted badly and to make matters worse she knew as little about what happened in that apartment as she did before her visit with Steve. All she'd done was put Steve on the defensive.

She took a deep breath and turned to leave the restroom. In the waiting room she found her mother reading a magazine while Braden played at a small table with his action figures.

"Where have you been?" her mother asked, not making any effort to hide her annoyance. There was no one else in the waiting room so there was no need to be concerned about appearances.

"I was with Steve, then I went to the restroom."

Her mother regarded her skeptically. "I'd like to go home. I can't remember the last time I slept. This whole situation has been very hard on me."

147

"It's been hard on all of us," Ana said.

"It would be a lot easier for me if your father was alive and if you weren't so busy with your own life and had time to think about me."

Ana was emotionally drained and in no condition to hold her own against her mother. "We can go now if you like."

"It's about time." She stood and collected her magazines, tissue box, and purse.

"Did you want to see Steve again before we leave?"

Her mother shook her head. "Let him sleep."

Ana stepped over to Braden and lightly touched the top of his head. He continued to play. Spiderman had just knocked the Riddler off the table and this apparently required Braden to produce a series of sound effects which resulted in the table being sprayed with spittle.

"Time to go Braden."

He looked up and smiled sweetly and she felt her heart melt. Thirty minutes with her mother hadn't caused any apparent damage.

As Ana drove, her mother reminisced about Steve as a child, about how creative and special he was. She spoke fondly of the time Steve had made her a bread board in wood-working class and how he'd given it to her for Mother's Day. The entire class had obviously made the bread boards for Mother's Day and Ana wondered who else her mother thought he would give it to. But her mother chose to remember this moment as a special gesture of love.

The memory Ana recalled with the greatest clarity involving her mother and Steve was when he was eight years old and had come home from a friend's overnight birthday party. He'd been rambunctious and with her patience strained, she snapped at him. Ana remembered the words as clearly as if they'd been spoken only seconds earlier. Her mother told Steve that she liked it when he went on sleepovers and that she wished he had a sleepover every night because she was happiest when he wasn't home. Steve had burst into tears and locked himself in his room which suited her fine. She never raised a hand to her children

148

but she had a knack for inflicting emotional scars.

"I could sleep for days," her mother said as Ana pulled the car into the driveway.

Ana smiled weakly. "I think we all could."

She knew that wasn't the reply her mother wanted to hear. She wanted it acknowledged that she held a special burden as the mother. That she'd been deprived of sleep longer than anyone else and that her pain was more severe than anyone else's. Ana was aware that she was being unnecessarily petty, failing to pander to her mother's needs, but she couldn't help herself sometimes.

"I don't know that I'll be able to sleep," her mother said, climbing out of the car and then turning back to face Ana. "I should probably take something but I'd worry that the hospital might call and I wouldn't hear the phone."

"Hopefully you'll be able to get some sleep. I know this has been hard for you." She had to dig deep for that comment but it had the desired effect.

"It's been hard. I wish your father was alive."

"Me too mom. Me too."

Her mother closed the car door and headed into the house. No goodbye. No thank you. Not even a wave to Braden.

Chapter 27

Ana parked in front of Rick's house on West 22nd. It was a nice neighborhood with houses that were older but well maintained. Rick's house stood out because it had been renovated and was more contemporary looking than rest of the neighborhood.

Rick met Ana and Braden at the door and let them in. The interior looked like the 'after' shots on those home improvement shows that Ana never watched. It had an open concept main floor with light oak hardwood floors, leather furniture, and stylish light fixtures. There was a huge flat screen TV mounted over the split-face travertine mosaic tile fireplace. The kitchen had the ubiquitous quartz countertops and white shaker style cabinets. She could smell dinner cooking and was reminded that she hadn't eaten all day.

Braden clung to her leg with one hand while the other clutched his Transformer backpack. She slipped off her flats, which was awkward to do with Braden attached to one leg.

"This is a nice place you have."

Rick smiled warmly. "Thanks. I made paprika chicken with

Greek yogurt and sriracha sauce. I hope that's ok."

"Ah sure," Ana said, looking down at her son, still firmly affixed to her leg. "It's not going to be too hot for Braden is it?"

"It shouldn't be but I picked up some Kraft Dinner just in case."

She reached down and picked Braden up and set him on her hip. "Why are you being shy?" she asked him. "You remember Rick."

She tried to turn his head to look at Rick but he hid his face in her shoulder.

"Don't be silly." She took a step further into the room. "Look at the big TV. Rick has to go to work tonight and you and mommy can watch one of your shows on it."

Braden kept his face hidden. She turned to Rick and tilted her head as if to say 'kids, what can you do?'

He gave them a quick tour of the house. She and Braden would sleep together in a spare room. Braden gradually began to warm to the situation and eventually Ana was able to put him down, which was good because the kid was heavy.

"So did you do all this work yourself?" she asked.

"A lot of it. It's different when it's your own house. I use contractors when I flip. I don't have time to do any work myself."

She knew he had a real estate business on the side and that was how he could afford luxuries like the sports car but she was starting to think he was more successful at it than he'd let on. They talked for a while about his real estate holdings and it turned out that not only did he flip houses, he owned a number of apartment buildings and a few commercial buildings. He was a regular Monopoly land baron.

"Why do you work as a paramedic? It doesn't look like you need the money."

He smiled. "I like the people I work with."

"No, seriously."

"These days I'm barely involved with the real estate stuff. I have a company that looks after the rentals and I haven't flipped a house in over a year. I like being a paramedic."

Braden had drifted away from the adults and found a spot in the living room where he could play with his action figures. Batman and Night Crawler were engaged in a life or death battle on the hearth of the fireplace.

They watched him play for a few minutes and she felt Rick put his hand on her shoulder. "How are you holding up?"

"I'm too tired to know." She turned to face him. "It's been hard but I'm ok. Really I am."

He smiled. "We should eat. I have to leave soon."

"It smells fabulous. You shouldn't have gone to so much trouble."

"This is nothing. You should see what I make on my days off."

Ana smiled. She could get used to this. Rick seemed more and more like the perfect man.

If only he'd let her muss his hair.

152

Chapter 28

Linda Thompson sat on the same leather couch she and Marko had shared two days earlier and took of a sip of Pinot Noir. She blinked away a tear and turned the page of a photo album. The pictures had been taken in the mid-nineties with a 35 mm camera before they'd owned their first digital camera and before anyone had imagined that one day people would take snapshots with their smart phones. In the family photos Andy was a baby and Marko looked blissfully happy. It broke her heart to know that she had deprived him of happiness for so many years.

It was 10:30 pm and the house was quiet except for the sound of jazz vocalist Cassandra Wilson drifting from the stereo. The song was a cover of a blues classic called Death Letter and it was the perfect accompaniment to Linda's melancholy mood. Her eyes had grown misty again and she blinked and turned a page in the album. She took another sip of her wine and stared at a photo of the three of them taken in the late nineties. Andy would have been two years old. They were at Linda's sister's wedding and Marko had asked a family member to take a picture of them since they were all dressed up.

In the photo the couple stood close together in front of a flower garden. Marko had one arm around Linda and he held Andy in the other. They were all smiling for the camera. Marko's smile was warm and genuine but hers held a hint of regret and sadness. Not everyone could see that but Linda knew it was there because she'd felt it. She hadn't wanted that life; the kids, the suburban home, the minivan, the backyard barbeques. But that hadn't stopped her from loving Marko.

Staring at the photo she was overwhelmed with regret and felt a deep aching loss. The tears came slowly at first but soon she was crying uncontrollably.

She didn't notice her son, Andy, come into the room until he sat beside her and put his arm around her shoulders. She'd never wanted to be a mother but she loved him. She cried on his shoulder and was grateful that he was there.

"I never stopped loving your father," she said, her voice hoarse from crying.

"I know."

The tears gradually slowed and she eased back and stared at her son. He'd become a handsome young man, good looking and slender like his father but much taller.

"I always thought we'd find each other again in our old age. I thought we could be a little old couple together. I know it's silly but I believed it."

"He would have liked that," he said. "I know he never stopped loving you."

She was struck by how he'd grown into an adult.

Andy started to tear up a little. "I miss him too."

Linda felt a twinge of guilt. She was the parent. She should be comforting him, not the other way around. "I know you do honey. He loved you with all his heart."

They talked for nearly an hour about Marko. They shared stories that were both funny and sad and they laughed and cried and comforted one another. Maybe this was the way it should be, Linda thought, with no roles to play anymore. She'd never felt close to Andy, probably because she'd never been comfortable with her role as a mother, but it was easier now that he was an adult.

Their conversation moved to other topics and they talked about school and his girlfriend Katie and his Aunt Ana. Ana was executor to Marko's estate and she'd asked Linda to help settle Marko's affairs and plan the funeral. Linda was happy to help and Ana was grateful, having little experience with the paperwork. Marko had been the one to look after the details of their father's death.

"I wish I'd know the last time I saw him that I wouldn't see him again," Linda said.

"I know what you mean. You just never imagine something like this happening. You just never know."

"You know," she said. "There was something strange about that last visit with your father."

Andy's eyes narrowed. "What's that?"

"It's probably nothing, but it was odd. He said he needed to check his email and wanted to use one of our computers but he didn't want to use my phone, the tablet, or the laptop. He used the computer downstairs."

"That's a little weird I guess."

"He was acting strange. I didn't think about it at the time but I wonder why he wanted to use that old computer." She turned to him. "Do you ever use it?"

Andy shook his head. "I have my MacBook. I tried to use it once when I first moved in but it's pretty slow."

"It's an old computer."

"That, and I hate to tell you this mom, but someone used it to watch porn, or at least they used to. It's loaded with malware."

"Oh?"

"As soon as you go on the internet you get bombarded with pop-ups for porn sites," he said.

Linda smiled awkwardly. "Well, I'm sorry you had to see that."

He scoffed. "I've seen it before. I'm not embarrassed by it or anything. It's a bit creepy to think of your step-father getting off on it though."

"You don't know that it was Dieter."

"Who else could it be?"

"I suppose," she said. If he thought it was creepy that his stepfather watched porn he probably didn't need to know about his mother's proclivities.

Andy nodded, like he was worldly and understood the baser nature of man.

"I want to check that computer to see what your father did on it," she said.

"We'll both look. Brace yourself though. You might see some stuff that'll embarrass you."

Linda smiled. It was sweet that her son thought that she might be offended by something as mundane as pornography.

Chapter 29

Andy Milanovic led the way to the basement with his mother following behind. The basement was finished but wasn't being used for anything except storage. The old recreation room was filled with abandoned furniture, boxes, and long forgotten exercise equipment. He took a seat at a desk in front of a fat CRT monitor. His mother stood behind him and watched as he booted up the CPU. There was no password protection on the computer and the familiar outdated Windows XP desktop image of a green field appeared on the screen. He set to work.

After a few minutes his mother asked, "Can you figure out what your father did when he was on the computer?"

He nodded. "Looks like he uploaded a video file."

He clicked the mouse. The CPU made a whirring sound and the media player opened and indicated it was loading the file. It took almost a minute but eventually the video started to play. The images in the video were dark and jumbled and showed two or three men and one woman loading boxed televisions and satellite receivers into a white panel van.

Andy stared at the images and felt his stomach drop. He recognized the woman in the video as Katie's sister, Toni. Presumably the video had been shot at the warehouse where his father and Toni worked.

His mother leaned over his shoulder. "What do you think this is?"

"I don't know."

"It looks like those people are stealing televisions," she said.

"It's hard to say," Andy said, staring at the screen.

She frowned. "Do you think this has something to do with your father's murder?"

Andy needed time to think. He needed to talk to Katie.

"I doubt it," he heard himself say, feeling for some reason like he was betraying his father.

"We should show this to the police."

"Maybe," Andy said.

"We can turn it over tomorrow. It might not have anything to do with what happened, but who knows, maybe it does."

Andy nodded.

"Is there anything else on the computer you can see that your dad might have looked at or loaded onto the computer?"

Andy shook his head. "No that's it. It looks like the only thing he did was load the video."

"That's strange," she said. "Why would he upload it on this computer and not tell me."

"I don't know, Mom."

There was a long silence.

"I'm sure it's nothing," she said.

"I think you're right," he said.

She kissed the top of his head. "Well, I'm going to bed. Don't stay up too late."

"I won't."

He stared at the computer screen and heard her walk to the base of the stairs and then stop.

"I love you honey," she said.

Andy's mother had told him many times that she loved him but he'd always suspected that she'd been going through the motions, saying things she thought a mother should say. For the first time in his life, he thought she meant it. Until that moment, he hadn't realized how desperately he needed that.

He heard her climb the stairs, unaware of the effect her words had on him. His eyes welled with tears, and then she was gone.

He watched the video three more times before he phoned Katie.

When she answered she was out of breath and sounded anxious. They usually texted one another when they were apart, especially late at night. They rarely talked on the phone, so the call, especially so late, had probably worried her.

He told her about the video and how his father had loaded it onto an old computer in his mother's house.

"Toni is on it," he said. "It looks like she's stealing from the warehouse."

Her tone was defensive. "She wouldn't do that."

"I'm just telling you what it looks like. There might be another explanation."

"There is."

"I hope so."

"Send it to me. I want to see it."

He disconnected the call and emailed her the video. A few minutes later she called back.

"Oh my God." The anger was gone from her voice. She sounded worried.

"I know."

"What should we do?"

"My mom wants to give the video to the police."

"She can't do that. My sister is on it."

"It might have something to do with my father's murder."

"It doesn't," she said.

"You can't know that."

"I know Toni would never hurt your dad."

"I'm sure she didn't, but someone did." Despite his assertion, he wasn't sure that Toni had nothing to do with his father's death. He knew she was paying for Katie's education and based on the video, it seemed clear how she could afford to do that.

There was a long silence and then Katie said, "Do you love me?"

"You know I do."

"You said you'd do anything for me."

The words stung. "I know, but -"

"Do you love me?" she repeated.

"I do," he said, barely more than a whisper.

"Will you do this for me?"

Andy closed his eyes. He felt like a paper doll being ripped in half.

"Yes," he said finally.

"I love you."

"I love you too." It was the first time since he'd found the courage to say the words that he struggled to repeat them.

"Don't forget to delete the email. We need to erase all traces of the file."

"Ok," he said but he knew it wasn't as simple as deleting the file. The police had sophisticated file recovery programs. He'd need to shred the file or wipe the hard drive clean.

"Text me when you're done."

"I will."

"You know I wouldn't ask you to do this if I thought Toni had anything to do with what happened to your father."

"I know," he said.

They disconnected the call and Andy wondered if love should make him feel this badly. He went upstairs. The main floor of the house was dark and quiet. His mother had gone to bed and his stepfather, Dieter, habitually went to bed early, often by 9 pm.

He made his way to his bedroom and found a USB flash drive on his desk. He decided he would keep his promise to Katie and remove the file from the computer.

But that didn't mean he couldn't save a copy for himself.

Chapter 30

Friday October 21

Ana stared at the plate of French toast that Rick had prepared like it was abstract art. She wasn't entirely sure what it was but it looked vaguely familiar. Regular French toast was obviously too pedestrian for Rick.

"It looks lovely," she said.

"It's infused with coconut milk and the bacon is smoked wild cherrywood," he said. "I get the bacon on-line from a little farm in Quebec."

Ana usually bought the no-name bacon from the grocery store but apparently there were gourmet bacon-farmers raising free-range piglets in tiny villages in rural Quebec and she could have been ordering exotic smoked bacons from them instead. It all seemed so pretentious to her.

It was also fucking delicious.

"Oh my god," she said. She was seated on a bar stool at the kitchen counter in Rick's house. "I feel like I'm having an orgasm in my mouth. You eat like this every day?"

He grinned at her from across the kitchen counter. "You can

too."

"No," she said automatically. "I could never cook like this." As she finished the sentence though she realized that wasn't what he meant. He meant that if she were in a relationship with him, he would cook for her all the time.

He smiled. "I bet you could cook like this if you wanted to."

She shook her head, pleased that he had allowed her misconception to go uncontested.

"Aren't you going to eat?" she asked.

"Absolutely. I wanted to take care of my guest first." He turned to the stove, finished preparing his plate, and sat beside her at the counter. "How was your night?"

"Surprisingly busy. My phone never stopped ringing."

She went on to tell him that her soon-to-be ex, Brad had called. He'd heard about Marko and Steve from Ana's mother.

"He's touring with his band in some hick town in Alberta. It turns out that he and my mother are Facebook friends and she follows his band on Twitter."

"It was good of him to call."

"I guess so." She decided not to mention that he started the call by complaining that she hadn't told him the news and then spent the rest of their conversation talking about his band. He didn't ask a single question about their son. "I also talked to Linda, Marko's ex-wife."

"How is she doing?"

She couldn't help but notice that he ate his bacon with a knife and fork. He probably ate pizza with a knife and fork too, she thought.

"As well as expected. She's going to help with the funeral arrangements. Marko made me his executor. Linda said she'd help. She's a finance whiz so it'll be nice to get her advice, plus I've always liked her." She ate a piece of bacon with her fingers, as God intended. "We're going to have lunch today to talk about it."

"That's great." Rick took a sip of pomegranate juice. "How's

Steve doing?"

"Not so good," she said and then told him about her visit with him at the hospital.

"It must be hard to have someone close to you struggle with addiction like that."

She sighed and stood. "I remember him before all this and it breaks my heart. He had so much potential."

She excused herself to go to the bathroom. When she returned Rick was standing at the living room window, looking out onto the street. He turned to face her.

"I talked to some of the fives last night, to see what I could find out about your brother's murder," he said.

"And?"

"The neighbors saw two men leave the building in a purple car."

"Did they get a good look at them?"

"Not really but it looks like one of the guys that did this is dead, shot in the head."

Ana remembered the story on the news about the other murder that night. "The body they found in the parking lot, he was one of the killers?"

"Yeah. He's some kind of juiced-up muscle-head. They found his car, a purple Sebring along with the TV still in the box, a few blocks from your place."

"Steve said the guy who beat him up was built like the Hulk."

"Sounds like the same guy. Apparently he was jacked."

"Anything else?" she asked, hopeful.

"It looks like the only thing these guys stole, other than the TV, was your brother's lap top and his cell phone. They didn't take anything else."

"The only thing stolen from my place was my tablet. I assumed they didn't have time to steal anything else because of Lukin."

"They only stole electronics."

"It doesn't sound like a robbery does it?" she said.

"What do you mean?"

"They were only interested in computer stuff."

"I guess so, but what else would they steal?"

"Marko had two other TVs. He had a stereo. They didn't even steal his wallet."

"Like you said, maybe they didn't have time to steal anything else."

"Steve said that what happened had nothing to do with him. He told me the killers were after Marko."

Rick scratched his beard. "And you believe him?"

"If they were after something on a computer or phone it seems more likely that Marko would have it."

"Does Steve even have a cell phone?"

"No. If he did he would sell it to buy drugs." She sighed. "I wish I'd listened to him yesterday instead of jumping all over him."

"You could talk to him again."

She nodded. "I'll go see him today and apologize."

Rick yawned and Ana remembered that he'd worked all night. It was nearly 10 am. He'd made breakfast for her after she dropped Braden off at school. "You should get some sleep."

He smiled. "I will. What do you have planned for today?"

"I'm meeting Linda for lunch and I need to pick Braden up from school. If there's time I'll swing by the hospital to see Steve before I get Braden."

Rick yawned again.

"I should let you sleep. Thanks for letting us stay here and for getting the locksmith taken care of. I appreciate it."

"I'm glad I could help. Are you staying at your place tonight?"

"I think it's best, for Braden. Maybe you can come over."

He moved close to her. "I'd like that."

"I'm sorry I've been such a mess lately."

"I'd say that under the circumstances, you're holding it together really well."

He stared into her eyes and she could sense that unless she did something to stop it, they were going to kiss. She reached out and ruffled his hair. It felt hard and crunchy with gel.

"Did it feel good to get that out of your system?" he asked, grinning.

"It did. Thanks."

"I'm here to please."

"How tired are you?" she asked with a flirtatious smile.

"Not that tired." His face moved closer to hers.

"Good."

They kissed. It was tentative at first. They'd been friends and coworkers for so long it felt awkward initially but it didn't take long for them to work past that.

Chapter 31

It was 11:35 am when Ana left Rick's place. She was running late for her lunch date with Linda but it had been worth it. The sex had been incredible - not as good as the French toast and cherrywood bacon - but almost. She sent Linda a quick text to let her know she'd be a few minutes late and noticed she'd missed a call. There was a voice message from her mother that she'd have to listen to later.

She drove over the Cambie Street Bridge and into downtown where she spent more time trying to find a parking space than she did actually driving to the restaurant. She eventually found a spot four blocks away. It was nearly 12:15 pm when she entered the restaurant. She spotted Linda at a table across from the bar.

"Sorry I'm late," she said, slipping her coat off and hanging it over the back of the chair across from Linda.

Linda smiled warmly. "No problem."

"I've never been her before," Ana said, taking a seat and looking around, feeling a little out of her element. The restaurant was retro hip,

167

reminding her of a big sixties-style diner but funkier. It wasn't the type of restaurant Ana would have chosen but she decided she needed to broaden her horizons and embrace new culinary experiences. It was exactly the type of place Rick would eat at and she had a feeling that she'd be eating out with him more often.

"It's close to my office and the food is good here," Linda said. "How are you doing? Are you holding up?"

"I'm ok. How about you and Andy?"

"Lots of tears but we're ok."

The waiter came and poured their coffee. She told them about the lunch specials, all of which sounded foreign to Ana. Reading the menu didn't help. Ana would have been comfortable with bacon and eggs or a roast beef sandwich and vegetable soup. Instead, she had to choose from things like octopus and smoked duck.

When the waiter returned to the table she ordered albacore tuna. She was familiar with tuna - it came in a can.

The two women talked. Despite the fact that they'd rarely seen each other in the past ten years, the conversation flowed effortlessly. They talked about Marko, their kids, current events and the weather. Linda looked gorgeous as always, wearing a tailored light wool business suit, probably Armani – not that Ana would know - and her red hair tied up in a messy bun that somehow managed to create the impression that every strand was in exactly the right place. Ana had done her best to dress up for the outing, wearing a newer pair of jeans with well-worn black flats and a chambray top she got at Old Navy for $30.

They talked about the funeral arrangements for Marko. Linda had been through the experience of planning funerals for each of her parents so Ana felt like she was in good hands.

Their meals came. Ana was surprised by how rare the tuna was and how little the food on her plate resembled the canned fish she used to make sandwiches. But it looked impressive. With new-found courage she ate a piece of the tuna and was pleasantly surprised.

"Something strange happened last night," Linda said.

Ana looked up.

"Andy and I were looking at old photo albums and reminiscing about Marko when I remembered something," Linda went on. "He came by the house on Tuesday. It was the last time I saw him. He said he wanted to return Andy's text book but I think he had another reason for the visit."

"Oh?"

"Just before he left he asked to use a computer. He said he needed to check his email but I'm pretty sure he made that up as an excuse. I offered to let him use my laptop, my phone, or a tablet but he wanted to use an old desktop computer we keep in the basement."

"Weird."

"I didn't think about it at the time but last night Andy and I were talking and I remembered Marko coming over. We decided to check the computer. It looks like Marko uploaded a video file."

"Really? Did you watch the video?"

Linda nodded. "It was dark and shaky but it showed a group of people, two or three men and a woman, loading TVs and other electronics into a van. I don't know for sure, but it looks like they were stealing from the warehouse where Marko worked."

Ana stared at her. "Oh my God."

"Do you think this has something to do with Marko's murder?"

"Steve told me that the men who came to the apartment were after Marko. Maybe he was right, maybe it had something to do with this video."

"The police haven't told us anything."

"Have you told them about the video?"

"I phoned them but there's a problem."

"A problem?"

"The video is gone."

"What do you mean gone?"

"We watched it last night but it was late and I thought I'd phone the police in the morning. Andy checked the computer in the morning but it kept crashing."

"What do you mean?"

"Every time he tried to open the file, text boxes kept popping up, multiplying, until the damn thing shut down. He rebooted it and tried again but it kept doing it. He thinks it might be a virus or something wrong with the operating system."

"You're kidding?"

"It's an old computer."

"I guess."

"Apparently it has a lot of malware on it. If only I'd saved it onto a flash drive or something last night."

"Maybe the police can pull something off the hard-drive."

"I called them. They didn't seem to be in a rush or anything. They're going to come and pick it up after five, when I get home. Andy didn't think they'd have much luck with it though."

"If Steve is right and the men came for Marko that might explain why the only things they stole from the apartment were his phone and his laptop."

"Didn't they take a TV too?"

"They did, but they left it in a car. The phone and laptop are still missing."

"You think they were after the video file?"

"They broke into my townhouse too. The same guys I think. The only thing they stole was my tablet."

"Oh my god."

"They killed my dog."

Linda looked horrified. "Oh, Ana, that's terrible." She reached out and put her hand on Ana's.

"It seems like they were looking for something someone might have on a phone or their computer."

"I can't imagine Marko getting mixed up in something like that."

"Me either, but I think that video could be important."

The waiter came and delivered the bill. Ana feigned reaching for it, letting Linda snap it up. She insisted that it was her treat, which suited Ana fine. Combined, Linda and Dieter made nearly seven figures a year while Ana was a struggling single-mother with a dead-beat husband and a massive child-care bill.

She thanked Linda for lunch and for all her help with the funeral arrangements. They stood and put on their coats.

"As executor, you'll need to talk to the HR folks at the warehouse," Linda said. "I can go with you if you like. There'll be paperwork for death benefits. You'll need to get a death certificate for that."

"Thanks. I appreciate your help."

Linda smiled. "It's the least I can do."

They left the restaurant and stepped onto the sidewalk at the intersection of Smithe and Homer. It turned out that Ana had parked close to where Linda's office was so they decided to walk together.

"It was good to see Andy the other night," Ana said. "The circumstances were terrible but it's been so long since I've seen him. I can't believe how old he is."

"You and I both."

"His girlfriend is cute," Ana said.

"Don't get too attached to her."

"Oh, why not?"

"I'm not sure she's a match for Andy."

"I don't know," Ana said. "They seem to really like each other."

"Don't get me wrong," Linda said. "I like the girl. I just think Andy is like his father and she might be a handful, if you know what I mean."

Ana wasn't sure what Linda meant but the girl did have tattoos and blue hair. "I like her look. I never had the courage to do anything like that when I was young but I secretly wanted to be a punk rocker."

"I had no idea."

"You'd never know it by looking at me. I look like a 'soccer mom'."

"Yes, but you pull it off nicely."

"Thank you."

"You know, Katie has quite a tragic story," Linda said.

"Oh?"

"Her father murdered her mother when she was 14."

"Oh my god."

"He set the house on fire while Katie was inside. She barely got out alive."

"Wow."

"She was in foster care until her sister came home from the army. Her sister had been overseas. After she came back, she got Katie out of care and took her in until she graduated high school."

"That's quite a story."

"I've never met her but the sister works at the same warehouse where Marko worked."

"That's quite a coincidence."

"Not as much as you'd think." Linda stopped in front of her office building. "Katie and Andy were dating. Katie's sister was looking for a job. Andy knew from his father that the warehouse was hiring so he told Katie and she told her sister who applied and got hired."

"Still, it's a small world."

They chatted for a while longer, said their goodbyes and made arrangements to meet again early next week. After Linda had left, Ana continued walking to her car, thinking about the computer file and how coincidental it had been that the computer with the video file had crashed. Maybe it wasn't a coincidence, she thought. Maybe Andy recognized someone in the video. There was a woman in the video and Katie's sister worked at the warehouse.

It was hard to imagine that Andy would destroy evidence related to his father's murder but if he was in love he might do almost anything.

When she got to her car, she remembered the voice message from her mother and pulled out her cell phone. Her mother's message had been left at 10:35 am, nearly three hours earlier. She played the message.

"Ana, where are you? Steve left the hospital. They don't know where he went. They said he was upset after he talked to you. He pulled out his IV, took his clothes and left. What did you say to him? Call me."

All at once Ana felt like she was fourteen years old. She'd ignored her mother's message for three hours. That sort of behavior wasn't going to earn her a 'daughter of the year' award.

Mostly though, she felt guilty about Steve. She wished she hadn't jumped to conclusions, that she'd been more supportive, and that she'd listened to him instead of judging him.

If Steve was right, the men who assaulted them were after something Marko had. She wondered if they broke into her house because they didn't find what they were looking for in Marko's apartment. Were they still looking for it? Was it possible that Marko had downloaded something onto Linda's computer that these people were willing to kill for?

Ana exhaled loudly. She wondered if she was being ridiculous, if she'd seen too many movies. Still, she couldn't help but think that the video file had something to do with Marko's murder.

She knew she should call her mother back but instead she used her phone to open an internet browser. She found a website with the telephone number she was looking for and called it.

A receptionist answered.

Ana took a deep breath. "Can I talk to someone in the HR department?"

Chapter 32

"Mr. Torvick will see you now," the Receptionist said.

Ana rose from her chair in the warehouse's modest reception area. The receptionist frowned and tilted her head slightly to indicate that Ana should follow her. She was a large woman who presumably hadn't been hired for her charming disposition. She led Ana down a short hallway from the reception area to the open door of a small office.

Mr. Torvick was younger than she expected, barely thirty years old. He stood when Ana entered the office but stayed behind his small, cluttered desk. He wore a wrinkled, long-sleeve dress shirt with no tie and casual dress pants.

"Ms. Marshall," he said. "Take a seat. How can I can I help you?"

Ana hesitated a moment, unsure if she should shake his hand but he sat quickly making it clear that no handshake was required or expected. She took a seat in one of two cheap vinyl upholstered chairs across from his desk.

"It's about my brother. He worked here," she said.

"Marko Milanovic," he said, nodding. "I'm sorry for your loss."

"Thank you," she said. "Did you know him well?"

"Honestly - not really. I knew his name and met him a few times - mostly to fill in forms. I haven't worked here long."

"I see."

"I understand you're the executor of Marko's estate."

It seemed ridiculous to refer to Marko as having an estate but she said, "I am. It's my first time and I'm not completely sure I know what I'm doing. I understand some paperwork is involved."

"There is. You'll need a death certificate before we can get much moving on our end. Have you applied?"

"Not yet. It's been a hectic time."

"I understand. There's no rush really. The families of the deceased often wait a week or more before worrying this kind of paperwork. You can take as much time as you need."

"The death certificate – I get that from the Province?"

He nodded. "You can do it on-line. I can help with that if you need."

"No, that's okay. I have family member who can help me with this."

"I can give you some forms to fill out, for the life insurance and so on. You can take them home and bring them back with the death certificate."

He gave her a package of forms that he had set aside in a manila envelope. He went through them with her, explaining the information that was needed for each.

"Thank you," she said. "I appreciate you taking the time."

"No problem. Let me know if there's anything I can do. When you have the certificate and the forms filled out, we can process everything."

He stood, signifying the end of the meeting.

Ana stayed seated. "Have there been any thefts here at the

warehouse?" she asked.

Mr. Torvick looked at her quizzically. "Not that I'm aware of but I don't know that I would know if there was. Why?"

Ana wasn't sure how to answer. She was prone to making comments to elicit a reaction but often had no idea what her next move should be once she'd opened a particular can of worms.

"Just curious," she said. "With the type of inventory you have, thefts must happen all the time."

"I wouldn't know but we have a security system and there are controls in place to prevent that. I'd be surprised if there was much, if any, theft."

"Well that's good to hear," Ana said.

"If you wanted to know more about that sort of thing you might want to talk to the General Manager or the Floor Supervisor. The Manager's not in but the Floor Super is."

"I'm not sure that's necessary."

"It's no trouble. I can call him." He picked up the phone. She could hear the phone ring on the other end. "We can ask him about Marko's locker as well. The employees all have personal lockers. You'll want to collect Marko's belongings."

Ana felt her pulse quicken. She hadn't thought of that. If Marko had a locker, he could have stored anything in it - including a video file.

♦

Gavin Taylor sat at the desk in his office trying to do paperwork but he was having a hard time concentrating. His desk phone rang. He tried to ignore it but it continued to ring. Finally, he scooped up the receiver and grunted into the phone.

"This is Curt Torvick," came the reply. "I have Marko Milanovic's sister in my office and I'm wondering if you have time to pop over and talk to her."

He sat up straighter. "-ah...what does she want?"

"She's looking after his affairs, death benefits and all that. She had some questions about the warehouse that maybe you can answer. She'd also like his things from his locker. I thought you could help with that."

Gavin mentally kicked himself for not thinking of Marko's locker. The police apparently hadn't thought of it either because they hadn't come to open it.

"We'll have to cut the lock unless she knows the combination," he said, hoping that would dissuade her.

"You can sort that out with her when you meet her."

Gavin swallowed hard. He didn't need further complications in his life. "Alright," he sighed. "I'm on my way."

Gavin left his office, took the stairs down to the warehouse floor, and then made his way to the administration offices at the front of the building. The receptionist greeted him with her usual grimace. For some reason she didn't like him, which was fine with Gavin. She was, in his opinion, completely unfuckable. He walked past her without a word and went to Curt's office.

He found him behind his desk, making awkward conversation with an attractive, athletic looking woman. She was wearing jeans and a loose fitting shirt. No cleavage or bare leg showing, but she looked good in a wholesome 'girl-next-door' kind of way. She was younger than he expected, probably mid-thirties. Marko was in his fifties and Gavin assumed his sister would be much the same age but she looked young enough to be his daughter.

Curt made the introductions. "Ms. Marshall, this is Gavin Taylor. Unfortunately, I have another meeting scheduled. Gavin, if you could help Ms. Marshall I'd appreciate it." He stood and she did the same. She was taller than both men.

"Pleased to meet you," he said, mustering as much charm as possible. He extended a hand. "How can I help you Ms. Marshall?"

"Ana," she said. She shook his hand assertively. It felt like she could crush bones if she wanted to. She had serious grip strength.

"Ana," he said. "What can I do for you?"

"Would you be able to give me a tour of the warehouse?" she asked. It was a strange request. There wasn't much to see as far as Gavin was concerned. "And Mr. Torvick said you might be able to open Marko's locker for me so I can get his personal belongings."

Gavin was torn. On one hand, he wanted to get closer to Marko's superhot sister but on the other, he didn't want to open that locker for anyone until he knew what was inside.

Curt interjected. "Ms. Marshall also had some questions about building security. Perhaps you could help with that as well." He motioned with his head to indicate that whatever conversation followed, it would need to occur elsewhere.

They stepped out of Curt's office and made their way down the hall to the reception area.

"Unfortunately," he said, "This isn't a good time."

"I understand. I should have made an appointment."

"You don't happen to have the combination to the lock on Marko's locker do you?"

She shook her head. "No, sorry I don't."

"No problem. We can cut the lock. Would you like us to box his belongings for you?"

"No, no. You don't need to do that," she said.

"It's no trouble."

"Still, I'd rather be here when you cut the lock. I know you don't have time for a tour now but is there any chance we can open the locker?"

"Sorry. I'd like to. Tomorrow maybe? I can give you the full tour, answer any questions you have, and we can open Marko's locker if that works for you."

That would give Gavin time to search the locker and then replace the lock.

"Isn't tomorrow Saturday?"

"I work Saturdays. No problem."

"Is early afternoon alright? Say around two?"

"That'll be fine," he said. "And I just want you to know that everyone around here...well, we feel terrible about what happened."

"Thank you," she said. He could see tears well in her eyes. She blinked and shook her head slightly.

Gavin knew that when some women were grieving, they'd fuck almost anyone. It made them feel alive in the face of death. The prospect made him optimistic. He had a chance. He was the epitome of 'almost anyone'.

They walked outside to the parking lot.

"I'll see you tomorrow," he said. "I'm sorry I didn't have time today...it's just...you know...I have this thing."

"No problem. I appreciate all your help."

"I'll give you the royal tour tomorrow."

The tour, he thought would include an up close and personal visit to his office. It was small but it could work. The important thing was to find a way to get her in there, preferably overwrought with grief.

She gave him a strained smile and nodded. He watched her long athletic legs as she walked to her car and wondered if she was into chubby guys.

He'd need to clean his office before tomorrow. Even a grieving woman won't get it on in a room that smells like stale vomit.

◆

After he watched Ana Marshall drive away, Gavin went back inside to search for Toni Little. He found her loading a trailer with another employee.

Gavin didn't usually hire women to work in the warehouse but he'd hired Toni because she'd been in the military. She was obviously a lesbian - just not the hot kind you see in porn. Toni was the butch kind that favored short hair, baggy plaid shirts and work boots. She was stronger and harder working than most of the guys on the floor but she also had a loose moral compass and it was that quality that made her an asset. Unfortunately she was also smart and ambitious, which was why Gavin needed to have her killed.

"What do you need Gavin?"

"I need to talk to you…. alone."

Toni shrugged at her coworker, as if to say, 'what can I do, the boss wants to talk to me.' They stepped away from the trailer and when they were a comfortable distance from it Gavin handed her the burner phone that Anton had given him.

She scanned the contact list. There was only one phone number listed, the one the hired killer had most recently used to contact Gavin.

"Is that it?" Toni asked.

"Pretty much. I'm counting on you."

She nodded and started to walk back to the trailer she'd been loading. After a few steps, Gavin called to her.

"What can you tell me about Marko's sister?"

Toni turned. "She's a paramedic I think. Why?"

"Just curious. What's she like?"

She shrugged. "I've never met her."

"D'you know anything about her…you know…whether or not she's single?"

"Are you seriously trying to make moves on Marko's sister, the day after his murder?"

"I never said that. I was just curious. I met her today. I thought you might know her…. that's all…you know…because of your sister and Marko's kid."

"I don't."

"She's coming back tomorrow to pick up his things. I thought

I'd give her a tour."

"What does that have to do with me?"

"Nothing. I just thought maybe you could tell me more about her."

"I can't." She shook her head. "Are we done here?"

Toni turned and went back to work. She was acting weirder than usual, Gavin thought. Probably having her period. She was super sensitive when it came to her sister. One time Gavin had told a joke about how girls from Surrey know when their mother is on the rag. The punchline was, 'they can taste it on their brother.'

It was a good joke because it was funny on multiple levels and he always got a big laugh when he told it. Except Toni. She didn't laugh. In fact she threatened to beat the shit out of Gavin if he didn't apologize, which made no sense because Toni's sister wasn't even from Surrey.

He didn't doubt though that she could beat the shit out of him.

He stood and watched her work for nearly a minute. Did Toni suspect that Gavin was responsible for Marko's murder, he wondered. Toni's sister was dating Marko's son. She agreed to murder a blackmailer but how would she feel if she knew the real blackmailer was Marko? Would she understand that Gavin had no choice but to have Marko killed? He didn't know.

Gavin wandered back to his office, feeling uneasy. He thought about Marko's locker and how lucky he'd been that the sister had asked about it before the police did. Now he could search it before anyone else

He'd worry about Toni later.

Chapter 33

Ana arrived at Braden's school and parked in the lot. Most of the parents waited in their cars at the curb for their kids but she preferred to go into the school to meet him in the classroom. It was too early to go in though so she waited in her car and scrolled through her emails. Dana had replied with a long message and Ana was reading it when her phone rang. She smiled when she saw the name on the display.

"Dana, I was just reading your email."

"How are you doing?" Dana asked, concern in her voice.

"I'm ok, all things considered."

Ana told her about Marko's murder, the break-in at her house and the latest revelation that Marko had downloaded a video file onto Linda's computer.

"Do you think the file has something to do with Marko's murder?"

"I'm looking into it."

"You're looking into it? What are you, Nancy Drew?"

"Nancy Drew had game."

"You do know that Nancy Drew isn't real?"

"Obviously. If she was real, she'd be like 90 years old or something."

"I think you should leave the 'looking into' to the police. Do they have the computer?"

"Not yet but Linda called them," Ana said. "Apparently the computer has a virus and keeps crashing or something. Hopefully they'll be able to recover the file."

"I'm sure they can."

"I think Andy might not be telling the truth. I think he might have done something to that file."

"That's crazy Ana. Why would he do that?"

"To protect his girlfriend's sister."

Ana explained her theory about the video and the woman shown loading equipment into the van.

"I can't image Andy doing something like that."

"I know, but you have to admit, the computer crashing is a pretty strange coincidence. His girlfriend's sister works at the warehouse and Linda said there's a woman in the video."

"You should probably leave the theories and crime solving to the police."

"Don't worry, I'm not going to go all 'Jessica Fletcher' or anything."

"That's good."

"But I am going to pick up Marko's things at the warehouse tomorrow. I'm thinking maybe he hid something in his locker."

There was a long silence on the other end of the line. Ana thought maybe they'd been disconnected so she said, "Dana are you still there?"

"I don't think that's a good idea Ana."

"I'm not going to do anything stupid. I'm just curious."

"You know what they say about curiosity?"

Ana knew. It killed the cat. And barking killed the dog.

She decided to change the topic. "You'll be happy to know I slept with Rick this morning."

"Do tell."

Ana was relieved to hear a lighter tone to her friend's voice. She missed their banter.

"I'm not that kind of girl."

"But you could be."

"Let's just say that I had more orgasms this morning than I had during my entire marriage to Brad."

"Oh my God. How many did you have?"

"Just the one."

Dana laughed

"But it was a good one," Ana said.

After all the terrible things that had happened, it felt good to laugh. They talked about Rick and his cooking prowess, his huge dimples, and his skills as an interior decorator. Ana felt some of the weight of the past two days lift.

Ten minutes later she noticed the time on her phone and told Dana she needed to get Braden. "I have to tell him that his dog is dead. I'm not looking forward to that."

"Kids are more resilient than we think."

"I hope so."

"They are, trust me."

"Thanks for calling, Dana. You're a good friend."

"I know. You're lucky to have me."

Ana disconnected the call and got out of the car. Telling Braden about Lukin was going to be difficult but nobody said being a parent was easy. She hoped Dana was right about the resilience of kids. If she was wrong, Braden was going to need therapy before he started first grade.

Chapter 34

Gavin turned up the corners of his cards and saw a ten and a jack, both spades. He was in the poker room of the River Rock Casino at the $5/$10 table. He'd taken out a series of new payday loans and managed to pull together $1,800, converting the cash quickly into poker chips.

He felt good. Things were falling into place. He'd opened Marko's locker and found nothing incriminating inside and if everything went according to plan, Toni would kill the hitman tonight, which would solve another problem. If Gavin got lucky at the table he could hire someone to take care of Toni, and all his problems would go away.

At least - most of them. He still had three ex-wives to contend with and a kid who wouldn't talk to him - but nobody's life was perfect.

"It's your turn to act sir," the dealer said to Gavin.

Gavin glanced around the table. It appeared that everyone had been waiting for him to act for some time.

"Raise," he said and slid two green chips over the line.

The next three players folded and action was on a young

Chinese woman wearing a baseball cap backwards over sleek black hair. She was pretty but Gavin wasn't into Asian chicks.

"$50 to call," the dealer told her.

She nodded, considered the bet and made the call.

The other players in the hand folded. The dealer turned over three cards. Gavin watched the Chinese woman closely to see how she responded to the flop. She wore large sunglasses and showed no emotion, giving nothing away. The three cards on the table were an ace, a seven, and a four- all different suits, none of them spades. It was a terrible flop for Gavin.

"I like that flop," he said. He didn't usually talk at the table when he was in a hand but she was a woman and Gavin felt he'd get a better read on her if there was some banter. "I like it so much I'm gonna continue here." He picked up four green chips, set them down on the other side of the line, and said, "$100."

She didn't say a word, staring back at him from behind sunglasses. Then she methodically counted the chips needed to call and slid them over the line.

The turn brought more bad news for Gavin, pairing the four on the board. He had no hope of making a straight now and he was drawing dead if she had paired the ace or better. If he checked though, it would show weakness. He decided his best chance to win the pot was to apply pressure.

"I know you were just floating the flop," he said. "But it won't work." There was over $300 in the pot and he knew it would take a big bet to convince her he was serious. He decided to fire a second barrel. "Your weak ace is no good."

She didn't flinch, in fact she didn't appear to be breathing. He may as well have been talking to a statue.

"$300," he said and pushed a small stack of chips over the line.

She remained still for nearly a minute, then looked down at her chips and silently counted out $300 and placed the chips into the pot.

Gavin felt sick. She had to have a strong hand if she was calling on every street.

The dealer turned over the two of clubs.

Gavin stared at her. "We both know that was a brick. The question I have to ask myself is, how big a bet are you willing to call?"

She remained perfectly still.

Most players had no qualms when it came to firing the first barrel. It was a standard play, a continuation bet. Fewer players had the balls to bluff by firing a second barrel. What truly required balls of steel though was a player willing to fire a third barrel, with complete air, knowing there was no chance of winning the pot except by convincing the other player to fold a better hand. It was the ultimate risk and reward - a triple barrel bluff.

Most players would have shut down by now but not Gavin. He had balls of steel.

He had over $1,300 left of his original $1,800 stack.

He stared at her, doing his best to intimidate her. "I'm all in," he said.

She called without hesitation as if she'd been expecting the shove, turning over ace-king and sparing Gavin the embarrassment of having to turn over his cards.

He tossed his cards into the muck. "Nice hand."

She smiled sweetly and stacked her chips. Gavin stared down at the felt where his chips had once been, chips that represented all the money he had to live on for the next two weeks.

He left the casino and walked to the parking lot in a daze. He'd busted in less than 15 minutes. The Poker Gods had fucked him over again. He got into his car, started the engine, and drove toward home.

Where else could he could go, he thought.

All he had in his wallet was one maxed-out credit card, a useless Blockbuster Video membership card, and a piece of paper that he'd written his account number on so he could transfer the $2,500 deposit for the hit man to kill Marko.

He drove over a bridge, crossing the Fraser River into Vancouver and gazed despondently out the window. What had he done to anger the Poker Gods? Why did they want to fuck him so badly?

It seemed like lately everyone was trying to fuck him and not in a good way.

Chapter 35

It was Fresh Meat Night at the No. 5 Orange.

Pete Pappas sat alone at a small table in the dark, mostly ignoring the amateur dancers on stage whose limited flexibility and lack of imagination was matched only by their enthusiasm. Normally Pete enjoyed Fresh Meat Night. In his opinion, the professional dancers often looked bored. The amateur girls on the other hand, really got into it.

He was distracted tonight though. He'd been picked up by IHIT in the morning and taken in for questioning for most of the day. They grilled him on and off for hours in a tiny interrogation room and fed him bullshit about an eye witness putting him at the scene of Marko Milanovic's murder. Pete stayed calm though, initially sticking to his story of being home alone on the night of the murders but eventually giving up the name of the married woman who would provide his alibi. Her name was Daria.

Pete had taken care of her abusive ex-boyfriend three years earlier and she owed him. Daria was married now and he told the cops that he was reluctant to mention her when he was first interviewed by the detectives. It wasn't the most original excuse but it was plausible enough and in Pete's opinion, originality was overrated.

Daria backed up his fake alibi and they released Pete ten hours after he'd been brought in. No one offered to drive him home so he was forced to take transit from the station in New Westminster back to Vancouver. He barely made it to the No. 5 Orange in time for his 9 pm meeting. Clearly he hadn't needed to rush. There was no sign of Gavin.

He glanced down at his personal cell phone - not the crappy flip phone Kevin gave him - and watched a YouTube video on how to hotwire a car. He'd watched it multiple times to make sure he could do it quickly when the time came.

Kevin had given him a random phone and laptop to fool Gavin. His plan was to give Gavin the backpack with the laptop and phone and wait while Gavin completed the wire transfer. After the transfer was complete, they'd go their separate ways. Except Pete would actually follow Gavin and kill him. If Gavin didn't pay, they'd still part ways and Pete would still kill him. Either way, Gavin was a dead man.

Pete had enough cash after last night's job to fix the Lumina's starter but unfortunately he'd been interrogated all day and hadn't had time to take it to a garage. That was why he needed to hotwire a car.

He couldn't exactly follow Gavin on the bus.

♦

Toni Little sat parked in her white Ford F150 on Main across the street from a bright orange strip club called the No. 5 Orange. The entire block was a no parking zone but the location gave her the best unobstructed view of the entrance. There was a cheap marquee sign mounted on the side of the building with plastic letters declaring 'Fresh Meat - Amateur Dancers - Friday 8:30 pm'.

Toni glanced at her watch. It was 8:55 pm.

She chose to park outside the Club, rather than go inside, so she could follow the man Gavin claimed was blackmailing him, when he left. As 'one of the guys' in a male dominated military she'd seen plenty of exotic dancers. She was gay, but she had no interest in watching straight women with no dance skills take off their clothes in a room filled with sad, lonely men.

Most people assumed Toni was gay when they met her, but for whatever reason, her sister Katie hadn't reached the same conclusion. Toni didn't make an effort to correct her sister's perception. She let Katie think she was straight and that her girlfriend, Shasta, was just a roommate. Shasta often asked her if she was ashamed of being gay and Toni assured her that she wasn't. Her sister, she said, was emotionally fragile and had weird romantic notions about the world. Toni didn't understand them but she thought it was best to let Katie hold onto those notions as long as she needed them.

Toni's relationship with her sister was based on guilt more than it was on love or anything else. Katie had been through hell and Toni felt obligated to protect her. She never really knew Katie growing up. Toni left home as a teenager and made her way in the world. She had effectively abandoned Katie, which sounded cold, but realistically they were fourteen years apart in age, had different fathers, and had only briefly lived under the same roof. When Toni left home, she didn't give much thought to the clingy, preschool-aged sibling she left behind.

But still, they were sisters. Blood was blood and Toni hadn't been there when her sister needed her.

She'd been overseas when their mother died. Toni hadn't seen or spoken to her mother for nearly six years before she was murdered and while her mother's death had been a shock, aside from that, she didn't feel much of anything when she learned the news. And so, she decided not to attend the funeral - if there was one - and stayed in Germany where she'd been stationed at the time. She only gave a passing thought to the skinny girl in the soiled dress who'd followed her around the house all those years ago. She wasn't even sure how old the girl was when their mother died.

Of course, if she'd done the math she would have realized that Katie was 14 years old.

But she hadn't.

She hadn't given it much thought at all.

It wasn't until she returned home, nearly a year later, that she discovered that Katie had been trying to contact her for months. It was through social media that the two sisters connected after years apart. Katie was in foster care and not doing well. Toni was overcome with guilt and set wheels in motion to become Katie's guardian. Katie lived with her for three years, until she graduated from high school and moved out on her own.

Toni pulled out the cheap flip phone Gavin had given her, the one that had supposedly come from the Russian Mafia. She knew Gavin was lying to her about the blackmailer. Katie had told her this morning about the video on Marko's ex-wife's computer. Toni managed to convince her sister that Marko's death had nothing to do with her or the video. Toni wasn't sure how Marko was connected to the video but she assumed it was the same video that Gavin claimed was being used to blackmail him.

At 9:00 pm sharp Toni typed a message into the phone. It took a long time without a proper keyboard but she managed to send the message:

Are you at the No. 5?

Step one, she thought, confirm that the target was at the location. There was a short delay and then the phone pinged.

Where the fuck are you?

Not a definitive answer but it seemed reasonable to assume the target was inside. Toni typed:

Something came up. I can't make it.

Step two, she thought, see how the alleged blackmailer responds to the news that Gavin wasn't coming. The answer came almost immediately.

You'd better fucking come

Toni sent her next message quickly, without giving it much thought.

Or what?

She stared at the screen and wondered if she'd pushed too hard. No reply came for a long time and then finally the phone pinged.

Who is this?

Toni winced. The last message was probably too assertive and didn't sound like Gavin. She typed:

It's Gavin

The reply:

Doesn't sound like it

Toni took a few seconds to think. There was no going back now. She decided she may as well provoke the target and see what happened. She typed:

I grew some balls fuckhead.

Nothing like poking a bear with a stick, Toni thought. The reply came back almost instantly.

You're fucking dead!

Toni kept her eyes on the front door of the Club, watching for someone to come out. A few seconds later a large bearded man carrying a backpack stormed out the front doors. He stopped on the sidewalk and began typing into a cell phone.

A few seconds later, the phone in Toni's hand rang. Toni didn't answer and it eventually stopped ringing. After a few seconds it rang again. The man outside the Club lit a cigarette and started pacing. Even with the windows closed Toni could hear him cursing.

The bearded man appeared to try again but this time the phone in Toni's hand didn't ring. She watched the man talk into his phone but she couldn't hear what he was saying. The conversation was short and when it was over the man slid his phone back into his hoodie and leaned against the wall like he was waiting for something.

Gavin's phone pinged, which was curious. The man outside the club hadn't sent the text but maybe the person he'd been talking to did. Toni read the message. It was from a different number.

Where are you?

Presumably she was supposed to know who the text was from. There was only one possibility that Toni could think of. It must be the legendary Russian gangster, Anton. Who else would have this number?

Toni typed:

Why do you want to know?

There was a pause and then the phone pinged.

Answer your phone. I'll call you.

Toni obviously couldn't talk to him. There was no way she could convince him that she was Gavin. She typed:

Bad time. Can't talk. Just text.

The reply:

WTF. Where are you?

Toni paused. The man Gavin claimed was a blackmailer was apparently working with Anton. It seemed hard to believe that Marko was working with either of them. Why did Marko have a video of the thefts, Toni wondered, and why did he download it onto his ex-wife's computer? Was Marko blackmailing Gavin, and if so, who was the bearded man and what was his connection to Anton, the alleged Russian gangster?

She replied:

None of your business

Toni watched the bearded man outside the Club pull out his phone and stare at it impatiently, like he expected it to ring. The phone in Toni's hand pinged.

Don't fuck with us

Anton wasn't revealing much in his texts. Toni wanted to know more about the money that the alleged blackmailer was supposedly demanding. She typed:

> I'm not going to pay

The reply came quickly:

> Bad idea

Toni stared at the screen for a moment and then typed:

> Why?

The phone pinged again:

> He'll kill you

Toni considered this. She decided that the $7,500 probably wasn't a blackmail demand as Gavin had claimed. Blackmailers didn't generally kill people if they didn't pay. They threatened to share their secrets. It seemed more likely that Gavin owed the bearded man money. But for what, Toni wondered. A gambling debt seemed likely but why would Gavin create an elaborate story about a blackmail video. Based on what Katie had told her, there was a video and Marko had a copy of it. He suspected there was some truth to Gavin's story. Gavin was probably being blackmailed, but not by the bearded man. And how did Anton fit into all this? She had an idea and typed:

> Your guy fucked up the job.

A few seconds later the reply came:

> Job was done. Pay him or he'll kill you too.

The pieces had come together. Gavin hadn't been lying when he said there was a blackmailer. It seemed likely that the bearded man had been hired by Gavin to kill the blackmailer and since Gavin wouldn't know where to find a hitman he'd gone to Anton for help. Marko Milanovic had a video of the thefts and he'd been murdered so it seemed likely that he was the blackmailer. The bearded man and Anton were clearly working together and Gavin either didn't want to, or couldn't pay the killer so he was trying to get Toni to murder the man he'd hired so he wouldn't have to pay him.

What an asshole, Toni thought. If anyone was going to get killed tonight, it should be Gavin. She couldn't see a downside to pissing these guys off. If she was lucky, Gavin might end up dead. She typed:

Tell him to go fuck himself. I'm not paying.

She grinned and turned off the phone.

Chapter 36

Pete's phone finally rang. He looked at the display and saw that it was Kevin.

"Hey," he grunted into the phone.

"Something's wrong," Kevin said. "I don't think that's Gavin on that phone."

"Who the fuck is it then?"

"I don't know."

"Maybe it's him and he's drunk or something."

"I don't think so. It's not just the tone of the messages. The text's themselves are wrong. Gavin uses abbreviations and numbers instead of letters to keep messages short. This guy types full sentences and uses punctuation. It's not Gavin."

"What the fuck? Someone stole his phone?"

"It's someone pretending to be Gavin. He knows what's going on. He knows who Anton is. He knows about the murder."

Pete scratched his head. "This is pretty fucked up."

"It almost seems like he wants us to kill Gavin."

"So what do we do?"

"Give him what he wants I guess."

"Kill Gavin?"

"Yeah. Be careful though. We don't know what Gavin or the guy on the phone is up to."

Kevin gave him Gavin's home address and they disconnected the call. Pete picked up the backpack and went around the block in search of a car to steal.

♦

Toni started the engine of the F-150 and turned down the volume on the radio. The bearded man was on the move. He was jumpy, looking over his shoulder like he was worried he was being followed. Toni stayed a comfortable distance behind. She decided she wasn't going to kill the bearded man but she was curious to see where he went and what he did next. She watched him make his way up the street, stopping and looking inside parked vehicles as if he planned to break into one.

She saw him slip into a small parking lot, a block or two from the club, and approach an older model sedan. The bearded man used a screwdriver to break the driver's side window by prying it between the top of the glass and the frame. He opened the car's door and crawled under the steering column. The window had been broken quickly and efficiently but once inside the car, the man didn't seem to know what he was doing. He fiddled under the steering column for at least 3 or 4 minutes before the engine finally started.

The man tossed the backpack he was carrying into the car, brushed glass off the driver seat, and settled in behind the wheel. The sedan emerged on Main Street with only one headlight working. Toni followed in her F-150.

The sedan headed out of the City and onto the freeway. Toni

followed the car as it took a Coquitlam exit and wound its way into a suburban neighborhood and parked. She drove past the car so she didn't raise suspicion, circled the block, and parked a few car-lengths back where she had a good view but was far enough away so she wouldn't be noticed.

And then she waited.

Chapter 37

George Richardson was living in hell. He'd always thought that he was the type of person who could get along with people, or at least tolerate them, but that was before Gavin Taylor entered his life. Now he felt like a prisoner in his own home.

George heard Gavin's car pull into the driveway and sighed. He retreated to his bedroom, as he always did when Gavin was home, and locked the door. His two sons, Noah and Levi, were in their bedroom down the hall. They were 7 and 9 years old. He prayed to Jesus that they were fast asleep.

George didn't get much sleep on the nights his kids visited because he was worried about their virtue anytime Gavin was home. The situation had reached a point where he seriously thought about having the boys stay with him in his room on air mattresses. But, then he'd have to explain to their mother why the boys didn't have proper beds to sleep on when they came over. And besides, there was no space in his bedroom anymore for air mattresses. He had a fridge in his room, not to mention all the other stuff he stored there because Gavin stole anything that wasn't locked up or tied down.

Fortunately for George he had two sons and not two daughters. While he didn't want his sons exposed to Gavin and his profanity and perversions, at least he didn't have to worry about him trying to molest one of them. If the website 'Ashley's Perv Dad' could be relied on, Gavin couldn't be trusted with young girls. Fortunately there was nothing on the website, or in Gavin's disturbing behavior, to suggest that his sexual proclivities included young boys.

George had to take small consolations where he could find them. He was at a loss for what to do about his situation despite all of the hours he had spent praying for divine intervention and guidance from above.

He had leased the Coquitlam three-bedroom house with a friend months earlier. George had been divorced, living alone in an apartment when a friend's marriage ended and the two men decided to rent a house together where their kids could have a bedroom to share and a backyard to play in. The other father had a son who was Levi's age which was ideal. George signed a one year lease and two men moved in and things had worked great until his friend reconciled with his wife and moved back in with her. George couldn't break the lease without a penalty so he agreed to find a roommate, preferably another single dad. He advertised on Craigslist, conducted interviews, and made the worst decision of his life when he selected Gavin as his roommate.

At first the problems seemed minor. Gavin left his dishes in the sink, he drank the soda George had bought for his kids, and he was unwilling to make any effort to aim with the slightest accuracy when using the toilet. It was as if he urinated with his eyes closed. It didn't take long for these minor grievances to give way to more serious concerns. The man stole anything of value he could get his hands on. He was late with his share of the rent every month. He watched porn constantly and didn't seem to think there was anything wrong with masturbating in the living room even when there were children in the house. The man had 'shot his business' on the very couch where his children sat to watch cartoons in the morning.

George had always tried to be a good Christian but Gavin made it increasingly difficult for him to turn the other cheek. He felt like Job. The obvious solution was to evict Gavin but he'd tried that and it hadn't worked. He simply refused to leave, telling George that he had connections with the Russian mob and that if George mentioned kicking him out one more time he could expect a visit from a man named Anton.

George heard the front door open and close, followed by the sound of Gavin going to the kitchen and opening the fridge in search of food that wasn't there. The fridge door slammed shut followed by the sound of the TV being turned on. George's face flushed with anger as heard the exaggerated moans of at least two people engaged in sexual congress drift down the hall, past the room where his children slept.

George turned on the TV in his own room and set it to Sports Center to drown out the sexual depravity in the other room.

Unfortunately he had never been good at confrontation.

George sighed and looked around his bedroom. It was crammed with nearly everything he owned. He stared at a bag of golf clubs and thought briefly about bursting into the living room with the driver and taking a swing at Gavin. Surely the Lord would forgive him. He'd been pushed further than any man could be expected to without breaking.

He knew, of course, that this was fanciful thinking. He would never murder another man and certainly not with a golf club. Murder was a sin but even if it wasn't, George was an accountant and a terrible golfer. He simply wasn't cut out for that sort of thing.

♦

Gavin sat on the couch and watched three nubile co-eds on TV go at it in their dorm room. On screen the young ladies had been trying to study but then decided they'd rather lick each other's pussies instead. He looked down with dismay at his crotch. It should be at full staff.

Girl-on-girl action always did it for him but his penis hadn't stirred.

He concentrated on the blonde girl on screen with the big boobs and touched himself through his Dockers hoping to get things started. He stopped when the front door opened and closed. Fortunately he didn't have his pants around his ankles yet. The last thing he needed was more grief from his roommate about jacking off in the living room.

He assumed that it was George coming into the house. Who else could it be? He thought George was already home but it was hard to know anymore because the guy was always squirrelled away in his room with his fridge full of food. Gavin hadn't noticed George's car in the driveway when he came in but that wasn't unusual because he usually parked around back.

Gavin stood. He couldn't see the door from where he was but if he took a few steps into the center of the living room he'd have a clear view. The only light in the room came from the glow of the TV.

"George buddy, is that you?"

He took a step forward and was startled to see a large figure barreling toward him. Before he knew what was happening he was hit hard in the chest and driven back into the couch. Pain radiated from his ribcage and something metal was rammed into his mouth.

"Eat this you cheap fucker," the man growled.

Gavin was confused and frightened. He felt his bladder let go. A huge bearded man loomed over him, gripping his shoulder with one hand and shoving the barrel of a gun down his throat with the other. Gavin had trouble processing what was happening. He was aware of pain in his chest, his shoulder, and his mouth. He'd chipped a tooth. And there was a warm, wet sensation between his legs. He could smell urine and for a moment he wondered how George would react when he discovered that his precious couch had been soiled once again.

"I want my fucking money," the man said.

Gavin felt the confusion and pain fade away.

All he felt now was fear.

203

♦

George called 911 on his cell phone.

He wasn't sure what was going on in the living room but he heard a stranger's voice and he could tell the man was angry, violent, and threatening. Both of George's kids were in the house and he needed to protect them.

"Police, Fire, or Ambulance," a man's voice said over the phone. "What is the nature of your emergency?"

George kept his voice low. "Police. I need the police. Hurray. There's an intruder in my house."

"Where are you sir? Are you safe?"

"In my bedroom. I'm ok for now. My kids are in the house. He's threatening my roommate. I think he may have a gun."

George wasn't sure about the gun but he thought the police would respond faster if he told them that. It wasn't really a lie. The man could have a gun. Jesus would understand.

"Are you able to leave the house safely?"

"No."

"Can you find somewhere safe to stay in the house?" the voice asked. "Are you calling on a cell phone?"

"Yes."

"What's your address?"

George gave it to him.

"I can stay on the line until the police get there if you like."

George glanced at his set of golf clubs. "No thanks. Just send the police."

He disconnected the call, went over to the bag of golf clubs and pulled out a five iron. He was armed now. He needed to get to the bedroom where his sons were sleeping. He couldn't leave them alone with an intruder in the house.

George stepped as lightly as he could and opened his bedroom door. He waited a moment before stepping into the hallway. Depending on where Gavin and the intruder were, they might have a clear view of the hallway or they might not. He peered out the door and down the hall to the living room. He could hear the intruder's voice but he couldn't see him. It appeared that they were near the couch in the corner of the room close to the kitchen. From there they would have no view of the hallway. George stepped out of his bedroom, armed with the five iron, and took slow steady steps down the hallway until he reached the room where his sons slept.

He paused and prepared to open the bedroom door. He could hear a woman having a remarkably long, apparently satisfying orgasm on TV. The sounds of ecstasy from the TV where juxtaposed by the gruff, menacing voice of the intruder. George could only make out parts of what was being said but he heard the man say that Gavin owed him money for a job he'd done and that he was going to kill him.

George's priority was protecting his children, not saving Gavin. In fact, he secretly hoped the man did kill Gavin.

He turned the doorknob and froze.

A voice came from the living room. "Is there someone else in the house?"

George stopped turning the doorknob and slipped across the hall into the bathroom, leaving the door to the kid's room closed. He lifted the five iron over his shoulder and prepared to swing. He heard the intruder and Gavin get up from the couch and start toward the hallway.

"It's probably my roommate," Gavin said. "His bedroom is down the hall."

George was appalled. Gavin's first impulse was to lead a killer right to him.

"Move," the intruder said.

George heard the man push Gavin who stumbled forward two or three steps. He waited, his heart pounding in his chest, ready to swing the iron when the two men stepped into view.

Gavin stumbled past the bathroom first, followed by a large bearded man. The bearded man held a gun in his gloved hands, pointed at Gavin's back.

George swung the five iron, chopping it down like an axe. The club clipped the bathroom door frame, losing some momentum, and came down across the big man's outstretched arm, driving the hand with the gun into his thigh. The gun fell to the carpet with a thud. The bearded man swore and stumbled back a few steps but stayed on his feet. Gavin dropped to the carpet and scrambled down the hallway on his hands and knees as George stepped out of the bathroom. He held the club low and swung it up, aiming for the man's head. There wasn't a lot of strength or speed in the swing but the iron made contact just under the bearded man's jawline and his head snapped back. The man staggered, swore, and then fixed his eyes on George.

"I called 911," George said, holding the iron up like it was a baseball bat, ready to swing again if necessary.

The bearded man was outside George's swinging range and there was no doubt in his mind that if the man decided to make a run at George he could easily disarm him and kill him. George was not a strong man. Without the element of surprise he had little hope of defending himself, even with a golf club in his hand.

"My kids are in that room," George said, sensing that intruder was weighing his options. He wanted the man to understand that he was prepared to do whatever it took to protect his kids.

As if on cue the voices of children came from behind the bedroom door. "Dad, what's going on?" and "I'm scared." And then the sound of crying.

The bearded man made his decision and turned and hobbled down the hallway, through the living room and out the front door.

"Holy fuck," Gavin said when the man was gone. "Thanks buddy." He stood and walked toward him like they were best friends.

He smelled like urine. "I never would have thought you had that shit in you," he said. "You were like fuckin' Liam Neeson man."

The boys were both crying now and one of them was trying to open the door. George reached out and held the knob so the door wouldn't open.

"Hold on boys," he said, soothingly. "Daddy will open the door in a second. Everything's ok." He could hear the porn playing in the other room and glared at Gavin. "I want you out of here," he hissed. "You pack up your things tomorrow and get out of my house."

Gavin held up his hands like he was surrendering. "Slow down, slow down buddy. No need to make rash decisions. It's been a crazy night but it's not my fault. This is a bad neighborhood."

The boys tugged at the door. It opened a crack and George pulled it shut. "Hold on boys. Everything is alright now. Go back to your beds and daddy will come in soon."

He turned to Gavin and said, "I want you to turn off that TV and get out of my way. I need to be with my boys."

◆

Gavin had never seen his roommate act like this before. He appreciated that the man had saved his life but at the same time, he was being a bit of an asshole. His roommate no longer held the golf iron, having dropped it to grab the door knob with both hands to keep his son's from coming out. Apparently he didn't want his precious boys to be exposed to the sound of people fucking on TV.

"Alright, alright," Gavin said, trying to calm him. "I'll turn it off."

George nodded and turned away from Gavin, his attention drawn back to the door knob. Presumably he was going to wait until Gavin had turned off the porn before opening the door to his kid's room. That was good for Gavin. He bent down, picked the gun up off the carpet and without hesitation, shot George in the head.

It was surprisingly easy. The gun was louder than he expected and the effect a lot cleaner. It made a small bullet hole in George's head and when he collapsed to the floor, it left only a trace of blood on the wall behind him.

The crying in the bedroom reached a crescendo after the shot. Almost instantly the bedroom door started to open. Gavin grabbed the doorknob and pulled it shut. "Stay in your room kids. This is your Uncle Gavin. Don't open the door. There's a bad man in the house. He'll hurt you if you try to open the door."

He glanced down at George, who lay slumped and motionless against the wall in the carpeted hallway. He let go of the knob, waited a second to make sure the kids had heeded his warning, and then went to the living room.

It turned out that it wasn't that hard to kill someone after all. All he needed was the right motivation and no time to overthink things. George had overheard things and Gavin didn't want him to talk to the police. There was no time and no other option, so he just did it. It was hard to believe that something that could be done so quickly and easily was worth $10,000.

Gavin looked around. His crotch was soaked and he reeked badly of urine, which was embarrassing but he had other priorities. He needed to hide the gun somewhere and he needed to do it fast. The police would arrive soon and they'd be crawling all over the house for hours. He wiped the gun clean of prints, went out the back door, and dropped the gun over the fence in the neighbor's bushes.

When he was done he went back inside the house and waited for the police. He'd need to come up with a story.

Telling the truth obviously wasn't an option.

Chapter 38

Pete Pappas stared at his reflection in the mirror and didn't recognize himself. The beard was gone. It was as if he were a Sesame Street muppet and someone had taken his eyes and nose and stuck them onto another puppet's face. He wasn't good looking before and shaving hadn't helped. If anything, it had made a bad situation worse. His skin was pale and pockmarked but at least he didn't look like an Islamic terrorist. More importantly, he no longer resembled the gun-wielding bearded man who broke into a Coquitlam house earlier that evening.

His head ached and his jaw was sore. The man with the golf club had barely clipped Pete under the chin, but the blow to his wrist hurt like a Motherfucker. He dabbed his neck with toilet paper to absorb the watery blood streaming down his neck from multiple razor nicks.

He wasn't looking forward to explaining to Kevin how he'd fucked up the hit on the warehouse supervisor but at least Kevin would see that he'd taken his advice on shaving.

Pete cleaned up the mess in the bathroom and flushed all the wet, bloody bits of toilet paper down the toilet. After he was done he changed his clothes - although his entire wardrobe consisted of the same thing - dark jeans, black t-shirts, and hoodies.

He left the apartment and walked to the stolen sedan he'd left in the parking lot with the engine running. It was strange to feel the cool October air on his naked face. He touched his cheeks self-consciously and climbed into the car.

He kept an eye out for cops as he drove to Kaitlin's apartment and abandoned the car a few blocks from her place, walking the rest of the way.

He needed to lay low but he also needed to talk to Kevin. He sighed. His career as a hitman was probably over. He wouldn't be surprised if Kevin fired him. It was a good thing he hadn't quit his job at the dollar store.

♦

When the bearded man emerged from the apartment complex Toni barely recognized him. He was no longer 'the bearded man'. He'd shaved it off and the effect was dramatic. If he hadn't gotten into the stolen sedan, Toni might have missed him.

Earlier that night, she'd watched as Gavin's shitbox Chevy hatchback pulled into a driveway in front of a two-story house in Coquitlam. She saw Gavin get out and go into the house. Shortly afterwards the man in the stolen sedan crossed the street and followed Gavin into the house. Toni wondered if Gavin had been expecting the man because he didn't appear to knock. He went inside as if he'd been invited.

The bearded man came out less than ten minutes later, hobbling, but moving quickly to the stolen sedan, the engine still running. Toni followed the sedan to an apartment complex in East Vancouver where, once again, the man left the engine running as he walked away from the car. This time he was gone for nearly half an hour and when he came out, he'd changed his appearance.

Toni followed the car once again and tried to make sense of what she had seen. Had the man killed Gavin, she wondered.

She could only hope.

Chapter 39

Saturday October 22

Ana woke and stared at the clock by the bed. She was confused. The clock must be wrong. It said 9:48 am, which was impossible. Braden never slept that late. She sat up, feeling a moment of panic before the realization sank in. Rick had stayed over-night. Braden hadn't slept in. Rick was with him. They were downstairs.

She fell back, letting her head sink into the pillow, and took a deep breath. She wasn't sure how she felt about the situation. Was it too soon for her son to know that Rick had stayed over? Was she scarring him forever? Would he think she was trying to replace his father with another man?

The more she thought about it, the more it occurred to her that her son probably hadn't given the situation much thought. He was only six years old and besides, Brad was never up in the morning so he had no reason to think Rick was replacing him, at least in that regard. If Braden saw his father in the morning it was probably because Brad was coming home from a night out, not because he got up early to watch cartoons with his son. Braden knew nothing of sex, so whatever concerns Ana had about Braden being exposed to her sex life were almost certainly misplaced.

She got out of bed, slipped on a robe and went downstairs.

"Mommy," Braden called, racing to her.

She scooped him up and kissed him all over his face and then pulled up his shirt and kissed his belly.

"Good morning munchkin," she said.

She put him back down and he immediately grabbed her hand and pulled her into the living room.

"Rick made my Bat Cave," he said. "Come see it mommy, come see."

She laughed, "Ok, ok, but then mommy needs her coffee. You know how mommy feels about coffee."

Rick was stretched out on the carpet in front of the couch with pieces of Lego scattered around him. The Bat Cave was nearly complete. She'd tried to build it when he got it for his sixth birthday last month but Braden seemed happy enough to play with the little figures and the truck it came with, so she'd never bothered to finish it.

"Very nice. You and Rick have been busy this morning."

She exchanged a quick smile with Rick.

Braden dropped to the carpet and crawled over to the Bat Cave. "Watch mommy. Bruce Wayne goes in the elevator, see, and then he turns into Batman."

Rick rose and said, "I'll make you a cup of coffee."

"Thank you," she said, then added, "Make it black."

She sat on the couch while Braden showed her the many features of the Bat Cave. She indulged him with the appropriate 'ooohs' and 'awes', showing as much interest as she could muster for a Lego Bat Cave.

Rick came with the coffee and sat on the couch beside her. She closed her eyes and took a sip, letting the coffee work its magic. She and Rick had stayed up most of the night, mostly talking, but sometimes not talking. She remembered that there had been at least some moaning.

Mostly though they had talked.

With Dana, she talked freely about her relationships but she'd never been able to talk about the job. She had started to talk about some of the things she dealt with at work with her therapist, and it had helped, but at the same time, she didn't believe that the therapist could relate to what it was like to see a young mother decapitated in a car, or a teenage boy dangling from a noose in his parent's garage, or a lifeless five year old who'd fallen from an apartment balcony.

But Rick was a paramedic. He understood things in a way that Dana and the therapist couldn't, and she found herself opening up to him completely. She even told Rick about the man who was crushed by a delivery truck. It had been one of Ana's first calls and it still haunted her. The man had been directing a truck to back up against a loading dock. The driver hit the gas when he meant to brake and the truck pinned him against the concrete wall just above the belt line. He'd essentially been cut in half.

The workers at the warehouse realized that if they moved the truck, the man would bleed out in seconds and die. The truck that would kill him, was also keeping him alive. There was nothing Ana and her partner could do.

The man was lucid and fully aware that he was going to die. Ana stayed with him while they called his wife so she could come and say goodbye. He was twenty six years old.

Eventually they moved the truck and Ana added her first glass jar to the cupboard. Over the next twelve years she added many more, never talking about them.

Of course, she might not have kept so much bottled inside, she thought, if she'd had an orgasm once in a while. Orgasms, it seemed, were a little like truth serum.

"Should I make us breakfast?" Rick asked.

Braden stopped playing and looked up, alarmed.

Ana smiled at him. "As wonderful as that sounds, we usually go out for breakfast on Saturdays when I'm not working. I promised Braden yesterday we'd go out."

"Great," Rick said, looking genuinely pleased. "I wrote a whole blog about the ten best places to eat breakfast in Vancouver."

"I'm sure you did..." Ana said. "But we like to go to McDonalds."

There was a flash of confusion and then a comical look of horror on Rick's face. He covered it up quickly with a strained smile.

"You don't have to come if you don't want to. Braden likes the playground and the hotcakes."

"No, no. It'll be fun."

Thirty minutes later they were out the door. They didn't go to the nearest McDonalds because not all McDonalds are equal. Some have better playgrounds.

When they got to the restaurant, Braden inhaled his hot cakes and went off to the playground, leaving Ana and Rick at a table in the parent section where they could keep an eye on him. Rick ate his Bacon n Egg McMuffin without complaint although he was clearly distressed to discover that it contained processed cheese rather than aged artisan cheddar. He was being a good sport about it though and even managed to eat the whole thing.

"Braden has a playdate this afternoon and I'm going to pick up Marco's things from his locker at the warehouse. Did you want to come?"

"I wish I could. I'd rather spend the day with you but I promised my brother-in-law I'd help him with a bathroom reno he's doing. I committed to it weeks ago."

She nodded, a little disappointed, but at the same time it was nice to know that he was the kind of man who helped his family, not to mention, the kind of man who knew how to renovate a bathroom.

"Tonight maybe?" she asked.

He reached out and touched her hand. "I'd like that. What time are you going to the warehouse?"

"2 o'clock. I have to pick Braden up at from his play date at 5. What time are you done at your sisters?"

"My brother-in-law is pretty hopeless but we should wrap it up by six."

"Text me when you're done."

"I will."

A disturbance in the playground required adult intervention. A little girl was hitting Braden because Braden was blocking access to the slide. The two mothers stepped in and when the situation was resolved Ana returned to the table. She took a sip of her coffee and finished the last of her Sausage 'n Egg McMuffin, which she thought was quite tasty.

"Anything more on Steve?" Rick asked.

Ana shook her head. "My mother is furious with me."

"It's not your fault."

She appreciated that he was taking her side even though she felt she deserved some of her mother's anger. Steve wouldn't have left the hospital, at least not that night, if she hadn't accused him of covering up for Marco's killers. She felt guilty about that but part of her knew that his return to the streets was inevitable and likely beyond her control.

She resolved to find Steve and to do whatever she could to get him into a program. She owed that much to Marko. It might be futile, but she needed to try. He was her little brother.

"On the upside, she won't talk to me, so I have that."

He grinned at her. "There's always a silver lining if you look for it."

She smiled back. They'd only been a couple for 24 hours, but already she could picture a life with him. She noticed that he hadn't used any hair gel that morning.

If that wasn't a sign of true love, Ana didn't know what was.

Chapter 40

Pete Pappas had had a bad night and his morning wasn't going well either. Never mind his complete fuck-up at Gavin Taylor's house, things hadn't gone well with Kaitlin last night and he was surprised by how rattled he was by that. Among other things, she was apparently not happy that he had shaved his beard. To make matters worse she'd heard about Chewy's death. She didn't know Chewy very well but he was an occasional customer at the bar where she worked and she knew Pete sometimes hung out with him. She didn't seem to think Pete had killed him but she suspected that Pete had been with him that night and that he was either in danger, in trouble, or both. Either way, she didn't want any part of it.

The end result was that Pete hadn't gotten laid last night.

He hadn't slept either. He phoned Kevin in the morning, using the burner phone Kevin had given him. Not surprisingly, he was not happy when Pete told him that things hadn't gone as planned. He wanted to meet Pete at his office at 1:00.

It was nearly noon now. He was still at Kaitlin's place, in the living room watching television, when her roommate, April, stumbled out of her bedroom. She looked hung over and didn't make eye contact with Pete, shuffling wordlessly to the small kitchen where she turned on the coffee maker.

April was built like an exceptionally tall ten year old boy. She was wearing loose-fitting shorts and a thin, dingy white t-shirt that did nothing to conceal her tiny breasts. Apparently there were men willing to fuck her. Pete had no idea why. She had short dark hair and a pretty enough face but he liked a woman with a little girth.

She came into the living room with her cup of coffee, sat on the couch, and finally looked up.

"Whoa, what the fuck happened to your face?"

"I shaved."

"No shit. What does Kaitlin think? Fuck, I can't even look at you. It's freaking me out."

Pete felt himself grow irritated, although to be fair, he'd been irritated before she opened her mouth.

"It doesn't matter what she thinks so shut the fuck up about it."

April started to say something but seemed to think better of it. She took a sip of her coffee and they sat in awkward silence.

The Noon News Hour came on. Pete watched anxiously. The home invasion in Coquitlam was the lead story.

"The Integrated Homicide Instigation Team is investigating the murder of a 42 year old man who was the victim of an apparent home invasion in Coquitlam last night," the pretty blonde newscaster said. "Coquitlam RCMP were called to the scene of a home on Alderson Avenue in the Maillardville area of Coquitlam last night at approximately 10:45 pm and found one man dead from an apparent gunshot wound to the head. The victim, whose name has not been released, was pronounced dead at the scene. Three other people, including two children, were present in the house at the time of the home invasion. One man was reportedly admitted to Eagle Ridge Hospital with non-life-threatening injuries and released hours later. The suspect is described as a heavy set Asian man in his late thirties or early forties with a thin mustache, wearing a red hoodie, dark jeans, sneakers, and a Seattle Seahawks baseball cap."

Video footage on screen showed the exterior of Gavin Taylor's house, close ups of police cars with their lights flashing, and curious and concerned neighbors huddled on the street.

"Sukh Dhaliwal is on the scene. Sukh, what are police telling us this morning?"

A good looking man in a windbreaker with the station's logo on the breast appeared on screen.

"Police are tight-lipped for the moment but we anticipate an updated statement soon."

"Are there any leads on the suspect in this case?"

"None, other than the description provided. The killer is described as a heavy-set Asian male, approximately 40 years of age."

"Are police saying anything about a possible motive, or if the victim is known to police"

"Coquitlam RCMP aren't sharing any information. The case has been referred to IHIT - the Integrated Homicide Investigation Team. In talking with neighbors there's no indication that the victim here had a criminal record or was known to police."

"Do we know anything about the victim?"

"The victim hasn't been identified pending notification of family but neighbors here suggest he may have been a single father, renting this house."

"What about the two young children who were present. Do we have any information about them or what they saw?"

"We've verified that there were two children in the house at the time of the home invasion. We haven't been able to confirm their identities, their connection to the victim or what they saw. They're in the custody of child services for the time-being."

"What are the neighbors saying about all this?"

"They're shocked of course and concerned. One neighbor I spoke to said she's lived in this neighborhood for twenty years and doesn't feel safe anymore."

"Thank you, Sukh," the blonde newscaster said. "That was Sukh Dhaliwal reporting live from the scene of a home invasion last night in Coquitlam. We'll provide updates as they come available."

The newscaster moved on to the next story - a house fire in Delta - but Pete tuned it out. He didn't know what to think. It had been Gavin's house on TV but he knew he hadn't killed anyone there. Both Gavin and the other man had gotten a good look at Pete. There was no way in hell anyone could mistake him for a heavy set Asian man in his forties.

Pete glanced around the room and realized that while he'd been watching the news, April had slunk back to her room. He heard a door open and turned to see Kaitlin come out. She was dressed in jeans and a sweatshirt. She seemed surprised to see that he was still there. Pete got up from the couch and came over to her.

"I'll grow the beard back," he said.

She shrugged. "Do whatever you want."

"I'm sorry Kait."

She stared up at him. "You don't even know what you're apologizing for." She shook her head. "Just go, alright."

He was obviously missing something. He didn't understand women.

"I really like you," he said and he meant it.

She looked bored or angry or sad – he wasn't sure. He didn't know how to read women.

"Good for you." She walked past him toward the kitchen. "You should go."

She was obviously upset about something. It had to be more than his shaved face but for the life of him he had no idea what it was.

"Ok," he said, because he didn't know what else to say.

He made his way to the door and looked back. She was in the kitchen, facing away from him, not bothering to look up. He decided he needed to leave anyway because he was meeting Kevin. He opened the door and went out into the hallway, feeling confused. He didn't always show it, but he really liked Kaitlin. He decided he would come back tonight.

Hopefully she'd be in a better mood.

Chapter 41

Toni Little was alert, her eyes fixed on the door to the East Vancouver apartment complex. She hadn't slept all night but that wasn't unusual for her. Once a soldier, always a soldier. She could stay awake for three solid days if she needed to.

She could feel the Walther PPQ 9 mm handgun she kept in an IWB holster against the small of her back. Toni had a number of handguns, most of them legal for target practice, but this one wasn't registered and had been a gift from a US soldier she'd met overseas. Americans, she thought, refused to adopt the metric system except when it came to drugs and handguns. Then they were happy to score a gram of coke or bust a cap with their 9mm.

Toni loved the PPQ. It had the best striker-fired trigger of any handgun she'd used and she loved the weight and feel of it. It had a five inch barrel and just like the Glock, the only safety was the trigger. No fucking around. Slide the clip in, cock it, and it was ready to fire.

Just before noon her phone rang. It was her girlfriend Shasta. Toni realized she should have called her, knowing she might worry. She felt bad about that. They talked and Toni assured her she was fine and would be home later.

"Love you," Toni said.

"I love you too," Shasta replied, not by rote, but with real conviction in her voice.

They disconnected the call and Toni thought about how lucky she was to find someone like Shasta. Straight people always wanted to know how she 'discovered' she was gay. It was a strange way to think of it, Toni thought. Did a person 'discover' they were heterosexual?

She'd always known she was attracted to women. There was no great epiphany, no crystalizing moment when she 'discovered' she was gay. When Toni met Shasta all she knew was that she wanted to be with her all the time. She would go to the gym when Shasta was there and suggest they go for a run on the seawall or out for a drink. She was attracted to her as a person and that ultimately led to a sexual relationship. It was a natural progression, not an end goal.

Of course, it didn't hurt that Shasta had a killer body.

There were two people in the world that mattered to Toni - Shasta and her sister Katie. She would do anything for either of them, even though they barely knew one another. Katie thought Shasta was just Toni's roommate. On reflection, Toni realized she'd kept Katie and Shasta separated on purpose. She'd always been good at compartmentalizing her life.

She was a sister in one compartment. Shasta's lover in another. A soldier in another. She was a distinctly different person in each of the compartments of her life and she liked it that way. Or at least, it was how she felt most comfortable.

Toni focused on the front entrance of the building. Her target was on the move, headed on foot toward Hastings Street. It was difficult to follow someone who was on foot when you were in a vehicle, but Toni stayed with him. The beardless man, as Toni now thought of him, joined a small crowd at a bus stop. She circled the block and found a spot to wait, ready to follow whatever bus he got on.

She had the radio tuned to a pop music station and the news came on. The top story was about the home invasion and murder of a man in Coquitlam. Based on the report, it sounded like Gavin had been murdered, which was good news. If that was the case, Toni could replace Gavin as the new contact at the warehouse and deal directly with Anton, running her own crew.

But then the newscast went on to say that there were three other people in the house at the time of the murder, including two children. This confused her. There had only been one car in the driveway, Gavin's. Toni had assumed that Gavin lived alone. Who were the other people? Did Gavin have kids? Was Gavin murdered or was someone else killed instead?

Toni pondered that as the radio delivered an even bigger surprise. The suspect was described as a 'heavy-set Asian man in his forties with a thin mustache, wearing a red hoodie, a ball cap, and running shoes'. The man Toni had followed and had seen go into and come out of the house, was in his late twenties, muscular, with a thick black beard, wearing a black hoodie under a black leather jacket, shit-kicker boots, and no hat.

What the fuck was going on?

The bus pulled up and the beardless man, who was definitely not a heavy-set Asian man in his forties, boarded. The bus pulled away from the curb and Toni followed in her truck, trying to make sense of it all.

Chapter 42

Pete arrived at the Hiro P Consulting office on Broadway just after 1 pm. The door was unlocked. Once again, Kevin was alone, although he was less enthusiastic to see him this time. He didn't shake Pete's hand or offer him a beer. He wanted to get down to business right away.

"Tell me what happened," he said.

Pete leaned against the same desk he had the last time he'd been in the office and provided a play-by-play explanation of what happened in Gavin's house. Kevin didn't interrupt.

When Pete was done, Kevin said, "The media is reporting that a man was murdered."

"Not by me."

"They also say the home invader was a heavy set Asian man, about 40."

"No idea how they came up with that. They both got a good look at me."

The door opened. Kevin hadn't locked it like he did last time. A muscular woman in a dark brown bomber jacket stepped in.

225

Kevin took a step toward her. "We aren't open."

The woman put her hands up and out to her sides like she was surrendering. "Sorry. I'm looking for Insight Systems."

Kevin stared at her skeptically. "They're on the eighth floor but its Saturday so I don't think they'll be there."

The woman nodded. Her hair was short and she carried himself in a manner that suggested a military background. "I have an appointment."

She didn't make any effort to leave and gazed around the office as if she had all the time in the world.

"Like I said, we're closed," Kevin said.

"What are you guys, some kind of IT firm? Hiro Protagonist. You must be fans of Stephenson."

Pete wondered if he was the only person in the world who had never heard of Hiro Protagonist. He sensed Kevin's irritation and took another step toward the woman, sending a clear message that it was time for her to go. "I think we made it clear that we aren't open."

She smiled. "Right. Maybe I can bring my computer in on Monday and you guys can take a look at it. I think I've got a virus."

"That's not what we do here," Kevin said.

Pete moved and stood beside Kevin, within inches of the woman, looming over her. "You need to leave now."

She stood her ground, showing no sign of intimidation. "No problem." She nodded. "Thanks for the directions. I appreciate it."

With that, she opened the frosted glass door and disappeared into the hallway.

Pete turned to Kevin and shook his head. "That was strange."

Kevin seemed lost in thought, running his hand over his chin. Pete stared at him but he didn't say anything. After a few seconds of silence, Pete locked the door. Kevin didn't appear to notice.

Finally Pete said, "So what do you want me to do?"

"Not fuck up," Kevin said, sounding distracted.

226

"What?"

Kevin stared at him. "Can you do that? Not fuck up?"

Pete involuntarily clenched his fists. "Don't be an asshole Kevin."

"Are you saying you didn't fuck up?"

Pete couldn't say that. He had fucked things up but even so, he didn't like Kevin's attitude. He wondered how Kevin would feel about getting his ass kicked.

"Fuck you," he said. "I don't need this shit."

"The door's there if you want it."

Pete stared at Kevin, weighing his options. Did he want to go back to the Dollar Store, the occasional B & E, and moving a little weed for chump change or did he want to get into a bigger game, even if it meant taking a little shit? He made up his mind.

"Look, I know I fucked up," he said. It physically hurt him to say the words but he managed.

"Good. You need to own that shit"

"The question is, what do we do now?"

Kevin shrugged. "Nothing's changed. Kill Gavin."

Pete hadn't expected that. He was thinking maybe he should lay low for a few days. "Do we even know he's still alive?"

"He's alive and he knows you're coming after him. He's killed someone now so he'll be desperate and dangerous."

"You think he killed someone?"

Kevin nodded. "I do. I think he shot his roommate with your gun after you left."

"What the fuck? How do you know that?"

"Common sense."

"I don't get it."

"Gavin gave the fake description," Kevin said.

"How do you know that?"

"Think about it. Who else would have?"

"I don't know but why would he give a fake description? Why would he kill his roommate?"

"Did you say anything to Gavin? Did you talk about him owing you money or mention killing the warehouse worker or anything like that?"

Pete thought about it. Like Kevin said, it was obvious. Gavin had killed his roommate because he'd heard too much.

"He gave the fake description because I can tie him to the murder of the warehouse worker," Pete said. "And now to the murder of the golf club guy."

Kevin nodded.

"So what's he going to do now?" Pete asked.

"Who the fuck knows?" Kevin stepped toward Pete. "He's a liability though. Find him, kill him, and we can put this shit behind us."

Pete nodded. Kevin was right. He needed to redeem himself. He needed to prove that he could be relied on to get the job done.

"You can count on me."

Kevin didn't look convinced. "Keep an eye out for the chick that wandered in here."

Pete nodded, knowingly. "You think she has something to do with this?"

"I don't know. Just watch your back."

After Pete left the office he went to the restroom to take a leak. Standing in front of the urinal he thought about what he needed to do. It was going to be a lot harder to kill Gavin now. For one thing he didn't have a gun. That meant he either needed to find another gun or find a different way to kill Gavin. Tracking him down was going to be harder too because Gavin knew Pete was coming for him.

And to make matters worse, he hadn't had a chance to get his fucking starter fixed so he still didn't have a car.

Pete shook and zipped up. He didn't bother washing his hands. Most mothers taught their sons to wash their hands after going to the restroom but Pete's mother was different.

'*Don't piss on your hands*' is what she always told him.

It was the only advice she'd given him that he'd paid any attention to. He hadn't gotten good grades, he hadn't gotten into a good college, and he hadn't married a nice girl.

But he didn't piss on his hands.

He went to the elevator and took it down to the parking garage. He needed to steal another car.

Chapter 43

Toni waited and watched as the beardless man left the Hiro P Consulting offices, went to the restroom, and took the elevator to the parking garage. She'd taken a chance by going into the Hiro P Consulting offices and while she wasn't sure she'd learned anything, sometimes you had to 'beat the bushes.'

She pulled the fur lined hood of her bomber jacket up over her head, aware that there may be cameras in the area, and took the stairs down to the garage, the 9mm in a leather holster inside her waistband. The parking garage was nearly empty. It was a professional building and most of the offices were open Monday – Friday. She scanned the lot and saw the beardless man approach an older model Buick. A few seconds later she heard a window smash.

Toni weaved in and out of cars, approaching the Buick. When she got close, she saw the man crouched under the steering column, muttering to himself.

"What the fuck are you doing?" Toni said, staring down at him.

The man turned awkwardly to face Toni. She aimed the 9 mm

at his head. The man looked more disoriented than frightened.

"Should I call the police or just shoot you?" she said.

He didn't say anything, eyeing Toni with curiosity.

"Get up," she said.

He hesitated but eventually stood. Toni stayed a comfortable distance back so she'd have time to get off a shot if the man came at her.

"I don't want to kill you but I will."

"What's this about?"

"Gavin Taylor. Marko Milanovic. Anton, the Russian mobster."

She could see in the man's eyes that the names meant something to him.

"If I wanted to kill you, you'd be dead." She motioned to the back door. "Get in the back."

The man hesitated but eventually moved to the door. Toni gave him room so he could open the door and slide into the car.

"Move over," she said.

He shifted until he was against the door behind the front passenger seat. Toni took a seat beside him, holding the gun firmly in her hand, her finger on the trigger.

She closed the door. "Put your hands on top of your head."

He did as instructed. "Who the fuck are you?"

"Gavin Taylor hired me to kill you."

The man nodded. He didn't seem surprised.

"But, Gavin Taylor is an asshole," she said.

He raised his eyebrows.

"You tried to kill him last night. I gather you fucked that up."

The man glared at her but said nothing.

Toni paused to collect her thoughts. She decided to lay things out as she understood them and watch the man's reaction.

"Here's what I know. Gavin Taylor is a supervisor at an electronics warehouse. He and some of the employees steal shit from

231

the warehouse for a man they call Anton. Marko Milanovic worked at the warehouse and shot a video of them stealing shit."

Toni paused. She was good at reading people, especially men under stress.

"Marko tried to blackmail them so Gavin hired someone to kill him," she went on. "Gavin had no idea where to find a hired killer, so he asked Anton. Anton hooked him up with you. Gavin thinks you're a professional killer but I know you're a low level fuck-up who can barely hotwire a car."

Toni could see rage in the man's eyes. He didn't like being called a low level fuck-up, especially by a woman, but that wasn't Toni's problem. Sometimes people had a hard time accepting the truth.

"So you killed Marko but then Gavin either couldn't or wouldn't pay you what he owes you. He probably can't. He has a gambling problem. Gavin doesn't show up to pay you at the No. 5, so you go to his house and....fuck, I don't know...somehow you kill the wrong guy."

The man's face grew red and his eyes narrowed.

"The radio said one man was killed but I don't think it was Gavin," she said. "The way I see it, the only person who would lie to the police about what the killer looked like, is Gavin. If you get arrested, you can tie him to Marko's murder."

The man kept his eyes fixed on Toni. He stared back, unflinching, letting her know he wasn't intimidated.

"So, the other man was a neighbor, a roommate, a friend, his brother? What?"

The man shook his head and started to move his hand toward his cheek, like he was going to scratch it.

"Put your hand back on your head," she snapped. "Or I'll Pulp Fiction it all over the windows. I'm not fucking kidding. They'll have to wet-vac your brains off the upholstery like you're fucking Marvin."

Without a word, the man showed an open palm and put his hand slowly back on his head.

"It doesn't matter who he was," Toni said. "All that matters is that you killed him."

"I didn't kill anyone last night."

He was talking. That was progress. "Who was he then?"

"I never said I was there."

"I followed you. I saw you go into the fucking house. I saw you come out, limping like a fucking pussy. Don't tell me you weren't there."

"What the fuck d'you want?"

"I want information. I want to know what the fuck is going on."

The man squinted. "I can't help you."

"That's a shame. I thought we could work together."

"Who the fuck are you?"

"I'm someone who was hired to kill you." Toni said, keeping the gun level and aimed at the man. "But, we could do this another way."

"And what way is that?"

"You kill Gavin and introduce me to Anton."

The man lunged at her. Toni pressed the trigger without hesitation and he stopped cold. The bullet struck him in the chest. She fired again, another shot to the chest and he slumped back against the door. Blood soaked into his black t-shirt and spilled out his mouth. He gasped and choked for a few seconds, clutching his chest, blood flowing over his fingers, and then his eyes closed and he stopped moving.

The report of the two shots had been deafening in the confined space of the car but Toni was accustomed to the sound of gunfire and was un-phased.

"Shit," she muttered under her breath. He hadn't given her a choice but still, it seemed crazy to her that people were getting killed over a few stolen televisions. What the fuck had she gotten herself into? Whatever it was, she was a killer now. She needed to move quickly and efficiently.

She checked the man's pulse to confirm he was dead and then

slipped his wallet from his back pocket. There was a few hundred dollars inside that she quickly pocketed. The man's driver's license identified him as Pete Pappas. Toni wiped the wallet with a paper napkin she'd found in the car and tossed it on the floor. She gave the interior a quick but thorough wipe and climbed out.

She slid the 9mm back into the holster in her waistband and closed and locked the door. The parking garage was eerily quiet. She put the hood up on her coat and walked briskly to the stairwell, keeping her head down. She hadn't planned to kill Pete Pappas but there was nothing she could do about that now.

Toni blamed television. It made people think they could do a lot of stupid shit that they couldn't do, like wrestle a gun away from a trained soldier in the back of a Buick. It was a plan that might have worked if Pete Pappas was bulletproof, but obviously, he wasn't.

Chapter 44

Ana, Rick and Braden drove back from McDonalds in her Sunfire. They'd taken her car because it was easier. The car seat was set up and properly secured in the Sunfire and, perhaps more importantly, the satellite radio was already tuned to the Pearl Jam radio station.

Rick was surprised that Pearl Jam, or any band for that matter, had a radio station completely dedicated to them.

"How many songs do they have?" he asked. "Do they just play the same ones every day?"

She explained that the station mostly played live recordings and every concert had a completely different set list.

"It seems a little over the top," he said.

She gave him a sidewise grin and rested her hand on his knee. "You have no idea," she said.

When they got back home, Braden raced to his Lego Bat Cave like it was an ice cream truck on a hot summer day. She didn't feel comfortable leaving him alone but she wanted to say goodbye to Rick with some privacy so they kept the front door open and stepped outside, into the carport. They could hear Braden playing with his toys, making a wide range of sound effects, all of them evoking some measure of violence. He was so sweet and yet all he seemed to think about was blowing things up and making the bodies of superheroes go flying through the air.

"I'm glad you came over," she said.

His hands rested on her hips. They felt like they belonged there.

"Me too," he said.

"Even though we had Egg McMuffins for breakfast?"

He pulled her close. "Yes."

"I think the Egg McMuffin should be 'our meal' from now on. Years from now when we celebrate special occasions we'll have Egg McMuffins and a bottle of champagne. It'll be our thing. What d'you think?"

"I think you have a twisted sense of humor."

"I've heard that."

He sighed. "I've got to go."

"See you tonight?"

He kissed her softly.

"Definitely," he said, parting slowly from the kiss

She told him she'd phone or text him after she was done at the warehouse and he said he'd let her know when he was finished at his sister's house.

"Have you heard from Andy?" he asked.

Ana had told him about the video and her suspicions that Andy may have sabotaged the computer. She'd tried to call Andy and had left him a message.

She shook her head. "He hasn't called back."

"I'm sure it's a coincidence that the computer crashed when it did. Maybe the video caused it to crash."

"I'm not going to accuse him of anything," Ana said. "I just want to talk to him."

They held hands for a few seconds in silence, both of them reluctant to let go. Ana hadn't felt like this since high school. What made it even more ridiculous was that Rick was a man she'd worked with daily for years.

Finally he stepped away from her and their fingers parted. After a few steps she called out to him.

"Stay away from Katie Perry. I was kidding about that. No free pass."

He turned and smiled at her. Last night she had told him that back in college she had slept with Matt Wood, the lead singer of a band called Jackknife Sugar-Truck. It was before she'd met Brad. In fact, she met Brad through Matt, who was unknown at the time, just a college kid playing local bars. But he was huge now, a bona fide celebrity, which led to the inevitable 'free pass' conversation.

The concept was that even the most monogamous couples were entitled to each have a free pass, a celebrity that they were allowed to have sex with, should the opportunity present itself. Rick had chosen Katie Perry. Ana initially picked Eddie Vedder but as gorgeous and talented as he was, she decided she wanted a rock star who was a little less serious.

She picked Dave Grohl.

"Katie can't hold a candle to you."

She gave him a full wattage smile and he turned and walked to his car. He glanced over his shoulder and she waved and then went back in the house.

She stared at the stand where the TV once was and sighed. The missing TV made her think of Steve and Marko and she felt an unexpected wave of grief wash over her.

Braden must have sensed something.

"What's wrong mommy?"

His words made her snap out of her thoughts and she smiled weakly at him. He looked up at her with earnest eyes.

"Nothing's wrong honey," she lied. "Mommy's fine."

He didn't look completely convinced.

"Be a big boy and go upstairs and get ready to go over to Riley's house. Mommy's going to drop you off soon."

He nodded and scampered up the stairs.

She checked her cell phone for messages but there weren't any. She found Andy's number in her address book and pressed call. It went quickly to voice mail.

"Andy, this is Auntie Ana. Can you call me back? It's important." She left her number and disconnected the call.

She looked up and saw Braden stumble-step down the stairs, armed with his backpack full of toys, his face bright with an enthusiasm she rarely saw in anyone over the age of six.

"Time to go honey," she said, hoping he could hold onto that childish enthusiasm for a few more years.

Chapter 45

Toni found the doors to the Hiro P Consulting office locked and the lights out. She was curious. Why had Pete Pappas gone there, she wondered. He didn't seem like the kind of guy in need of innovative business solutions.

She took the elevator back down to the lobby and walked casually to her truck which was parked across the street from the building. She settled into the driver's seat, took her phone off silent mode, and noticed that she'd missed a call while she was in the parking garage. It was from Gavin.

If there had been any doubt about whether or not Gavin was alive, there wasn't now.

Toni called him and Gavin answered on the second ring.

"Yeah – what?"

"Gavin, this is Toni."

"What the fuck? What happened last night?"

"What are you talking about?"

"You were supposed to take care of things...you know...with our friend."

"It's done."

"What's done? Nothing was fucking done last night."

"Last night?"

"The fucking guy showed up at my place."

"You're kidding?"

"No, I'm not kidding. What the fuck happened? You were supposed to take care of it."

"I did, this afternoon."

"You were supposed to take care of it last night."

"I couldn't do it last night. I lost him."

"You're fucking kidding me."

"I'm not."

"Bullshit."

"It's not bullshit. I followed him to his apartment. When he left, I lost him in traffic so I went back to his apartment and followed him this morning. I took care of it a few minutes ago."

"It's done?"

"It's done."

"Good, the fucker deserved it. He shot my roommate. That could've been me. Fortunately, I know how to swing a golf club."

Toni did her best to sound empathetic. "Jesus Gavin. I had no idea. Are you ok?"

"No. I'm not ok. He almost fucking killed me."

"Shit."

"I've got cops all over my place. It's a fucking gong show. I had to go to the hospital to get checked out. I've been with the cops all morning. They're still at my house."

"I heard about a home invasion on the radio. That was you?"

"Haven't you been listening? Yeah, that was fucking me. I almost got fucking shot. I could be dead now."

"There were some kids in the house or something?"

"Yeah, yeah," Gavin said dismissively. "My roommate had his fucking kids over."

"Did they see what happened?"

"No. It was late. They were in bed."

"That's good."

"What the fuck? Who gives a shit about the kids? Did you hear me? I almost got killed last night."

"Yeah, well, thank God you're alive," Toni said, hoping Gavin didn't notice the lack of conviction.

"You should have warned me. I didn't even lock my front door. The fucking guy walked right in. You could have told me he was coming."

"I didn't know he was coming."

"Tell that to my dead roommate."

Toni decided to let the comment slide. She knew Gavin was lying to her. Pete had denied killing anyone in the house and Toni thought there was at least a possibility he was telling the truth. There was a good chance, she thought, that Gavin had shot his roommate.

"What does Anton look like?" she asked.

"What?"

"Anton, what does he look like?"

Gavin sounded annoyed. "What does that have to do with anything?"

"Is he an older guy?"

"Fuck no. He's like, late-twenties, early thirties maybe."

"Short guy?"

"No. What the fuck are you talking about? He's tall. Really tall. Good looking guy."

Gavin's description of Anton sounded like a perfect match for Mr. Hiro Protagonist. "Where are you now?" she said.

"What is this? What's with all the questions?"

She had questions she wanted answers to but she realized that her approach wasn't working. She needed to let the conversation flow naturally, something that would be easier to do in person.

"Are you at home? Are you done with the police?"

"Would I be talking like this in front of the cops? What the fuck? I'm in a Tim Hortons parking lot. I'm on my way to work."

"You're going to work?"

"I'm meeting Marko's sister. We're going to open her brother's locker. I thought I'd give her a tour... you know... show her around the warehouse."

"I'm near the warehouse. Maybe I'll swing by."

"Whatever. I gotta go. I'm late as it is."

Toni disconnected the call and was about to make another when she noticed two police cars approach the building across the street with their lights flashing. She started the ignition.

Her next phone call would have to wait.

◆

Twenty minutes later Toni drove into a drive-thru and got a coffee and a ham sandwich on a rock-hard bun. She hadn't eaten since late afternoon the previous day and she was starving. What she really wanted was a blood rare steak and an ice cold beer, but the sandwich would have to do. She parked and ate.

When she was done she slid Gavin's cell phone out of her bomber jacket pocket and dialed a number. It rang multiple times but no one answered. An automated voice gave her the option of leaving a message so she did.

"Pete's dead. Call me back."

A few minutes later, the phone rang. She recognized the number as the one she'd just dialed.

"Anton?" she said into the phone.

"Who is this?"

"It's not Gavin."

"Obviously. Who is this?"

"Did you get my message?"

"I did, but I have no idea what you're talking about."

"We both know that's not true."

"I'm going to hang up."

Toni knew he was bluffing. He wasn't going to hang up. "I met you today," she said. "You were with Pete, at Hiro P Consulting."

There was a long pause. "You still haven't told me what you want."

"We all want the same things in life don't we? Too bad your guy fucked up last night."

"I have no idea what you're talking about."

"Poor Pete. He wasn't cut out for this kind of work."

"Is that so?"

"It is. I didn't want kill him but he didn't give me a choice. I'm hoping it doesn't affect our relationship; that we can still work together."

"I don't know who you are or what you're talking about."

Toni paused. She'd already killed someone today. As the saying went, 'in for a penny, in for a pound'. She took a deep breath. "I'm willing to finish the job your guy tried to do last night."

"Assuming I even knew what you're talking about, which I don't, what's your interest?"

"He's an asshole which could be reason enough, but I also figure with him out of the way, I'll be the person you deal with at the warehouse."

There was a long pause before he said, "Alright, I think we can work something out."

"Good, and just so we're clear, I know your name's not Anton. I know you're not part of the Russian mob."

"Only an idiot would think I was part of the Russian mob."

"Agreed. So, do we have an understanding?"

243

"We do."

"Good," Toni said and disconnected the call.

She started her truck and drove east to the warehouse where Gavin Taylor was planning to meet Marko's sister Ana.

Chapter 46

Katie McGuire was a mess. She'd been crying on and off all morning.

More on than off.

Things with Andy hadn't been the same since the other night, after the video. He said everything was fine but it wasn't. They usually texted each other whenever they weren't together. They'd spent part of everyday together for 46 straight days – she kept track – but last night he said he was going out with friends instead of being with her. He hadn't called her all morning. He hadn't sent a single text.

She'd sent him eleven and he hadn't replied to any of them.

She tried to be casual:

Hey, what's up?

She showed interest:

How was your night out with the boys? Hope you're not too hung over today. ♥ ☺ ♥

She was informative:

Running a few errands. Back in 45 min.

She tried to be clever and random:

You can make a necklace out of macaroni but I wouldn't recommend it.

She was needy:

Call me

She made sure he knew that she cared:

Miss you. Love you. ♥ ☺ ♥

And she'd been repetitive:

Call me.

Call me.

Call me.

Call me.

Call me.

Maybe he was passed-out drunk, she thought. That would explain why he hadn't answered any of her texts. Maybe he'd lost his phone.

She stared at the wallpaper photo on her phone. It was a picture she'd taken of him at English Bay. In the headshot, his face was tanned and his smile broad. It had been a windy day and his usually neatly parted chestnut hair was windblown and perfectly mussed after a day of swimming and sunbathing.

She felt like she was going to cry again.

All because of that stupid video.

She wished she hadn't asked him to delete it but what could she do? She didn't want her sister to lose her job or get into trouble but she also didn't want to lose Andy. They were meant for each other. They were soul mates.

She hadn't realized it was so complicated to delete a video file. She thought it could be done with a simple mouse click but apparently, it wasn't that easy. Andy said that when someone deleted a file, it didn't actually remove it from the hard drive, it simply hid it from the operating system.

He said he'd made his mother think the computer was infected with a virus by writing a script for what he called a 'fork bomb' and putting it on the desktop disguised as the video file. The 'fork bomb' itself didn't do any permanent damage to the computer or its files but it caused the computer to crash in seconds. He said the fork bomb was intended to convince his mother that the video file couldn't be retrieved and then, after she left for work, he wiped the hard drive using something called DBAN. He told her it took almost the whole day. When the computer was turned over to the police, the hard drive was wiped clean and none of the files could be retrieved, including the video.

He told her all this yesterday but he didn't sound like himself. He sounded distant. Sad. Like he resented her. Like she'd betrayed him and he couldn't bear to talk to her, let alone be with her.

She sat on the couch in the living room watching television but couldn't concentrate. She stared up at the painting on the wall, the one Andy thought was cool, the one Dakota, her roommate, had called 'Cutting.'

When Dakota wasn't home, Katie frequently went into her room and looked through her stuff, reading through dozens of notebooks filled with doddles and poetry. The over-riding theme to both her poetry and her artwork seemed to be that the world was harsh and cruel and that to cope, all you could do was turn your pain inward. Dakota believed that she deserved every scar she'd inflicted. If you can hurt me, she seemed to think, why shouldn't I hurt myself?

Fuck that, Katie thought. I would hurt you, before I hurt myself.

She got up from the couch and went to the kitchen and returned with a thin, sharp steak knife. She stood in front of the painting Andy had admired so much. Maybe he'd rather be with a girl like Dakota, she thought. Dakota would never ask him to make a sacrifice for her. She would never expect anything from him. She would smile and pretend to be happy and then retreat to the bathroom with a razor blade and her tears.

Katie attacked the painting with the knife, tearing into the fabric, knocking it off the wall. Tears streamed down her face and she fell to her knees, stabbing it over and over again. When she was done, she stood and went to each of the other paintings on the wall and tore into them, savagely ripping them apart.

When she was done, she dropped the knife and collapsed on the couch. A dozen paintings lay strewn about the room, slashed to pieces. She thought of Andy and his murdered father. Both she and Andy had parents who'd been murdered. It should have drawn them closer together but instead, the stupid video had driven him away.

Why did the video matter so much to him? Didn't he understand that they were soul mates? Didn't he see that they were bound by tragedy?

It wasn't like he knew the truth about Katie.

No one did.

Katie's father hadn't set the fire that killed her mother. Her father had beaten her mother - that part of the story was true - but she was alive when Katie came downstairs, after her father left. Her mother might have survived if Katie had called an ambulance, but then again, maybe not.

Katie didn't call 911.

She hadn't necessarily intended to murder her mother. She just wanted someone to rescue her. So she set fire to the curtains over the sink and watched as it spread quickly up the wall. She took one last look around the kitchen, at the overturned table and chairs, at her mother sobbing on the floor, and went back upstairs to her bedroom to wait.

Suicide never entered her mind. She believed in her heart that she would be saved, first by the fire department, and then by her sister. Toni would come back for her, Katie was sure of it. She'd always admired her older sister. As a small child she remembered following her around the house. They had a special bond that other people wouldn't understand.

She took a deep breath and selected Andy's name in her phone's contact list. She needed to talk to him. If she lost him, she would spiral out of control.

He was her salvation.

The phone rang and he answered, sounding groggy and hung over.

"Hey," he grunted.

She felt her heart skip a beat, relieved that he'd finally answered the phone. "Andy. It's good to hear your voice."

He groaned.

"Are you ok?"

"Rough night."

"I need to see you."

There was a long silence.

"I need to see you," she repeated.

"Ah – I don't think that's a good idea."

Her heart pounded. He was going to break up with her. She knew it.

"I'm coming over."

She wasn't going to let him break up with her on the phone. If she could see him in person she could apologize. She could make it right. She could tell him that she shouldn't have asked him to delete the file. She'd made a mistake. He would see how sincere she was. He would realize how much he loved her.

"I don't -"

She cut him off. "Don't say anything. I'm coming over."

She disconnected the call, turned off her phone, and went to the bathroom - not to cut herself, but to shower.

I would hurt you before I would ever hurt myself, she thought.

Chapter 47

"There's a lady waiting for you in the lunch room," one of the material handlers said to Gavin when he arrived at the warehouse.

"Thanks, buddy," Gavin said.

He called all the South Asian men at the warehouse 'buddy' because it was easier than learning their names. He used to call them all Apu, after the character on the Simpsons, but apparently that was racist. Gavin had learned this when he was required to take workplace sensitively training a few years ago. In his training they had encouraged him to call people by their given names and that he refer to people from India and Pakistan as 'South Asians' and not 'Punjabs' or 'Pakis'. Apparently calling them 'cow kissers' and 'goat herders' was politically incorrect as well.

Whatever you called them, Gavin thought, there was a boatload of them working at the warehouse.

"No problem SPF," the man said with a grin. His teeth were very white.

For some reason a lot of the South Asian men called him that.

He suspected it was an insult, which bothered him, but he didn't have time to think about it now. He went up the stairs to the lunchroom. It was 2:15 pm.

He found Ana Marshall sitting alone at one of the tables. She had her head down, typing into her phone.

"Ms. Marshall?" he said, extending his hand. "Sorry I'm late."

She looked up. He was disappointed to see she hadn't put much effort into her appearance. Would it kill her, he thought, to wear a little make-up and show some cleavage? She was fit and toned, but not overly muscular, reminding him of an Olympic beach volleyball player.

She stood. "No problem. Thanks for doing this."

She was two or three inches taller than him but he didn't mind. It didn't matter how tall a woman was once she was flat on her back.

"It's been a crazy day. My house was broken into last night and I had to give a statement to the police."

Maybe she'd feel sorry for him and want to ease his pain.

"Oh my God, that's terrible."

"I don't know what the world's coming to...I mean...what happened to Marko....that was just awful. And then a home invasion at my house."

"You were home when they broke in?"

He nodded. "I chased them out with a five iron but not before they shot and killed my roommate."

Her face went pale. "Oh my God. You don't need to do this. You should be at home, with your family or something."

"I want to do this. There's nothing I can do at home. I just feel bad that I was late and kept you waiting."

He could tell she had a new found respect for him. They had both been victims of violence. If he was lucky, maybe they'd find comfort in one another by doing it on his desk.

"Don't worry about that."

He clapped his hands together. "So do you want me to show

251

you around?"

"Ah, sure. If you don't mind."

"It'll be my pleasure," he said.

It didn't take long to conduct the tour. There wasn't much to see. He showed her rows of floor-to-ceiling heavy-duty storage shelves loaded with boxes, wrapped in plastic and stored on pallets. He showed her the loading bays with trailers backed up to them while workers in hard hats and safety vests, more than half of them South Asians and almost all of them men, loaded trucks bound for destinations throughout Western Canada.

"That's about it," he said over the sound of a beeping forklift behind them. "There isn't much to see."

"With all the inventory you have, you must have a really good security system."

Gavin gave her sideways glance. "We've got cameras everywhere. The warehouse never closes so we don't have an alarm system. We have staff here 24/7."

"Do you always load these big trailers?" She pointed at one of the loading bays. "Do you ever load smaller vehicles, like a van?"

Gavin felt his pulse pound in his neck. He tried not to flinch. There was no way that was an innocent question. He needed to draw on his poker skills, to stay calm and make sure he gave nothing away.

"Just the trailers," he said.

"Could any of your employees steal anything?"

"No," he said as decisively as he could. "They'd get caught. We have cameras and we monitor the inventory."

"Do you ever have thefts?"

"No, never," he said. "Nothing like that." He needed to change the subject. "Would'ya like to see my office?" he asked.

"Ah – sure – I guess."

He smiled and led her up the stairs to his office, near the lunchroom. He'd tidied up and gotten rid of the garbage can, the one he'd puked in a few days earlier. He'd actually switched the can for one in the accountant's office. It wasn't like the lingering odor of stale vomit was going to negatively impact her sex life.

"This is where I get my work done. It's really the nerve center for the whole operation."

She nodded without enthusiasm and showed no interest in venturing beyond the door.

"We can go in and chat for a while if you like. Get to know each other a little better."

"Ah- no that's fine. I think if we can just open Marko's locker and I can get his stuff that'd be good. I have to pick my son up soon."

"Yeah, sure, of course. I understand. How old is your son?"

He had no interest in kids but he knew that if you wanted to fuck a single mom, you had to pretend that you did. He couldn't help but notice that she'd bounced back admirably from childbirth. There wasn't an ounce of fat on her.

"He turned six last month."

"That's nice." He wanted to prolong the conversation but he wasn't sure where to take it. He had a kid but he didn't know anything about raising one.

There was an awkward silence.

"Does a woman named Toni Little work here?" she asked.

Gavin frowned. "Why d'you ask?"

"My nephew's girlfriend. It's her sister. I thought maybe I could say hi."

"Yeah, well….she's not here at the moment."

"That's too bad. Was Marko close to anyone here? I mean, did he have friends, anyone he was close to?"

Gavin did his best to smile warmly.

"People liked Marko. He was a good worker but he mostly kept to himself."

She managed a weak smile. "I know Marko enjoyed working

here."

She was almost certainly lying, he thought. It was a shit job and she had to know that.

"He was trying to get my brother Steve a job here," she added.

What kind of game was she playing, he wondered. Did she know Marko was blackmailing him? He was worried, but at the same time, he had a half-chub stirring in his pants. It was like they were playing a naughty game of spy vs. spy.

"I didn't know that," he said. "But if he's as good a worker as Marko, we'd be lucky to have him."

"I'll talk to him and see if he's interested."

"That'd be great. What about you?" he asked. "What d'you do?"

It was chilly in the warehouse and he couldn't help but notice that her nipples were hard. He saw a look of disgust on her face and desperately tried to redirect his gaze but it was too late. The damage was done. She'd caught him staring at her breasts. Some women might welcome the attention but Marko's sister wasn't one of them. He knew instantly that he'd wasted his time cleaning his office.

"Look, I've got to get going soon," she said.

He nodded, accepting defeat. He wasn't getting laid today. "Why don't you go to the lunch room and I'll get the bolt cutters."

"Thank you," she said, all the warmth gone from her voice. "I'd like to use the restroom. Where would I find one?"

He pointed her to the restrooms and watched her walk away.

He heard a female voice behind him. "Gavin, you fucking pervert, don't be so obvious."

He turned and saw Toni. "Don't tell me you wouldn't like to lick that carpet," he said.

Toni smiled, which was weird. She hardly ever smiled, especially when he said something crude. "You're a pig," she said, still smiling. "And seriously, who talks like that? Lick her carpet? What are you, 12 years old?"

"Men are pigs. You know that."

"That may be true but you take it to a whole other level." Her smile disappeared. "We need to talk."

"I need to get some bolt cutters. We can talk on the way."

They started down the stairs.

"Some of the Pakis here call me SPF," Gavin said. "What the fuck is that about?"

Toni stared at him like he was an idiot.

"What?" he said.

"Sun Protection Factor. Because you're white. You need to wear suntan lotion. They think it's funny that you can't go outside in the summer without suntan lotion."

"Is that supposed to be an insult?"

Toni shrugged. "Does it bother you that you're white?"

"No."

"Then I guess it's not."

Gavin nodded, satisfied. He wondered why he hadn't been able to figure it out himself. The irony was that he never used sun tan lotion. He hated the sun and never went outside long enough to get a sunburn.

They reached the bottom of the stairs.

"Marko's sister wanted to know about our security cameras, whether or not we ever loaded equipment into a van, and whether or not we had thefts here," Gavin said. "And she asked about you."

"About me?"

"One and the same."

"And she asked specifically about merchandise being loaded into a van?"

"She did."

"It sounds like she knows about the video," Toni said.

"No shit."

"She knows about it but she hasn't seen it."

"How d'you know that?"

255

Toni tilted her head slightly. "I assume you're in the video."

"You don't know that."

"If you weren't in the video you wouldn't have asked me to kill someone blackmailing you with it."

She had a point, he thought. "Okay. I'm in the fucking video. That doesn't mean she hasn't seen it."

"If she's seen the video, she can identify you. Does it seem like she suspects you of anything other than being the pervert you are?"

Gavin thought about that. "I don't think so. You're right. She hasn't seen the video."

"So if she knows about the video, we have to ask ourselves, how is she connected to Pete Pappas?"

"Who the fuck is Pete Pappas?"

"The man I killed today. The man you said was blackmailing you."

"Oh." Gavin grabbed a set of large industrial bolt cutters from a tool rack and swung them so they rested on his shoulder. "None of that matters. What we need to do is find out what she knows."

"You don't need to do anything anymore," Toni said. "I'm in charge now."

"What the fuck are you talking about?"

Toni stared at him. "That's what I want to talk to you about. I'm in charge now."

"Fuck you."

Toni didn't blink. "I talked to Anton. We reached an understanding."

"I don't believe you," Gavin said, but he could hear the doubt in his voice. "And where's my fucking phone? I want it back."

"It's my phone now. You don't need it anymore."

Gavin started to say something but stopped. Toni was a woman, but she was a scary fucking woman.

She turned abruptly and walked away, leaving Gavin standing

alone with bolt cutters in his hand. It felt to him like he was holding his limp dick. He couldn't believe Toni's attitude but this wasn't a time for confrontation. That could come later when Gavin had a gun in his hand. In the last 24 hours he'd learned that killing people wasn't nearly as hard as it was made out to be.

The handgun was in his car. He'd gone back for it after giving his statement to police, pulling it out of the neighbor's shrubs right under the cop's noses. They didn't suspect him of anything. He was the victim and a hero for saving those two kids.

Thank God he'd been there with a golf club to save the day.

Gavin wondered if a person told a lie often enough, if it became the truth. As it was, he almost believed his own bullshit. In a few days, who knew, he might not be able to tell the difference between his lies and reality.

Chapter 48

Ana Marshall leaned against a table in the warehouse lunchroom, waiting for Gavin to return with the bolt cutters. She'd gone to the restroom and had been waiting for almost ten minutes. It was nearly 3 pm so she had plenty of time to pick up Braden, despite what she'd told him.

Her phone rang. She glanced down and saw that the call was from Andy. She looked around the empty lunchroom and decided to take the call.

"Hey Andy, thanks for calling back."

"What's up?" He sounded like he was barely awake.

"Are you ok? You sound a little under the weather."

"Rough night last night. You said it was important."

"I wanted to ask you about that video you and your mom found on the basement computer."

"Oh." He sounded guarded. "What d'you want to know?"

"She said it showed some workers at the warehouse loading TVs and other merchandise into a van."

"Yeah."

She paused and then said, "Was one of those workers Toni?"

There was a long silence.

"Andy?" she prompted.

"Yeah."

"Was one of the people in the video Katie's sister?"

"What makes you think that?"

"I think that's why you deleted the video."

There was another long silence.

"It's okay Andy. I understand. You love Katie."

"It was an old computer. It was loaded with malware."

"I get it. You didn't want Katie's sister to get in trouble."

"No, that's not it."

"C'mon Andy. Level with me. We're talking about your father here."

He sighed. "It's not like that. Katie talked to Toni. They weren't stealing from the warehouse."

"What were they doing then?"

"She said they were helping one of the local stores by letting them pick up some merchandise in a van early because they ran out of stock. She said it wasn't illegal but they could get in trouble. She might lose her job."

"D'you believe that?"

"I don't know. Katie said Toni's boss was right there so it must have been alright."

Ana felt her heart beat quicken. "Are you saying her supervisor is in the video?"

"Yeah. Katie said Toni was just doing what she was told."

"What does he look like, the supervisor?"

"He's fat I guess."

"Brown hair?"

"I don't know. It's hard to tell on the video. He's a messy

looking fat dude."

Ana felt adrenalin course through her body. "His name is Gavin. I think he might have something to do with your father's murder."

"Do you really think the video has something to do with Dad's murder?"

"I do. You need to try and remember everything you can about what you saw in that video."

"Why?"

"To tell the police."

"I don't need to tell them. I made a copy."

"You made a copy?"

"Yeah. I saved it on a flash drive."

"That's great, Andy. Can you sent it to me... or... no –wait – I'll come over. Can you show it to me?"

"Yeah – I guess so."

"You're at your Mom's?"

"Yeah."

"I'm coming over. What's the address?"

She knew Linda and Dieter lived in Point Grey but she'd never been there before. Andy told her the address and she repeated it back to confirm, writing it on her hand with a pen she found in her purse.

"I shouldn't have deleted that file," he said. "My mom's gonna be pissed."

"It's okay Andy. You did good. I'm on my way."

Ana disconnected the call and looked up to see Gavin standing a few feet away with a set of bolt cutters in his hands. She had no idea how long he'd been there.

"I have to go," she said and started to walk past him.

He moved in front of her, blocking her exit. "You should stay."

She heard voices and a small group of men entered the lunchroom behind Gavin. The men ignored them and settled into seats at one of the tables.

"It's a family emergency," she said. "I can't stay."

Gavin looked around helplessly as more men, and a few women, streamed into the lunch room and began taking seats. It must be the 3'oclock coffee break, she thought.

She didn't hesitate. She slipped past him, moving quickly out of the lunch room, down the stairs and out of the building. She raced to her car, unlocked it, and sped out of the parking lot. As she drove away she saw Gavin stumble out of the building, the bolt cutters still in his hand.

♦

"Fuck!" Gavin screamed as the Sunfire sped away.

"I think he might have something to do with Marko's murder."

She knew.

He needed to move quickly. Fortunately, he knew where she was going. She'd said the address out loud.

Still carrying the bolt cutters, he jogged along the sidewalk to the staff parking area at the back of the building. He got winded quickly and had to stop jogging and walk part of the way to his car. He saw Toni's truck parked beside his car and peered into the cab. The cell phone Anton had given him was on the passenger seat.

Gavin swung the bolt cutters like a baseball bat into the passenger side window of the truck. The heavy steel jaws struck the glass and the window shattered, some of the glass bouncing back and hitting Gavin in chest. He smashed out the remaining glass and reached in and grabbed the cell phone.

He got into his car and drove out of the parking lot. A few minutes later, he was on the road and stopped at a red light. He opened the flip phone to scroll through the text messages.

"Tell him to go fuck himself. I'm not paying."

He hadn't trusted Toni but it was still a shock to see her betrayal

261

so clearly played out in a series of texts. Toni hadn't lost the killer last night like she'd said. She'd tried to have Gavin killed.

That ungrateful bitch, he thought. After all he'd done for Toni, hiring her at the warehouse, recruiting her for the theft ring, treating her like his second-in-command even though she was a woman, and then hand-picking her for the important task of eliminating Marko's killer. Instead of appreciating all that, Toni had lied to him, betrayed him, and tried to have him killed.

Of course, Gavin intended to have Toni killed too but she didn't know that.

He heard a car behind him honk and looked up to see the light had turned green. He tossed the Judas Phone onto the passenger seat and accelerated, changing lanes without signaling.

He had to stop Marko's sister and then kill Toni. It was a good thing he had gone back for the gun. He was going to need it.

Chapter 49

Ana parked on the street in front of Linda and Dieter's house. There were multiple cars in the driveway including a rusted navy blue Toyota that looked out of place. She'd thought that Rick's house was impressive, but this house, and the entire neighborhood it was in, made Rick's place look like a humble shack.

She rang the doorbell and Linda answered. She was dressed casually but Ana knew looks were deceiving. Her jeans and blouse probably cost more than Ana spent on clothes in an entire year.

"Ana," Linda said, genuinely surprised.

"Didn't Andy tell you I was coming over?"

"No, but that doesn't matter. Come on in."

Ana stepped into an elaborate foyer and slipped off her shoes, leaving them by the door.

"Come into the kitchen with me," Linda said. "I was prepping for dinner. Can you stay?"

"No. Sorry. I have to pick Braden up soon from a play date."

She followed Linda into a huge modern kitchen. There was a cutting board on the counter where Linda had been chopping vegetables. Two pots simmered on the stove.

"Can I get you a drink?" Linda held up a glass of red wine. "I always cook with wine. I don't necessarily put it in the food, but I always cook with it."

Ana smiled. "No thank you. I can't stay long." She wanted to watch the video and get it to the police as quickly as possible. "Is Andy home?"

"He is. He's upstairs with Katie." She gave Ana a conspiratorial look. "I think something is up with those two."

"Oh."

"I don't think all is well in Romance Town, if you know what I mean."

"Really?"

"There was a lot of tension when she came to the door and they've been upstairs for 15 or 20 minutes," Linda said. "I think Andy might be breaking up with her."

"That's a shame."

Linda shrugged. "Sometimes it's for the best. Do you want me to call him?"

Ana winced. "I don't know if we should interrupt."

"Maybe not," Linda conceded. "Why don't you sit down and make yourself comfortable. You're making me nervous standing there like a security guard."

Ana moved awkwardly to a bar stool at the counter. "Sorry. I guess I can wait for a little while."

Linda cut carrots and added them to one of the simmering pots. "Dieter's upstairs in our room, watching the game."

"I never pictured him being a big football fan."

Linda laughed. "He is, but not that kind of football. He's watching a soccer game. Don't ask me which one because I have no idea. I took the TV out of the living room. I got tired of seeing him flopped on a couch, watching it all the time. We only have one TV now, in our bedroom, so he watches it there."

Ana was about to say something but before she could she was interrupted by heavy footsteps coming down the stairs and the sound of someone crying.

"Leave me alone!" It was a female voice, young.

"Katie..." Andy called after her, exasperation in his voice.

It appeared that Linda's assessment was correct. All was not well in Romance Town. Andy had clearly broken things off with the blue-haired girl and she obviously wasn't taking it well. Ana's instinct was to give them privacy but Linda had a different idea, scooping up her wine glass and drifting from the kitchen into the living room to the foyer where she could watch the proceedings. Ana felt compelled to follow but stayed a reasonable distance behind so she didn't feel like a voyeur.

Katie was at the door with her hand on the knob. She turned to face the top of the stairs and screamed. "I hate you! You said you loved me. Liar!"

She swung the door open and stopped. A man stood in the doorway with a gun. Katie backed into the house with her hands up.

Gavin Taylor held the gun level, pointed at the girl, but his eyes were fixed on Ana. "Nobody move or I'll blow her fucking head off."

Ana was tempted to duck out of sight. She was far enough away from Gavin, lingering back in the hallway near the kitchen, but it was too risky. She had no doubt that he was capable of killing someone. He looked deranged.

"You, upstairs," he called to Andy. "Come down slowly."

Katie, who had already been crying, was hysterical now. Gavin held the barrel of a small gun inches from her head.

Ana heard Andy slowly descend the stairs.

"You," Gavin shouted to Ana, "Don't think about trying anything. Come here so we're all together."

"What do you want?" Linda asked. She sounded confident, in control.

He motioned with a nod of his head at Ana. "She knows what

this is about."

Linda turned to Ana.

"He wants the video that Marko took."

"It's gone. We don't have it. We turned the computer over to the police," Linda said.

"According to Ms. Marshall here, someone made a copy of the file."

"What?" Linda said.

"He overhead me talking on the phone," Ana said. "He knows Andy made a copy."

Linda turned to Andy who nodded reluctantly to indicate that it was true. Katie glared at Andy, betrayal in her eyes.

"Is there anyone else in the house?" Gavin asked.

No one replied. Ana knew that Dieter was upstairs. Hopefully he would hear what was happening and phone the police.

"Is anyone else home?" Gavin repeated.

Linda shook her head. "No. This is it. This is all of us."

Chapter 50

Gavin Taylor stood in the center of the living room, facing the leather couch where the teenage boy and the three women sat wedged together. The three women were different ages but they were all hot, which was distracting. Marko's ex-wife had a 'Julianne Moore vibe'. She looked good, even if Gavin wasn't usually into older chicks. The young one had been crying but her tattoos gave her a 'bad girl' look and there was a hot little body underneath the tight, strategically torn Ramones t-shirt and short plaid skirt she was wearing.

He thought of the three women as Ginger Spice, Sporty Spice, and Baby Spice.

He'd taken their cell phones and set them on the dining room table so no one could covertly send a text, post a 'help me' message on Facebook, or call 911.

He had no plan though and hadn't expected there to be so many people in the house. Keeping an eye on four people wasn't easy. Gavin had shot someone at close range but he had no idea how accurate he would be with the weapon at a distance of more than three feet. It was a small gun and he had no idea how many bullets it held or how many were left. For all he knew, the gun was empty.

"If it's the video you want, just take it and go," Ginger Spice said.

Gavin was about to tell her to shut the fuck up when he heard a voice behind him. "What's going on here?"

He spun around and saw a tall thin man about 60 years of age, standing at the entrance to the living room. Without thinking, Gavin pressed the trigger. There was a shot and the man looked confused for a moment, then grabbed his throat and started choking, blood streaming from his neck.

"Oops," Gavin said.

Ginger screamed and bolted from the couch. The man dropped to his knees, gasping and spitting blood. She raced to his side. Gavin turned the gun toward the other three on the couch. He was most concerned about Sporty Spice. She stared at him like she was a pit-bull and he was a mail-man. He needed to maintain control.

"Don't move," he said.

It was difficult to keep an eye on the couch in front of him and the wounded man and Ginger behind him, so he backed up until he was parallel to the man on the floor. Ginger cradled his head, saying his name, Dieter, over and over again.

She glared at Gavin. "He's dying."

"Yeah...well, he startled me."

"We need to do something. Help him."

Gavin made a face. "There's not much I can do."

"He needs an ambulance. He needs to get to a hospital."

Gavin wondered if she had lost her grip on reality. The guy was a goner, couldn't she see that? It was time to move on.

"You know, this is kinda your fault," he said. "If you'd told me he was in the house, he wouldn't have startled me and I wouldn't have shot him."

"I'm a paramedic," Sporty Spice said from her place on the couch. "I can help him."

Gavin suspected it was a ploy to get close to him so she could make a move for the gun. He had no doubt that she could kick his ass, although to be fair, Baby Spice could probably kick his ass too and she couldn't weight more than 110 lbs.

The man's raspy breathing stopped.

"You can't help him Sporty." He didn't bother to explain that he'd nick-named the women after the Spice Girls. "No one can. Sometimes you gotta let 'em go."

"You bastard!" Ginger screamed. She pulled the man's head close to her chest and hugged him tight, tears streaming down her old-lady face.

Crying was not a good look for a mature woman.

"It's over, Ginger. There's no point crying over spilt milk. You need to go back to the couch now."

She stared at him but didn't move so he stepped toward her and pressed the gun to her head. That seemed to work. She carefully laid the man's head on the tile and stood, her blouse and hands covered in blood. He followed her back to the living room and watched her sit on the couch between Sporty Spice and the teenage boy, moving like she was in a trance.

Shooting Dieter in the throat had been an accident but Gavin couldn't help but be impressed by his aim. Murdering Dieter changed things. There was no need to worry about the video file anymore. He'd just shot a man in front of four witnesses. In light of that, stealing a few televisions wasn't much of a crime. The video could show him lopping off the heads of school children for all it mattered now.

He needed a plan and the first step in that plan needed to be finding a way to tie them up, starting with Sporty Spice.

Chapter 51

Ana lay on the floor with her wrists and ankles bound together. A strip of duct tape covered her mouth. Katie and Andy lay beside her, similarly bound. Gavin had sent Andy to the basement with instructions to come back with something he could use to tie everyone up. He threatened to kill the three women, starting with his mother, if Andy didn't come back in less than sixty seconds with some rope, some duct tape or something else that would do the job.

Andy did as he was told. He returned with plenty of rope and a roll of duct tape.

Gavin forced him to tie Katie and Ana up and once they were bound, and mouths taped shut, he had Linda do the same to Andy.

With the three of them secure, he forced Linda onto the couch and had her open her laptop and log into her on-line banking.

Linda obeyed his commands without emotion. All the fight in her seemed to be gone. She sat on the couch, facing the three of them on the floor. Gavin stood behind her with the gun held close to her head. Linda tapped at the keys, dried blood still on her fingers, while

Gavin stared at the screen.

"Holy shit," he said and whistled. "Is that your balance?"

Linda didn't respond.

"Transfer it all, every fucking penny into my account. Can you do that?"

Linda remained silent but tapped at the keys on the laptop. Gavin stood behind her, looking over her shoulder. He prompted her every once in a while, and when the time came, he read his account number out for her to enter. For some reason he had his account details written on a small piece of paper in his wallet.

Ana shifted her weight. The ropes around her wrists weren't loose, but they weren't that tight either. She was certain she could wriggle her hands free if she worked them back and forth hard enough but it was impossible to do with Gavin standing across from them.

When the transaction was complete he grinned. "You did good Ginger. Now I need you to search for countries that have no extradition treaty with Canada."

Ana couldn't see the screen but she assumed Linda had pulled up a list on the computer. Gavin leaned in, peering over Linda's shoulder, studying the screen. He told her to purchase an airline ticket for him to fly to the Dominican Republic that evening, using her credit card.

"I don't know why I didn't think of this before. I've been busting my hump my whole fucking life. All I needed was a gun and a computer and I'm rich."

When the tickets were booked and sent to a wireless printer, Gavin used the remaining rope to tie Linda up. She was docile and made it easy for him. Ana wished Gavin would get close enough to her so that she could make a move, but he was wary and kept his distance. He seemed to know that if anyone was going to put up a fight, it would be her.

He was right about that.

271

"Okay Baby Spice," he said. "It's your turn.

She squirmed and made muffled sounds under the tape.

"Your sister is a rat and you're going to be the cheese."

♦

Gavin had Baby Spice sit on the couch so he could take a few pictures of her using her iPhone. She relinquished the password when prompted with the gun. After he'd taken a few pictures he sorted through them quickly, looking for the best one. Her eyes were puffy from crying and there was silver duct tape across her mouth in all of them, but she looked especially vulnerable in one photo. He chose it for his text message to Toni the Betrayer. It was an important message so he took the time to use punctuation.

I'm at Marko's ex's house. They have video from the warehouse. It looks like I will have to kill them all. Katie is here. Oh well. Shit happens. -GT

He sent the message along with the photo of Katie.

He couldn't help smiling. Despite the absence of a plan, things were working out better than he expected. Shooting the tall gawky man had been a mistake but the outcome had been good. Once he accepted that he no longer needed his shitty job and his shitty life, it opened his mind up to other possibilities, like a bank transfer and a permanent vacation. Fuck his ex-wives and his ungrateful daughter. Fuck his crappy warehouse job and the fucking Russian mob squeezing him every chance they got.

His phone pinged.

I'll kill you if you hurt her

Gavin grinned. Toni wanted to kill him already so the threat was redundant. He replied:

Why didn't you tell me your sister was such a hottie? Looking forward to tapping that. lol ☺

He thought the happy face was especially hilarious. Toni would lose her mind.

Baby Spice's phone rang. Toni's photo appeared on the screen.

Gavin answered. "Toni, girl, how's it going?"

"I'm going to fucking kill you."

"That's no way to talk, after all I've done for you."

"Don't you dare touch her."

"Ohh sorry Toni. It's too late for that. Your sister may be small, but you'd be surprised how much she can take."

"You're a dead man. You're a fucking dead man."

"We'll see. Say, do you know where Marko's ex-wife lives? You should join us. We've got some of the Spice Girls here. Your sister is Baby Spice. You can be Scary Spice."

"You're not funny Gavin. I'm going to find you."

"I'm counting on it. I'll even text you the address."

Chapter 52

At least thirty minutes had passed since Ana heard Gavin on the phone with Katie's sister.   She thought of Braden. The realization that she might never see her son again, tore her apart. It was well after 5 pm and she was late to pick Braden up from his play date. Rick would also be wondering why she wasn't answering his texts or calls.

It had been over an hour since Gavin had taken them hostage. He'd been edgy, ever since he'd talked to Toni on the phone. He kept Katie close, pulling her around with him everywhere he went. He kept checking windows and wondering aloud if anyone else had heard a sound.

Whenever Gavin was out of sight, Ana worked the ropes around her wrists. He'd made a mistake not tying their hands behind their backs. They were getting loose, from twisting and turning. In a few minutes she might get her hands free, as long as Gavin stayed out of sight.

◆

Toni Little parked the F-150 in the alley, a few houses down from Marko's ex-wife's house. She hadn't needed Gavin to provide the address. She'd picked Katie up there on two occasions when Katie's Toyota had been in the shop. She'd never gone inside but she knew where the house was.

She also knew Gavin would be waiting for her and that Katie would still be alive. He needed her for protection. As long as he had a gun to her head, Toni was helpless and he knew it. The only way she could save her sister, and probably herself, was if he could surprise him.

Toni got out of her truck. She didn't bother locking it. There wasn't much point with the passenger window smashed. The last remnants of daylight were fading. She made sure there was a full clip in the 9 mm, tucked it into the IWB holster, and then made her way up the alley to the house where her sister was being held.

◆

Gavin was in the kitchen, staring out the window over the sink. It gave him a partially obstructed view of the driveway and the street. He kept Baby Spice close. He'd untied her legs so she could walk but left her hands tied and her mouth taped shut.

From the kitchen he couldn't see much of the living room and that worried him. Ultimately, he would need to decide what to do with Marko's family. He could leave them alive and tied up. After all, once he was in the Dominican Republic, it didn't matter what they told the police.

Or he could kill them all. If he did that, there was no risk of anyone getting free and calling the police before he escaped. The question was; did he have what it takes to kill three innocent people? He'd never killed a woman before, or a teenager.

Of course, 24 hours ago, he hadn't killed anyone.

275

He'd murdered George in cold blood but George was an asshole who was trying to evict him. He'd also shot and killed Ginger's husband but that had been an accident. He didn't feel bad about it, but at the same time, he hadn't done it on purpose. He hadn't had time to think about either murder. They just happened.

It was getting dark and that worried him. In hindsight, his plan to kill Toni may not have been a good one. He could have simply left the country without staging a standoff. He knew that he'd regret that though. He really wanted to kill her.

Besides, there was no point in second-guessing himself, he thought. In some ways it was like playing poker. He needed to stick with the line he'd taken. He needed to trust his instincts. He needed to play out the hand.

♦

Ana finally worked her hands free and was about to pull the tape off her mouth when she noticed a woman in jeans and a bomber jacket come up the basement stairs. She held a gun and moved quickly and quietly across the room. Ana tucked her hands under her back so it wasn't obvious that she'd removed the ropes from around her wrists. She couldn't be sure whose side the woman was on.

The woman approached Ana and the others, a finger pressed to her lips like a librarian. Loose rope lay on the floor beside Ana. She hoped the woman didn't notice.

"Where's Katie?" the woman whispered.

Ana motioned with her head toward the kitchen.

"Is Gavin with her?"

Ana nodded.

"I'll be back. Stay here."

With that, the woman, who Ana assumed was Toni, moved silently across the floor toward the kitchen.

As soon as she was gone, Ana pulled the tape off her mouth and started untying the ropes around her legs.

♦

Toni took careful steps, entering the dining room and slipping quietly into the kitchen. Gavin was waiting for her though. He stood of the other side of the kitchen counter, near the window, holding Katie close to him, the gun pressed against her forehead. She looked terrified, her mouth covered with duct tape.

Toni held the 9mm level with both hands and pointed it at Gavin.

"Nice try Toni," Gavin said. "Put the gun down."

"I can't do that."

"Should I go ahead and shoot her now then?"

"If you do, I'll kill you."

"Sure, but she'll be dead and you'll have to live with that."

"If I put the gun down, you'll kill both of us."

"Not true." Gavin smiled. "I'll kill you, obviously, but there's no point in killing her after you're dead. If I'm going to kill one of you, do you want it to be you or her?"

"There's no reason to kill either of us."

"You betrayed me."

"That's not true."

"They almost killed me."

"I didn't know they were going to do that."

"Fuck you. I read the texts. Don't fucking lie to me."

"I didn't know what they were going to do. I was trying to rattle their cages. You didn't tell me what was going on."

"Bullshit. Put the gun down or I'll fucking do it."

"Alright, alright." Toni set the gun on a baker's rack, her palms turned out, arms at her side.

Gavin pointed the gun at Toni and fired but nothing happened.

Toni reacted quickly, grabbing the 9mm off the baker's rack and swinging around to face Gavin. Katie ducked under the counter and Gavin struggled to keep hold of her. Toni fired.

The report was loud but she expected that. She fired again. Both shots struck Gavin high in the chest. He staggered back a step and tried to point the .22 at her, as if he hoped it had been miraculously reloaded, but he couldn't hold his arm steady. Blood bloomed across Gavin's shirt. Toni took three steps forward and unloaded a third shot from close range. The bullet struck Gavin in the head and he collapsed to the floor.

Blood was everywhere; on the counters, the cabinets, and the window over the sink.

Katie crawled around the counter, crying. Toni helped her to her feet and hugged her. After holding her for a few seconds, they parted and she pulled the duct tape off her sister's mouth. There was blood in Katie's bright blue hair and spattered on her face and t-shirt. She glanced down at Gavin on the kitchen floor. A large pool of blood spread out from his body. The .22 Ruger lay on the tile beside him.

Toni set the 9mm down on the kitchen counter and untied the ropes on Katie's wrists.

Chapter 53

Ana untied her legs and once she was free, turned to Linda and Andy and pulled the duct tape off of their mouths. She started to untie Linda's wrists when Linda said, "Leave it for now. Call 911 instead."

Ana nodded. It made sense. Call for help, then untie them. She decided to use the landline phone rather than a cell so that even if the call got interrupted, the dispatcher would know where the call had come from. There was a portable phone on the end table beside the couch and she picked it up and dialed 911.

That was when she heard the first shot from the kitchen, followed quickly by a second, and a few seconds later, a third.

"Police, fire, ambulance. What is the nature of your emergency?" a female voice spoke into her ear.

"Police," she said in a hushed tone. "Home invasion. At least one person has been shot and killed."

The voice on the phone started to ask a question but Ana set the phone down. That was all they needed to dispatch the police so there was no point wasting time on the phone. With the recent flurry of gunfire, surely the neighbors would call 911 as well. They apparently hadn't heard the shot that killed Dieter but these shots were louder and in rapid succession.

She moved toward the kitchen and positioned herself against the wall at the entrance to the dining room. She couldn't be sure who'd been shot – Gavin or the woman in the bomber jacket - but she could hear Katie crying so she knew the girl was alive.

The woman in the bomber jacket stepped out of the kitchen and Ana pounced on her, knocking her off balance and driving her to the floor. She managed to crawl on top of the woman and pin her to the floor, face down. The woman held a gun in her outstretched hand. Ana dug her knee into her arm, just above the elbow.

Ana screamed, "Let it go, let it go, let it go!"

The woman released the gun and Ana leaned forward to grab it.

"Don't touch it," a voice said.

Ana looked up. Katie had followed the woman out of the kitchen, her clothes spattered with blood. She had a gun too, the smaller one that Gavin had used, and she pointed it at Ana.

"Get off her," Katie said.

"The police are coming," Ana said. "I called 911."

She turned her head to both sides. "They aren't here now are they?" She motioned with the gun. "So get off her."

Reluctantly, Ana stood.

Katie bent down to pick up the other gun. When she had both guns, she held up the smaller one.

"This one's empty," she said, and dropped it on the floor. "But this one's not." She pointed the loaded gun at Ana. "Go sit on the couch."

◆

Toni got up off the floor and stared at Katie, confused. She didn't understand what her sister was doing. As far as she was concerned, it was over. She'd saved Katie. Gavin was dead. She could live with that.

"Give me the gun Katie," she said gently.

Katie shook her head.

"It's over," Toni said. "It'll all come out now. I'm okay with it."

"I'm not ok with it."

Toni turned her head to Ana, sitting on the couch, and the other two on the floor. "They know about the video. That gun you're holding, it was used to kill someone today. The police will figure that out."

"Not if we kill them," Katie said. "Not if we kill them all."

Toni stared at her, not comprehending. She was her little sister. She was young and innocent. She couldn't be suggesting that they murder three people in cold blood.

Katie went on, her voice eerily quiet. "We can tell everyone that the fat man killed them all and he was about to kill me, when you killed him."

"But these are innocent people."

"He's not innocent," Katie screamed, pointing the gun at Andy. "He lied to me. He said he loved me."

Her hand shook, her finger on the trigger, the gun aimed at Andy's head.

"Don't Katie," Toni said. "He's not worth it."

Katie turned to look at Toni, despair in her eyes, and then she raised the gun to her own head.

"Maybe I'll do this instead," Katie said, her voice a whisper. "Then he'll know – he'll know what he did."

Toni felt tears in her eyes. "No...Katie...don't...don't do it."

"He'll never forget me then, will he?"

"Don't do it Katie," Andy said from the floor.

She turned to face him, the gun still pressed to her head. "Do you love me?"

"Yes."

"Liar!"

"No, it's true. I love you. Don't do this."

Toni stepped toward her sister. "Give me the gun Katie."

"He's lying," she said to Toni. "He's a liar. I would hurt you before I would ever let you hurt me!"

Toni knew what was going to happen. She could see it in Katie's eyes, but she couldn't react fast enough. Katie pulled the gun away from her own head and pointed it at Andy. The shot was loud. Andy cried out and blood spread rapidly down his shirt just below his shoulder.

♦

Ana watched, horrified, as Katie turned and fired the gun. She bolted up from the couch and lunged at Katie. Toni moved toward her sister at the same time and Ana drove hard into both of them. The three of them crashed to the floor.

Ana heard Linda scream. Andy had been hit and was bleeding badly.

She felt Katie squirm underneath her, trying to break free. Toni got to her knees and was trying to pull Ana off her sister but Ana grabbed Katie's legs and tried to crawl up, to get to her head, to her outstretched arm and the gun.

The whole scene played out, simultaneously moving in slow motion and high speed. It was a blur of confusion, but at the center of it all, Ana focused on one thing - the gun. Finally, she felt metal and began to pry the gun from the girl's hand.

She was so focused on the gun that it took a few seconds to realize that someone was shouting at her. There were multiple voices, hard and urgent, screaming at her to put her hands on head. She looked up and saw at least four police officers with their weapons drawn.

She let go of the gun and did as she was told.

It was over.

Chapter 54

Friday November 4 (two weeks later)

Ana stood at the podium in the funeral home, looking out at the crowd of mourners. There were fewer than fifty people in attendance, which made her sad. It was disappointing that Marko wouldn't be missed by more people. She couldn't help but wonder how many people would attend her funeral one day.

Marko's killers were either dead or brought to justice but there was surprisingly little comfort in that. He was gone and knowing who killed him couldn't change that. It all seemed so senseless. Six people had died, including Marko and Dieter - and for what? A few stolen televisions?

There was an absurdity to everything that had happened that might have been funny if it weren't so tragic.

If Ana closed her eyes she could visualize the two cops performing CPR on Marko as if it were happening now, right in front of her. She could picture Steve, badly beaten, unconscious, naked, and bloody on the bedroom floor, or most horrifying of all, she could clearly recall Dieter's confused and terrified eyes as he clutched at his throat, gasping for air as blood spilled through his fingers. Not long ago, she would have taken those images and forced them into glass jars, hiding them away for as long as she could in that locked cupboard in her mind.

But those days were gone.

It was painful for her to let those memories roam free but she'd learned it was better to live with them every day, than it was to lock them away. Locking them up seemed easier, mostly because it worked – at least, until it didn't.

Until the jars broke. And they always did.

It was just a matter of time.

Her eyes scanned the small gathering. Linda and Andy sat together in the front row. They had postponed the memorial service until after Andy had recovered and could attend. He remained stoic beside his mother, his innocent face somehow looking older and world weary. His eyes were vacant, fixed on the stained glass window behind Ana. He'd lost two fathers in less than a week and had been shot by a girl he had loved.

Ana's mother and Steve sat next to them in the front row. Steve had agreed to get a haircut and promised to go to rehab but Ana wasn't optimistic. Steve had made promises before and Ana could tell that he was high. She decided she wouldn't give up on him though, no matter how many promises he broke or how many TVs he stole.

Beside them sat Brad and Braden. Brad postponed his band's tour of rural Alberta so he could attend the funeral, disappointing tens of fans. Remarkably, he'd assumed he could crash with her for a few days, but the fact that Rick had practically moved in convinced him to find a different couch to surf.

Rick was in the front row as well, next to Braden. They exchanged eye contact and she felt reassured. Her gaze shifted from Rick to Braden. Her little man was dressed in a suit and was trying to look brave but didn't fully understand what was going on. She smiled reassuringly at him and he smiled back, looking uncertain.

Ana started the eulogy.

"Marko was the best big brother a girl could have," she said, her voice cracking. "He was a wonderful and dedicated father to Andy, a loving husband to Linda for years, and an incredible friend and coworker to many people in this room."

She paused to collect her thoughts. She knew now that Marko had a tumor that would have killed him in six months. The autopsy had confirmed what Marko had known, but had kept to himself. If he hadn't tried to blackmail Gavin, and Gavin hadn't sent two thugs to murder him, he'd be dead anyway in a few short months.

"Marko was the kind of man who'd do anything for the people he loved no matter how difficult it was." She thought of how Marko had gone to extreme lengths to try, however misguidedly, to get Steve off the streets. "In fact, he even taught me how to drive, which I can tell you, wasn't easy." She was relieved that there was modest laughter from the audience. She took a deep breath. "Marko gave me lessons when I was sixteen." She smiled at the thought. "He had this Ford Pinto..."

There was a spattering of laughter from the audience as people in the room recalled Marko's infamous orange Pinto.

"He'd always let me drive past the houses of boys I liked, and trust me, there were a lot of them. Whenever I got a glimpse of one, I'd make him duck his head down, so they wouldn't see him. The poor guy spent most of his time in the car with his head under the dashboard."

She smiled at the memory. It seemed long ago but she remembered it vividly, like it was yesterday.

She told the story of Marko using her as collateral for a gas can and, with growing confidence, told three additional stories that had the crowd laughing warmly.

"Marko called me Bean." She closed her eyes to hold off tears that seemed inevitable. "He read me a picture book when I was little called 'Have You Seen My Jellybean?' I loved that book and I made him read it to me, over and over again.

"For those of you not familiar with this literary classic, it's the tale of a princess who loses her jelly bean. She tries to get the king and the queen to help her find it but they're too busy ruling their kingdom. The court jester helps her though. Together they go around the castle asking if anyone has seen her jellybean. But everyone they approach needs the princess's help instead. There's a kitten tangled in wool and a maid who needs help folding the royal bedding. The princess helps them but she doesn't find her jellybean. The big twist at the end is when the court jester suggests that maybe she had the jellybean with her all along. She searches her clothing and finds the jellybean in a secret pocket in her dress.

"Marko tried to tell me later, when I was older, that the jellybean was a metaphor for happiness. You found it by helping others."

Ana's voice cracked and she felt tears in her eyes. She composed herself for a moment, determined to finish.

"I told him he was full of shit. I said I liked the book because there was a princess in it. And jellybeans. What more could a girl want?" She blinked a tear from her eyes. "But maybe he was right. I don't know. What I think though is that Marko was my court jester. He taught me a lot. I'm not sure he was always happy, but he was happiest I think when he was helping others."

She choked on the last few words, finally letting go of the tears she'd been holding back. Before she knew it, Rick was by her side, gently guiding her back to her seat. She sat and Braden crawled onto her lap.

The minister said a few words, none of which registered in Ana's brain, and then the slide show started. Photos of Marko appeared on screen, accompanied by music. It was a slide show Ana had seen dozens of times. She and Linda had spent countless hours, poring through photo collections, putting it together.

People laughed as the slide show progressed, reacting to photos of Marko as a baby and growing up - the bad haircuts and outdated clothing - the moments of his life. A photo of Marko, taken in the mid 1980's, appeared on screen. He wore boat shoes without socks, a skinny leather tie, and a Members Only jacket, standing proudly beside his orange Pinto.

She stared ruefully at the photo on the screen and wondered how Marko could have shown such terrible judgment by blackmailing his boss and how he could have been naïve enough to think that getting Steve a job would solve the problems of a drug addict. She focused her gaze on the orange Pinto, the skinny leather tie, the Miami Vice boat shoes, and the goofy grin on Marko's face, and she realized it wasn't difficult to understand.

He often said he was a simple man with simple needs. He believed there were simple solutions to complex problems. She'd never had faith in people like he had. Sometimes she thought his influence could change her, make her less cynical and help her see the best in people.

She smiled at the thought.

There wasn't a hope in hell - but it was nice to think so, at least every once in a while.

About the Author

Jeff Norburn is the author of two novels, "Mustang Shuffle" and "Triple Barrel."

He lives with his wife Melody in Quesnel, British Columbia. His two grown children live in Victoria and Vancouver BC.

When Jeff isn't writing, he spends much of his spare time playing poker. He warns readers though that while there are some poker scenes in Triple Barrel, the novel should not be used as an instructional tool. Anyone modelling their game on Gavin Taylor's can expect to lose a lot of money.

Jeff is currently working on his third novel, tentatively titled "Slow Roll"

On Social Media:

Twitter: @jeffnorburn

Facebook: Jeff Norburn - author

Cover Design and Artwork

Daryl Stephenson

http://www.caricatoons.ca/

Made in the USA
Lexington, KY
04 November 2019